THE RETURN OF
SGT. HAWK

"HIT THE DECK!" SGT. HAWK BELLOWED.

The Japanese splashed into the green water of the shallow stream. After the first American shot was fired they opened up. The exploding shots reverberated through the dense, steamy jungle.

Hawk was among the men closest to the stream. As he lay in the sandy soil he heard the bullets whizzing past him and crashing into the trees. The Japanese, with their wildly gyrating limbs seemed to be upon him.

Without thinking, he jerked the trigger of his Thompson. The muzzled flash lit his face beneath the dark shadow of his helmet. Yeah, he thought, war is sure enough hell!

1

A NERVE-SHATTERING ROCKET SHRIEKED JUST ABOVE THEIR heads, slicing into the ocean in a harmless display of power. The unexpected landing by the American forces had put the Japanese into a general retreat all along the Beachhead. The mad scene seemed like anything but an enemy withdrawal to the attacking Marines.

The bright tropical morning was as dark and grey as mid-winter with the overcast fumes of battle. The gloomy cloudiness shuddered continuously with the falling of both friendly and unfriendly fire. A blast from a lesser distance would cause the dirty sky to blow and rush like a raging river, breathing an evil heat down on the benumbed men.

They lay there on the beach in an unearthly silence while other Marines lay slaughtered beside them and still others charged beyond them toward the deadly front. Some fidgeted and flinched at the harsh, uncompromising sounds, limitless in their intensity, that battered their ears and their innards. Most of them cowered there on the sand, praying for the enemy barrage to cease. At least one man cried. They were all dazzled by the incredible spectacle that had revealed their own frail mortality—and, at the same time, their savagery.

Sergeant Hawk strode out of the smoky cloudbank between them and the front. He was not attuned to their feelings. The horror of the scene registered little upon him. He only saw *his* men—stationary objects in an urgent and fluid phantasmagoria. He stopped and stood in front of them. Several of them stood up. He watched a young boy's face hovering painfully over the bloody sand. The young Marine threw up all of his shock and fear.

Hawk impatiently slung his Thompson over a naked shoulder. A fuel drum, bobbing in the surf, had been perforated by machine-gun fire and doused him with gasoline. He had thrown away his shirt and now his lean, muscle-knotted body looked harder and fiercer than the men decked out in their elaborate combat gear.

"Anybody here got some tobacco?" he asked, ignoring the thousands of roaring and buzzing sounds that swam around him. Someone handed him a block of black chewing tobacco and stepped back among the men. No one spoke to the sergeant, no one stood near him as he paced slowly between the two ragged lines of men. The Marines squinted at one another as they watched him bite off a plug of tobacco. None of them had enough saliva in their fear-dried throats even to consider such a thing. They watched as he spun around and stood over their frightened comrade. Hawk pushed back his helmet and went to one knee beside the ailing Marine. His heaving had subsided somewhat.

Hawk's dog tags threw a soft, dangling shadow

across the young man's anguished features. Just over the boy's hunched back, the sergeant could see the mottled pink half of a marine, neatly sliced in two.

"We gotta get movin'. You okay?" he asked the boy.

The marine raised and lowered his head, indicating that he was ready now. His tongue protruded and he couldn't see to close his mouth. Hawk nodded back at him and gripped him heavily under the arm. The sergeant stood and dragged the boy up with him. The men lying on the sand got up.

"This way—follow me," said Hawk, motioning casually for the men to follow him into the terrifying forest of flame and phosphorescent smoke. The casual signal made the hearts and breathing of the men hesitate, but they began to follow him.

The sharp, nose-wrinkling smell of burning flesh forced them to tighten their lips in disgust. Some tried to hold their breath, but the odor only became worse when they released it. Hawk unslung his Thompson and bent forward from the waist. Sensing the paralyzing dread that had seized his young followers, he took the point himself.

Japanese mortars walked along the edge of the forest. They scooped heavy chunks of earth skyward and poured them down in granules. These blasts were distinguishable from, and preferable to, the obliterating shocks of the random artillery shells. Hundred-pointed stars erupted when one of the artillery shells struck the sand. The far-flung blasts of rocky dust pelted Hawk's bare skin and embedded themselves there.

A red flash blinded the men. It was difficult to tell whether the flash came from in front of or behind their eyelids. They all collapsed under the irresistible concussion. Hawk fought the great pushing force that buffeted his body and managed to remain on his feet. He saw somebody's arm and leg fly into oblivion. The Marines had been bracketed by the mortars, and he knew that the next round would fall among them. He pulled them to their feet, one at a time, and pushed them forward.

"Off the beach, there's cover up ahead!" he shouted. There was no need to shout; no one could hear him, including himself. They ran to a mold-covered ridge that marked the end of the beach and the beginning of the jungle. The men huddled there, cringing, whining, and clinging to their helmets.

The order was *to* move forward. Every reserve of common sense in every man there told him to stay down, to wait right where he was. Hawk raised his eyes above the ridge. They were two fiery blue slits beneath his camouflage-covered helmet. Fear and common sense had long ago been pounded out of his thick skull. Still, it took great effort for him to order his men forward.

He rolled over the top of the ledge and bounced to his feet. White sand blanketed his sweating back. He ran in a crouch, somehow avoiding the fountains of earth and steel erupting in every direction. He leaped over a smoldering stump and went to one knee. The men following him halted and scattered nearby. Interlocking tornadoes of shrapnel clanged above their quivering heads. Hawk's piercing gaze scoured the hellish jungle. The trees were scorched and gnarled, looking like amputated tombstones choking in wisps of smoke and dust. The feathery curtain of cordite that clung to the ground burned the eyes and obscured the vision.

Then he spotted them. Caution was useless now.

Action was required merely to survive. A contingent of inhumanly brave Japanese were daring their own barrage in a charge toward the beach. There was no place to hide from them, no place to run. Sergeant Hawk held back the trigger of his Thompson. A mad lightning bolt shuddered from its muzzle, and from its breech a dozen spent casings spewed into the air.

"Open up on them weeds, the goddam place is full of 'em!" he bellowed. The men fired dutifully. Some kept their heads down and pointed their rifles without looking where they were shooting. The unenthusiastic volley forced half a dozen grey-clad figures to spring to their feet and dash back into the misty recesses of the forest.

The retreat surprised Hawk. The enemy seldom backed down. Times were changing; the Japanese must finally have come to realize that they could not win the war. He felt a little disappointed, the way a man feels when the character of an old friend changes. His chest pounded, his head throbbed, and his fist held a crushing grip on the submachine gun. He wanted them to fight; he wanted to kill them.

It made him uneasy. The enemy was losing their savage zeal for this madness, yet his still burned brightly. His concern for their slackening spirit was premature.

The other Marines cautiously picked up their heads, looks of suspicious relief in their terrified white eyes. Hawk trudged through the brush the enemy had evacuated, looking about for signs of a trap. Failing to find anything, he pumped his arm, and once again the men began to follow him.

A nervous skirmish line moved inland. Parts of it

would occasionally surge ahead of other parts. The adventurous souls who had stormed ahead would then stop and wait for the others to catch up. The squad ran, stopped, and crouched. They looked around, stood up, and repeated the whole procedure. The maneuver was interrupted by a series of far-flung explosions.

The ground vibrated under the weight of dueling Japanese artillery and American naval guns. The Marines fell where they were and waited for the storm to cease; deafened, blinded, their sense of touch numbed by the vibration, they lay in another world waiting for sensibility to return. It ended at last, without harming them, and they again had to move forward.

Hawk signaled a halt on the brink of a shallow draw. Below him dead enemy troops were piled three deep, their charred limbs horribly entwined and reaching. No sign of their killers remained. They had either died with them or moved along. The stench was not yet overpowering. The bodies had not begun to bloat. The blood that covered both them and the earth was still a vivid red. Hawk ran his tongue along his upper teeth as he looked about. He motioned the men forward, down into the draw.

They slid down the side of the ravine and walked across its body-carpeted floor. Flies darted gleefully between the black and green nuggets of their fellows that gathered at each eye, mouth, and nostril. Several of the men stumbled on the once human cushions that filled the bottom of the ravine. Their boots were slick with flesh and blood, making the climb up the far side of the draw a difficult one.

That was where a runner from battalion caught up with them. He was a young fellow in a shiny, coverless helmet, wearing dungarees that looked freshly laundered. His shirt was tucked in and, for some reason, he still had a pack on his back.

"Sergeant Hawk? We've punched a hole in the Jap lines to the west of here. Companies A and B have already taken the barrio. All of Company D is to halt this operation here and return to the open corridor over on the west. We need you at the barrio." The messenger spewed the entire message out without taking a breath.

Hawk looked at the youngster for a moment, then slung his Thompson over his shoulder and spat disgustedly onto the ground. Corporal Joe Canlon had been standing nearby. When he heard the news he broke into a wide smile, exposing an ugly disarrangement of teeth.

"Best news I ever heard," said the corporal, slapping the messenger on the back. Joe was in no great hurry to be killed. He was the only man who had been with Hawk before this campaign. He knew that the easiest way out was always the best.

"Awright," Hawk finally conceded. He eyed the messenger's pack. "You got a extra shirt there, private? I'm kinda superstitious about gettin' one off some dead fella."

The messenger shuffled anxiously. He didn't want to give up a shirt. But Hawk didn't want to be devoured by mosquitoes—and, before the boy returned to battalion, the sergeant was proudly donning his new shirt.

Hawk signaled for the men to take a break. Joe Canlon shook a Japanese cigarette from its package and bit one end off. The corporal and the sergeant sat down together on the black grass. The crisp ashes smeared their clothing.

"Goddamn Philippines," said Joe. "Goddamn Army.

I thought they gave the Army the easy campaigns. We coulda got slaughtered back there." He stuck a pasteboard holder onto the end of the cigarette and lit it.

The invasion of the Philippines was to be handled strictly by the Army. All official versions of the campaign left the Marines unmentioned. But at only the last moment the Army general in charge of the invasion of Lamare, General Kravanart, had agreed to let a couple of battalions of Marines join in the amphibious assault landing. Both the Marine Corps and the Navy felt that the soldiers needed the experience and the spirit of the leathernecks to give them some indication of how things were to be done.

General Kravanart hadn't been too keen on the idea. There were plenty of experienced Army infantrymen around who could show them how it was done. Saipan was fresh on his mind, where the Marines had accused the Army of cowardice and managed to steal the whole show. He didn't like Marines or the Marine Corps philosophy. They considered themselves great fighters merely because they were willing to absorb such outrageous casualties.

He finally agreed to let a small number of Marines take part in the landing. They would help soften the beachhead and probably be wiped out in the process. Their role in the campaign after the landing was a tenuous one.

That was all fine with Joe Canlon. He was ready for a trip down to Australia any time. Joe began speaking again in his throaty boxer's voice. He had a habit of grunting for a second or two before any words came out. It was his wind-up, his way of forewarning the world that he was about to say something momentous.

"Damn Army." Canlon shook his ponderous helmet. "They get one rough deal and we gotta be in on it. I thought this was gonna be easy."

"What makes you say this ain't easy?" Hawk asked, spitting between his knees.

2

_____

THE MEN REACHED THE CORRIDOR TO THE FILIPINO village before dusk. It turned out to be a corridor through the dense jungle as well as a corridor through enemy lines. A and B companies had captured the narrow roadway in the chaos of the Japanese retreat. The enemy had left a few strategic sections of it unguarded, and that was all the fast-moving Marines needed.

Apitong trees and groves of bamboo grew tightly against the edges of the muddy path. Splattered dead men from both sides of the conflict lay in the ruts in the center of the road. Tanks and jeeps rolled over them. The hollow-eyed Marines cursed the drivers when they hit an American corpse. They turned away when they hit a Japanese. Hawk's squad came out of the woods and onto the trail to be confronted by one of these hapless bodies. It had been run over so often that it looked like nothing more than a dirty maroon blanket.

Hawk pushed back his helmet and pulled at his straight, narrow nose. The men couldn't take their eyes from the grisly sight. There were dead and there were dead, and that one was especially dead. Hawk knew that death had no degrees.

"That's sweet," one of the men said. The roaring passage of a Sherman tank forced the men back off the road. The tall treads clanked against their sprockets and driving rods and the men stared mutely into the pulsating machinery.

"Hey, buddy, how about a ride into town?" Hawk shouted up at the observer perched in the tank's hatch.

"Liloila? Sure, hop on," the Army tank sergeant answered. The men clambered onto the big green dinosaur. The whirring treads splashed them with blood, mud, and guts before they reached the hamlet. They hopped off on the outskirts of Liloila as darkness fell.

The town looked, for the most part, like any other Filipino barrio, but this was the only one any of the Marines had ever seen. Mud and grass huts were thrown up as shelters against the elements. There were a few more elaborate structures of wood and tin. At the end of the main street was a line of shops made from one long building. There was a facade resembling a Spanish mission on this building, but behind the facade the building was only wood. It had an awning and a wooden sidewalk across its front. The most unusual feature of the town, however, was a row of frame houses sitting up on concrete blocks. They were made of shiplap, or 105 siding, and were of the same construction as the houses in Hawk's native Mississippi. The roofs were of tin, there were no singles. The houses gave the place a homey, American appearance. One home even had a front-porch swing.

Liloila had been spared the ravages of open combat. There was the odd bullet hole in the side of a house, a shattered pane of glass here and there, but nothing had been seriously damaged. Hawk learned later that the enemy had abandoned the town without a struggle: very unusual for the die-hard Japanese. The Marines threw themselves down on the ground in the evening coolness. Mosquitoes swarmed over them. They ignored the inconvenience; they were still dazed by the speed with which they had penetrated seven miles into the interior of Lamare.

Hawk sat with them, content to rest there until his company commander or a lesser authority found him. He sighed deeply as he watched the bustling soldiers. The only thought on his mind pertained to the finding and securing of cigars. They were hard to come by.

A platoon of grimy dog soldiers came up the path Hawk had just traveled. They escorted a group of civilians, mostly women. Several children and one or two men accompanied them. Half of the group were Filipinos, the rest were Americans or possibly Australians or Europeans. The light-colored dresses of the women contrasted with the darkness that grew in intensity. They flowed like ghosts before the black background of the forest. Above them the forked fingers of palm leaves swayed against the greying sky. Hawk watched the women pass through half closed eyes. He enjoyed the dreamlike quality of the peaceful scene.

Most of the non-Filipino civilians entered the frame houses that lined the road. They entered them slowly, afraid of what they might find.

"Sergeant Hawk? I'm Lieutenant Jackson, your new platoon leader."

Hawk looked up. A handsome little officer of about twenty-five was talking down to him. The officer carried his helmet, exposing a head of thick black hair. Hawk stood and Jackson shook his hand. "It doesn't look like we'll get to kill any more Japs tonight," the lieutenant said.

"No, sir, it don't. What's next for us, Lieutenant?"

"I think we're through for a while. General Kravanart is kind of jealous of Marines." The officer pulled a cigarette package from his pocket and gingerly slid one out with two fingers. "I think he wants to slow us down to make the Army look better. Colonel Heller is the ranking Marine officer on Lamare now, and he's pretty upset about it. But there's nothing he can do. We'll probably stay here for a couple of days and then we might even go back to the ships. Unless the Army really gets bogged down."

"Well, they're movin' right along. That don't look likely, sir."

Jackson raised his eyebrows in agreement. The two men looked at each other. Jackson's first meeting with his acting platoon sergeant left him dissatisfied. The sergeant was a bit older than Jackson, and that was always unsettling. He had a confident, almost belligerent Delta accent; his eyes tunneled through the lieutenant's head whenever they focused on him. Hawk would not be an easy man to lead.

"This your first campaign, sir?" Hawk asked.

"It might as well be. I was in on the last day at Tarawa, and that's about all the action I've seen." Jackson smiled good-naturedly. "I'll rely heavily on your experience, Sergeant Hawk," he said seriously. "Just don't try to take over."

Hawk nodded. "Gotcha, sir." He didn't smile or try to continue the conversation. The lieutenant felt a creeping awkwardness as he put on his helmet and nervously met the cold stare of the sergeant. He could see the icy blue color in his eyes smoldering in the dark. The eyes looked like two searchlights buried in the head of a corpse.

"Carry on, Sergeant. Bed down wherever you can find a comfortable place. Tell the men to stay out of the dwellings." There was a casual salute.

"Aye...sir," Hawk mumbled, forgetting to return the courtesy.

* * *

JOE CANLON and another man named Chuck Lasker decided that the best place to sleep that night would be under one of the frame houses. Hawk didn't try to stop them. The house was vacant and Jackson's orders only forbade entering the houses.

Lasker was an innovator. He was a half-crazy forever-happy boy from Illinois. He was tall and thin and he always had a good idea and the energy to go through with it.

Lasker strung mosquito nets along the raised bottom of this particular vacant house. Not satisfied with just this amount of insect-proofing, he built smothered fires out of green branches, causing smoke to billow from beneath the house for over an hour. He and Canlon then buried the smoking fires and their squad had an insect-free haven for the night. There were minor interruptions; every officer in the South Pacific converged on the scene and fell to ordering men to put the fire out. Things went smoothly after it became common knowledge that the house was not on fire.

Ironically enough, Hawk didn't even benefit from this incident. He didn't like crowds, so he didn't sleep under the house. He put a mosquito-net bag over his head, fastened his jacket, and settled down for the night on the ground near the roadside. He had almost dozed off when he saw the warped nose of Joe Canlon hovering over him.

"What are you doin' out here, you dumb cracker?"

"Sleepin'. What's it look like, you ignorant yankee?"

"You'll get the malarias out here," Joe urged in his dumb voice.

"Crackers don't get malaria."

* * *

THAT NIGHT the men heard the steady crackling of small-arms fire between the brutal, punctuating explosions of artillery. The Army was moving inland and the Japanese were running.

Lieutenant Jackson didn't show the next morning. It was rumored he had gone to a meeting of all the platoon leaders. Hawk didn't know, or especially care, where he was. Things were quiet and he was willing to take advantage of that for the time being.

The owners of the house that Lasker had chosen to cook returned that morning. Canlon saw to it that the men removed their paraphernalia from beneath the building. This wasn't all that was required, however, to satisfy the owner. Mrs. Jennings was indignant about the smoky odor that permeated her home.

"You won't be bothered by bugs," Canlon consoled her.

She demanded to see his superior and, since just about everyone in the armed services was superior to Joe Canlon, he chose Hawk to iron out the difficulties.

Later in the morning, the sergeant trudged up the wooden steps, knocked on her door, and waited impatiently on the front porch for her to answer it. The grey-haired, emaciated Mrs. Jennings met him at the screen door.

"Sergeant James Hawk, ma'am. The corporal tells me you got a complaint."

"I certainly do. What is the meaning of your trying to burn my house down, Sergeant? The Japs were here for two years and they never did anything so monstrous."

"Sorry, ma'am. Won't happen again. We didn't know y'all'd be comin' back. Won't happen again."

"Well, see that it doesn't. Now, I don't want to give you the wrong impression." Her tone eased a bit; she had a Midwestern accent. "We were glad to see you boys drive those devils off...but, my goodness, without a man around, we'd never be able to repair any of the damage. And just get a whiff of this place."

"We'll fix anything that gets busted. Don't worry none about that, ma'am. There's plenty of no-accounts around to do that for you." Hawk touched his helmet and turned away in what was almost a graceful escape.

"Now, don't get me wrong, young man. We're Americans and we're awfully glad to see you—especially since all that dreadful noise has stopped. But, you see, my husband is a prisoner of war and we're on our own here.

You're a Marine, aren't you? Well, what are you doing in the Philippines?"

"I wisht I knew, ma'am." Hawk flashed a rare and brilliant smile from beneath his dirty, beard-covered face.

"Would you care to come in? Those nice gentlemen from the Army gave us tea and coffee and—just everything you could want. Won't you come in?" She opened the door wider. "Let me fix you some tea."

"Well...uh...thank you." Hawk was never one to be unneighborly. The screen door squawked shut behind him. The furniture inside was covered with sheets. Hawk removed his helmet and ran his fingers through his tangled, sandy hair. "Downright cool in here, ain't it?" he observed, making no mention of the smoky odor.

"Isn't it, though? We haven't had a chance to clean up. It doesn't usually look this way. We left in such a huff, you know," she said, running about and lifting sheets from the furniture. Hawk smiled, again cracking the grim exterior of his face. Women were so silly. "Sit down, if you can find a place."

"I imagine I can."

"Mr. Calvert, Mr. Calvert, come in here and meet Sergeant Hawk," she called to the next room. A slight young man dressed in white shirt and pants sauntered into the living room with his hands in his pockets. "When I told you there were no men around, I didn't think of Mr. Calvert—he's so unhandy, with his hands, I mean. He's not much help around the house either—a bachelor, you know. Are you married, Sergeant Hawk?"

"Glad to meet you, sir," said Hawk, shaking the hand of the civilian. He had a very weak grip. Then hands slipped apart. "No, ma'am, I ain't."

"How do you do, old sport. It sounds like you've given these Nipponese a time of it out there." Calvert smiled amiably enough and replaced his hands in his pockets. The two of them sat down. Calvert crossed his legs.

"Yeah, ain't it the truth."

"You're from New Orleans, aren't you, Sergeant?" Mrs. Jennings said.

"No, ma'am."

"Georgia?"

"No, ma'am."

"I thought so. Mr. Calvert is from Boston. That's a long way from Georgia. You two may need me to translate for you. Now, my husband was from Missouri."

"What brings you here, Mr. Calvert?" Hawk asked as Mrs. Jennings left the room to prepare tea.

"I'm afraid I became caught up in things." Calvert forced a rather nerve-wracking laugh. He had a small, thinly boned head, but there was a large nose sticking out of it. The nose tripled in size when he laughed or smiled. "I'm an architect. I just happened to be here when the Japanese invaded. I was working on a project and staying with Major Jennings."

"Architect, huh? You make blueprints for houses and shit like that, huh?"

"Uh—yes, quite so. Primarily, I dealt with commercial properties, most recently with the military. As I said, I just happened to be here..."

"That's right," Mrs. Jennings called from the kitchen. "So was my husband. The dirty things took him prisoner, though. He's either in Cabanatuan or Fort O'Donnell or some other godforsaken place. Not Mr. Calvert, though. He's been here with us for two years. Isn't that right, Mr. Calvert?" She said this accusingly to Calvert, and in a tone that would not allow him to deny it, if such were his intentions.

"Yes, yes indeed." Calvert's smile faded and he looked quietly at the floor.

"My husband was a Marine. A major," Mrs. Jennings chattered on. "I suppose they had to take him. They probably considered him dangerous. But they took several American engineers, too. All civilians. They were men, of course. Not Mr. Calvert, though. He's been with us for two years." Hawk smiled at Calvert, but the young man didn't see it. Had he seen it, he might have liked the sergeant better. "No, not Mr. Calvert," repeated Mrs. Jennings, bringing the steaming tea into the living room. Hawk thanked her.

Calvert remained silent. The menacing, inhuman presence of Hawk intimidated him. He had been through things Calvert had not. The grim Marine continued to answer all of Mrs. Jennings' questions with short sentences when a single word wouldn't do. There were an endless number of things to talk about, but Calvert couldn't think of a single thing to say to the Marine.

The screen door creaked open. "Well, who is our visitor?" A young woman entered the room.

"Amelia, this is Sergeant Hawk. He's in the Marine Corps," Mrs. Jennings proudly informed her.

"How *do* you do, Sergeant." The young lady held out her hand and Hawk stood and took it between his thumb and fingers. She turned and saw Calvert sitting almost behind the door. "Why, Daniel, I didn't see you back there, sitting so quietly."

"You may have mistaken me for a Jap. Your mother has been painting me a yellow color all morning."

Amelia laughed. "Mother, have you been at it again?"

"Oh, Mr. Calvert's so sensitive." Mrs. Jennings laughed nervously and put her hands on her knees.

The young woman turned back to Hawk, who still held her hand. His parched eyes drank in her beauty. She had a smooth white face with a complexion that fairly shone. Her large, long-lashed eyes were luminous green. Auburn hair the color of new copper fell to her shoulders.

"I must say that you boys are doing a splendid job, Sergeant. It took you a while to get here but, when you did, you didn't waste any time. I never thought things would return to normal. You must have had a terrible time. The Japs are such brutes." She took her hand away and walked lightly across the room to stand beside her mother. Hawk stood gazing at her.

"Yes, Miss, we did, for a while." Hawk sighed deeply. "Well, I guess I better be gettin' on back out there. I think there's probably a lieutenant lookin' for me right now." He stood and gulped his boiling tea, then took two heavy steps toward the door, shaking the whole house.

"You come back this evening, Sergeant. I want to give you some information about Major Jennings. You may run into him later on," Mrs. Jennings said, jumping to her feet.

"I doubt we'll be in the Philippines much longer, ma'am, the way things is goin'. But I'll drop by if I'm still around," Hawk assured her. They heard the porch steps complain as he stepped off them.

"Wasn't he a handsome young fellow?" Mrs. Jennings asked Amelia.

"Yes. He didn't have much to say."

"Probably shy. Shy and quiet, with a prominent bone structure. Very handsome," the perky mother said to herself as she returned to the kitchen.

"Yes, bony and quiet, like a skull, don't you think?" Calvert quipped.

Amelia laughed and put a hand on his shoulder.

* * *

THAT EVENING, Sgt. Hawk returned to the Jennings residence. Mrs. Jennings wasn't there. She had been asked to go down to the beachhead with several American intelligence officers. They wanted to find out what she had learned of the Japanese over the last two years. Mr. Calvert felt poorly. He was in his room with a touch of his old malaria. Hawk thanked Amelia for this information and turned to go. Then a sudden cloudburst swooped down on the jungle with all the unleashed fury of an artillery barrage. Water poured from the corrugated roof of the house. A glassy beaded curtain of dripping rain hung along the edge of the porch. The Marine slouched solemnly on the steps and watched the palm trees bend back and forth under the force of the gale. Amelia Jennings insisted that he wait out the storm on her front porch.

"Yes, ma'am, that's kinda what I had in mind," he said. She brought him a cup of coffee as he waited in the porch swing. The falling of individual raindrops was no longer distinguishable on the tin roof of the porch. A uniform clanging roar was broadcast from above as the peaceful gloom of the late afternoon changed into a threatening black night. Amelia carried a radio out onto the porch. It was too heavy for her, but she had already set it down before Hawk noticed what she was doing.

"I hope you don't mind my visiting with you," she said. Her voice was somewhat muted by the noise. "This thing is supposed to be working again."

"Oh, no, ma'am," Hawk said politely. He supposed she wanted to be friendly, and he was grateful for that. He knew it wouldn't be proper for her to invite him inside, and the family seemed very proper.

She sat down on the porch swing within three feet of him. Hawk shifted uneasily. He hadn't had a bath in several days and he had been wallowing in every variety of filth. The girl didn't seem to notice as she fiddled with the dials on the radio. She was trying to get the channel with the Voice of America. Hawk could only see the glowing orange tubes in the back of the set from where he sat. They cast a dim, fiery glow on the underside of the tin roof.

"Mother may not be back tonight. She so wanted to see you again," she said distractedly. Finally the proper station was located and they listened silently to General MacArthur's "I shall return" and "I have returned" speeches. This was followed by an incomprehensible weather report. Hawk turned the set around to face himself.

"Tokyo Rose has probably got a better program," he said, twisting the dials. He didn't much care for radios, or entertainment of any sort, but he wasn't going to listen any longer to the weather report.

"I know," she laughed, "but I was afraid it might offend you. She's very funny."

"Nah, I'm pretty tough to offend." They leaned closer to one another and their hands almost touched. Hawk glanced over at her eyes, huge and glowing in the dark. His stomach sank for a moment. "Sure is coming down," he said. "I guess you're used to it."

"Yes, it's that time of the year." Her voice was small and hollow against the thunder.

"So your Dad's up in Luzon somewhere?" Hawk felt awkward. Spray from the splashing drainage was slowly saturating his sleeve. He was sitting closer to the outer edge of the porch than comfort allowed, but he didn't mention it. They remained at opposite ends of the porch swing.

"Yes. They were kind enough to let the Red Cross deliver a letter from him last year. Let me get it for you." She got the letter and, with perhaps a little too much expression, read it to the sergeant. It described conditions in the camp where Jennings was being held. The men were given no drinking water. The floor of their prison was of concrete and it sloped into a drainage ditch along the back wall. The Japanese threw buckets of water into the cell to wash the excrement from the floor. If the men wanted a drink they had to dip their hands into the ditch immediately after the floor was washed. If they didn't act fast enough, the filthy water drained off, and they ran the risk of a horrible, thirsting death. Most of them were wasting away with typhoid, malnutrition, dysentery and malaria. She put the letter down.

"They're demons. First to do such things, then to permit a man to tell his family of it. They're *fiends*." Hawk held his helmet in his hands. He studied the stitching of its canvas cover.

"Well...Japs figure it's a disgrace to surrender. They figure you get what you deserve," he said quietly. Very little shocked Sergeant Hawk. He had seen men on both sides do unthinkable things. He had even done a few himself. Still, it was the girl's father; she had a right to be outraged.

"I hope he survives," she sighed at last. "Perhaps you'll be among the men to liberate him."

"Yeah, I'd like that."

"You're a lot like him. It must be the Marine Corps training. You're both strong and quiet."

"Yes, ma'am—or just tired all the time."

"Were you over here when the Japs took the Philippines?"

"No, ma'am."

"I'll bet you were at Guadalcanal?"

"Yes, ma'am."

"We cheered you, you know. I think the whole world did." She laughed sadly. Tears were falling from her eyes. "We cheered you like kids at a football game." He cleared his throat and continued to study the intricacies of his helmet. "They said that they had you surrounded, completely cut off?"

"They was tellin' the truth about that. I was in the Raiders then. The Marines was cut off from the Navy, and we was cut off from even the Marines. Them Raiders—they was some good ol boys." His deep voice sliced through the clatter of the rain on the roof. He couldn't begin to tell her of it, so he didn't try. It all sounded different now that the danger had passed; it didn't sound as if it had been that bad, but it had.

"When we quit hearing about Guadalcanal, we knew that you must have won. We knew that someday you would come back here." She turned the volume up on the radio. They were playing an American torch song. Hawk listened sadly to the plaintive cries of the female singer. The music was supposed to make you sad.

"Oh, the dirty bastards. I hope you've killed some of them?"

"My share, I guess," he answered, with a mixture of shame and modesty.

"I'm glad. You must think that I'm terrible talking this way. I wish Mother was here. We could all have a normal, pleasant conversation."

"We're doin' all right. I reckon I'd rather talk to a pretty girl any day. It wouldn't matter what she had to say."

"How nice of you to say that." She smiled. "Mother likes you very much. She misses Father so. When you walked in this morning it was as if he had come home."

The poor bastard won't be coming back, Hawk said to himself. Mrs. Jennings wasn't even kidding herself.

Hawk suddenly felt Amelia's hand touch his. He managed to appear to not be startled. She gripped it firmly. "Thank God you're here now. It's been a nightmare."

He didn't try to hold her hand. "Them Japs are pretty ornery, I guess."

"They were courteous—to us. I can't complain. It was just the whole oppressive situation. If it hadn't been for Mother and Daniel, I'm sure I would have gone crazy."

"Yeah. I hope he's feelin' better. That malaria can sure take the starch out of you."

She continued to cry softly, drying her eyes with her

handkerchief. Hawk tightened his lower lip against his upper teeth and slid hesitantly toward her. He carefully lifted his arm around her and rested his hand on her shoulder.

"I think it'll be better from now on," he said.

"Mother says that Daniel *always* has something. If it's not malaria, it's his back, or this or that. But he's really very charming. He's very witty, didn't you think?"

"Sure, he's a real cut-up."

"She's so mean to him. I wish she wouldn't be that way. She hates him because they took Father and left him."

"Yeah, probably."

Amelia looked over at Hawk. She seemed to notice for the first time that he was sitting next to her and that his arm was around her. He looked down into her deep velvet green eyes.

Her wide little mouth twitched and she whispered, "Has anyone ever told you that you have pretty eyes, Sergeant?"

"Not lately."

"Well...you do. My, I have gone on, haven't I?" She sat back against his arm with a new control over herself. The song on the radio ended. The mood was broken. Hawk leaned away from her. "Yes, I hope poor Daniel gets over it. They say it stays with you forever. That's what I've heard. We're going to be married, did you know?"

3

THE NEXT DAY, HAWK WAS CALLED TO A MEETING OF THE
platoon leaders. The Marines were getting back into it.
They were to push eastward and clear the forests of the
fanatical defenders who had resisted all attempts to
destroy them. He spoke briefly with Lieutenant Jackson.
The departure was to be the following morning. Hawk
was appointed platoon sergeant. He led two squads
down the main road through Liloila and brought them
together with his old squad. Canlon was made acting
squad leader of the old squad. A man named Pidge
Shaeffer was made corporal. These promotions never
became permanent.

Amelia Jennings recognized the slouching swagger
of a Marine walking away from her. He was far ahead of
her on the muddy street, but he was easily identified by
the vicious aura that surrounded him. Sergeant Hawk
stood out even in this congregation of killers.

"Sergeant Hawk!" she called, and ran toward him.
He turned and watched her knock-kneed approach.

Women—they even ran funny. She had a huge, floppy hat on her head.

"I knew that was you," she gasped as she caught up with him. "How do you like my new hat? A flirty Army captain gave it to me. It came from Brisbane. It's pretty, isn't it?"

"Yeah. Damn sure is."

"It makes me look like Barbara Stanwyck, doesn't it?"

"Naw—more like Loretta Young."

"Oh, Loretta Young." She bent her hand at the wrist. "What do you know about Loretta Young?"

"What do you mean, what do I know? I met her one time at the Hollywood Canteen. Me and ten thousand other jerks."

"You *met* Loretta Young? What did she say? What did she look like?"

"I told you. She looked like you. I couldn't hear much of what she said on account of all the racket." She took hold of his sleeve with two fingers and made him stop walking.

"I've been thinking—you should come by our house again. Come by often. What else is there to do around here? We should get to know each other."

"That'd be nice. 'Fraid we're headin' out tomorrow, though. Probably won't be back." It was Hawk's luck. Females were in short supply in the South Pacific, and usually they were surrounded by officers ready to defend their honor against such lowborn creatures as enlisted men. He accepted disappointment as an inevitability, however; it didn't really bother him.

"Oh?" Her long lashes covered her eyes as she looked down. Her wide little mouth drooped at the corners. "Oh, I didn't know. That captain said that you Marines would just be sitting around for a while, and I thought..."

"Don't pay no attention to no fella in the Army. They're all full of...baloney." He read the hurt in her face. "But I don't know—hell, we'll probably be back."

"Yes, I hope so. I...well, I thought you would be here a while. Will you write, then?"

"Sure." Hawk had never written a letter in his life.

"I'll write to you, too." He looked down at the road, and then at her.

"I thought you was gettin' married, kid?" he said in a low voice.

"Not for a while. We haven't set a date. Not until the war's over. Maybe we won't even get married. Poor Daniel."

"Yeah, well...y'all take care of yourselves."

"James?" She jumped up on her toes like a ballerina and kissed him on the cheek. "You will write, now?"

* * *

THE NEXT DAY the townspeople were out early, waving homemade American flags. Hawk marched his squad by the Jenningses' house. He stood on the ground below the porch as his men filed by. How all-American they all looked, Mrs. Jennings commented—boyish Pidge Shaeffer, gangly Chuck Lasker, dopey Joe Canlon. Other happy Americans were on the porch with the Jenningses. They cheered Sergeant Hawk as if he were some witless quarterback skipping off to the big game, instead of a kill-crazed, hate-maddened combat Marine on his way to almost certain destruction. But he liked them. He didn't mind fighting for them. He had never once regretted volunteering for his vocation.

"Give them hell, old boy!" Calvert shouted.

"Write to me!" Amelia called.

"Yes, yes, do write to us," said Calvert.

"Be careful!" Mrs. Jennings squealed. "Watch out for the sneaky little devils!"

Within a few hours, the men had stepped off into that horrifying abyss known as the combat zone. It was quiet at first, like it always was—at first. They were several miles east of Liloila when it happened. Night had already fallen.

No one you talked to could explain it. It was just one of those shockingly sudden things that happens sometimes. By the time the next morning arrived, the American forces had been driven back to the beach, overwhelmed by a massive Japanese counterattack. They backed through the forest, trying desperately to cover their retreat. They took enormous losses in the treacherous swamps and tangled jungles. Colonel Heller, when he first realized what was going on, ordered the Marines to stand their ground—to show the Army how it was done.

They held out a bit longer than the Army, all right. In an hour's time, an entire Marine battalion literally disappeared, chewed to pieces. Colonel Heller was confident, however, that *his* midnight stand broke the strength of the Japanese attack. Whatever happened, Hawk's decimated platoon lay entrenched six hundred yards from the Pacific Ocean when dawn hit the treetops. Liloila was again seven miles behind Japanese lines. No civilians had been evacuated. Sergeant Hawk didn't know this at the time; he found out later in the day.

General Kravanart was in charge of the invasion of Lamare, commanding both Marine and Army troops. Colonel Heller, the ranking Marine commander, was furious about the counterattack. He let it be known that this would never have occurred if Lamare had been a Marine operation. His outspoken opinions did not endear him to Kravanart. The general was beginning to hate the Marine Corps more than he hated the Japanese.

Fortunately, the General's headquarters were located right on the beach. The lightning counterattack did not reach him. There would be no need to move his little portable building and, in fact, there wasn't any place to move it where it would be farther from the front. He spent the harrowing night aboard ship, just in case his troops were driven into the sea. He was pretty upset the morning after the attack; some fools had taken his generator during his absence, to provide lighting for the hospital tent. He was without his air conditioner. You just couldn't function in this sweltering heat without an air conditioner—it was ridiculous. He vowed to remedy the situation, but he forgot the vow after a midday mortar barrage, and once again retired to the safety of the ships.

The Japanese had spent every ounce of their strength in the counterattack. It was a tremendous success, but it fell just short of being a brilliant victory. The Americans had not been driven into the sea. They had a foothold and were still fighting back. The enemy had used up all of their reserves and most of their supplies and their lines were hopelessly thin. The endless flood of GI's and equipment continued to pour out onto the landing beach. By the end of the following day, the weary Japanese had to give up a couple of miles of hard-won territory.

The Marines wanted to capture Liloila. They had been placed in the sector facing the enemy defenses which surrounded the town. The enemy built a formidable line of defense a few miles south of the town. The American lines again crept five, seven, ten miles inland, but they never approached Liloila. The town and the entire eastern edge of the island were being bypassed.

Colonel Heller approached apoplexy in his efforts to get Kravanart to liberate Liloila. The general was adamant: the Army would continue to move forward on all fronts; the Marines would remain stationary and "contain" the enemy in the forests around Liloila. The Army had fairly easy going, because the main concentration of enemy troops was around Liloila and the eastern shores of Lamare. The Marines had easy going, too, because they were not on the attack at all. The problem was that nothing in particular was being accomplished, or, as Colonel Heller put it, "Nobody's getting killed." A week passed.

Sergeant Hawk's platoon was dug into a ridge about three hundred yards from the enemy's Liloila fortifications. A clever individual had named the line of pillboxes, spider traps, and tank ditches the Iron Gopher Line. The Marines could see the heavily dug-in Japanese across a little valley. Hawk was sitting placidly in a machinegun pit, scratching the sand fleas that played across his filth-encrusted body, when Lieutenant Jackson jumped down into the hole.

"It smells terrible in here," Jackson commented.

"Yessir. Water just drained out. Fills up ever' time it rains," said Hawk. His fatigues were already beginning to rot at the stitches.

"I lost three more men in that goddamn mortar barrage this morning." Jackson threw his helmet into the mud floor and it hit with a splat. "I can't understand why we're just sitting here. I want to get out there and get some Japs."

Hawk looked up at him from beneath his brooding brow. "We'll get some. We can't take the Iron Gopher ourselves, Lieutenant. We gotta have the Army in here. The Japs could roll right over us if they took a notion. They got a lotta shit out there."

"I know, I know. But just *sitting* here—it doesn't make sense."

"Yessir. I gotta admit, it's mighty peculiar."

"It's the Army. It's General Kravanart. He *wants* us stuck here doing nothing. He wants the Japs to snipe us and shell us till there's nothing left. Then he can send in the Army and say the Marines couldn't hack it."

Hawk snorted. "Ever'body knows better than that. Nobody's that goddamn stupid. The Marines can do anything, if you let 'em. Maybe he's got a plan. Who knows?"

"No, he's just being an asshole. The infantry is ahead of us by at least seven miles all along the front lines. He wants us to die here."

"We ain't dyin'. He'll probably move us out real sudden-like."

"I wish he would." Jackson's young, naive eyes lit up. Sweat poured from his forehead. The temperature in the hole was over a hundred and five.

* * *

ANOTHER WEEK PASSED. The situation evolved from the unusual to the incredible. The Army's front line was fifteen miles ahead of the Marines. Jackson attempted to trace the rationale behind this mystery. The explanation all led to one source, one man: General Kravanart. And he wasn't saying much about it other than that things were going well and according to plan.

Three weeks after the counterattack, the Marines were still in the same positions. Light daily casualties drained them. The heat and disease weeded out those less than fit. The remaining men, the fittest, grew thin, bearded, and dirty, and continued rapidly to weaken and deteriorate. Men deteriorate physically much the same as an inanimate object does. The rain rots their unshingled roofs, the sun buckles their unpainted sides, and the moving earth eventually cracks their very foundations.

Sergeant Hawk grew angry. He didn't mind occasional casualties or the eternal sitting in one place. He had put up with that before. He didn't even mind eating the captured enemy rice and fish heads. He had done that before, too. But Liloila contained American civilians. They could have been rescued within one or two days of the counterattack. By now, they had probably been hauled off to an internment camp—if they were still alive.

He began thinking of Amelia Jennings: the smoky fragrance of her front porch, the rainy night on the swing, the way she held her knees together as she sat there and the way she looked at him when he had told her he was leaving. He was anxious to get back to

Liloila. He spat out his last plug of chewing tobacco. That's what you get for being a no-account sergeant, he told himself. You can't run your own life; you have to wait on some jackass to tell you what to do. On that day, he first subconsciously decided to use any excuse to find the girl.

He stood up and peered from beneath the coconut-log roof of the machine-gun pit. The rising sun was slowly raking the valley treetops with yellow streaks. He sensed it before he really saw anything; the Iron Gopher Line was vacant. He cranked the field telephone. Lieutenant Jackson was at his side in a few minutes.

"Well, god damn," Jackson kept saying. He swept the empty line with his field glasses. "Let's take 'em, Hawk. Let's move the platoon up there."

"Sir...Colonel Heller might oughta be contacted— and the general," Hawk added reluctantly. Then he smiled at Jackson and said, "Or at least the skipper."

Jackson smiled back at him. Of course, he'd tell the captain; somebody to dump the responsibility on. "Why, hell yes, I'll tell the captain," he laughed. "That's proper procedure, isn't it? Get me the company commander."

He was willing. But Jackson didn't get to be the first to move into the Iron Gopher. Other units in another company had noticed that it was vacant. Colonel Heller had been notified. General Kravanart was kept in the dark, lest he spoil the party. Heller gave the order to move in. He set a dangerous precedent by doing this. The remainder of the campaign was to be plagued by serious breaches of discipline and blatant flaunting of authority.

The Marines crossed the Iron Gopher and kept

going. They were amazed at the extent of the underground fortifications they found there. What was even more amazing was why anyone would give them up. The Marines went perhaps a mile beyond the Iron Gopher, meeting no resistance. Heller set up the order to halt the advance and dig in.

The Marines went mad with rage. This was a war in which winning ground won battles and winning battles ended the war and sent you home. Everyone knew that Kravanart must have finally heard about the advance and thrown a monkey wrench into the operation. Hawk ended up on a ridge much like the one that he had just spent three weeks on. The Japanese leisurely set up a line of defenses in front of him, across a valley that looked much like the first. The defenses became known as the Little Gopher Line, and the stalemate continued for another three days. Jackson swore he would write to Roosevelt and have Kravanart's stars.

Dysentery, malaria, and typhus became tougher to deal with. The heat got to one or two men every day in spite of the lack of activity. One day Jackson came to Hawk's trench. His eyes were wide and the skin was stretched tightly over his cheekbones.

"The skipper says we're going up to the Little Gopher," he gasped. "I...I don't think he got the go-ahead. I think he decided to do it on his own. What do we do?"

"We'll need artillery," Hawk growled. He was sitting motionless in the dark hole like a bloodless slug.

"He says he can get it. He thinks Heller will back him once we start moving. He's got the support of every rifle and weapons platoon in the company. He said the major over in F company is in on it, too." Jackson caught his breath and slumped against the side of the hole. "You know damn good and well that we can take the town."

Hawk's face showed no expression. "Then let's do it," he said. He had never been in a situation like this before. A war that nobody was trying to win, he thought; how ridiculous can you get? He called Pidge Shaeffer up from the line.

Shaeffer was in his mid-twenties but he could have passed for sixteen. He had red lips, large darting eyes, and a beardless face. He was a wiry man with quick reflexes and the temperament of a trampled cobra. He was also the best scout in the company.

"Pidge, we're talkin' about a push." Hawk didn't look at him as he spoke. He looked out over the Little Gopher Line. "Think you could get on down to the Jap lines for a look-see?" Shaeffer grunted. "We don't need no complicated recon, I'd just like somebody to check it out before we go wadin' into something." Shaeffer nodded. The sergeant knew Shaeffer was a perfection-ist. He would do a good job regardless of how little or how much was asked of him. "You want anybody to go with you?"

Pidge shrugged.

"Okay, get back here pretty quick." Shaeffer bobbed his helmet and hitched his Reising submachine gun across his shoulder. Most of these weapons had been thrown away or recalled years before. Pidge clung to his.

Jackson saw the young scout snake down the ridge on his way to the enemy. "Where's that man going?" he asked Hawk.

"Recon, sir."

"He'll give the attack away."

"The artillery will do that anyway, sir," said Hawk.

"There won't be any pre-attack artillery, Sergeant."

Hawk shifted his eyes toward the lieutenant. "Does that mean there ain't gonna *be* any artillery, sir?"

"Possibly. I don't know." Jackson shrugged impatiently. "You know the situation, Sergeant. I've told you everything I know about it."

"Yessir."

That might have been considered an invitation, or at least an opportunity, to withdraw from the upcoming insubordination. Hawk didn't recognize it as such. If he had, he still wouldn't have done any of it differently.

The attack was set for 0630. Shaeffer was back by 0400. He and Hawk puzzled over a map. They were at the bottom of a slit trench with a poncho over them to cover the light of a kerosene lantern. Little clumps of mud were smeared on the plastic coating of the map.

"Son of a bitches are all over here," Shaeffer indicated. "Here they got a half-dozen machine guns. Back here is a row of five or six mortars, little ones, fifty millimeters."

Hawk studied the map. He climbed out of the trench and crawled over to Jackson. "Looks pretty rough up there, sir," he reported.

"What did you find out?"

Hawk showed him the map.

"Maybe our platoon can spearhead the attack. We know what to expect. If we hit a soft spot, we might be able to get behind some of this shit."

"Where?" Hawk pointed to a concentration of rifle pits in front of the mortars.

"If we can get through there, we can knock out them

mortars and roll up the flanks on the machine guns," said the sergeant.

"That's a damn good idea. Maybe a squad could do it." Jackson stood up straight, filled with enthusiasm.

The sergeant had seen good ideas get a lot of men killed. "Well, there's no need in gettin' carried away, sir."

"Get me six men with rifle grenades. I don't even need a squad. I'm going in there in thirty minutes."

Hawk ran his finger up and down his nose. "Uh...I don't want to tell you your business, sir...but a section..."

"Then don't. You'll stay here. I don't want you second-guessing me in a combat situation."

Hawk didn't answer him.

Jackson knocked out the mortars a half-hour before 0630. Some time after that he took care of most of the machine guns. Neither he nor his six men were ever seen or heard from again. Sergeant Hawk was the officer's only heir, and his estate consisted of first platoon, Dog Company. The sergeant had to lead the unauthorized attack on the Little Gopher. His men faced the weakest part of the enemy defenses; they could break through and save countless Marine lives. The Japanese were caught off guard. They had no artillery, no mortars, and, in one sector, no machine guns.

Hawk led his men through the furious rifle fire to the position Jackson had assaulted earlier. The Japanese retreated and let him have the indefensible sector. First platoon mounted the Little Gopher fortifications without a single friendly fatality. Elsewhere, the attack was not so easy. Machine guns caused a fifty percent casualty rate over in F Company.

The starving, numerically overestimated Japanese fell back from the Little Gopher rapidly. They dispersed throughout the eastern jungles, maintaining no definite line of defense. Hawk didn't stop at the Little Gopher. He led the platoon into the jungle. Three men disappeared and three more were killed. A sniper got one of the old squad members through the head. A trip wire and a tape measure mine got the other two. They were flankers, so no one else was near them, or the casualties would have been greater.

Ignoring these setbacks, the sergeant pressed on, closing the gap between the American lines and Liloila. He knew that he had led his men dangerously far ahead of the other attackers, but he refused to stop until something forced him to.

They ran into a group of Japanese along a little stream. The enemy was of something less than platoon strength. They were probably originally from a labor battalion of some sort, for they put up a weak showing. They launched a poorly conceived attack. Shaeffer was at the point. He warned the marines, but there was no time to do much in the way of preparations. A gang of bullet-shaped helmets came sliding quickly and quietly from the woods across the stream, materializing from nowhere, like disembodied spirits.

Someone shouted, "Hit the deck!" And then it was on. The Marines threw themselves down. The Japanese splashed into the green water of the shallow stream, keeping their knees high as they ran. After the first American shot was fired they opened up. The exploding shots seemed much louder than they should have because of the dense, cramped jungle. It kept a lid on the noise, causing it to reverberate in the ears of the combatants.

Hawk was among the men closest to the stream. As

he lay in the sandy soil, he heard bullets that sounded like arrows swishing inches above his helmet. The men in the alien uniforms with their wildly gyrating limbs seemed to be upon him. He shuddered reflexively and brought a knee up under himself. Without thinking, he jerked the trigger of the Thompson. The flickering muzzle flash lit his face beneath the dark shadow of his helmet. The nearest attacker threw both arms behind his back, clapped his hands behind himself, and tumbled into the slimy water. His rifle landed on top of him. Hawk picked another target, ignoring the erupting spouts of dirt and lead that encircled him. The muzzle of the submachine gun leapt angrily and two more of the Japanese fell screaming over one another. He looked urgently about the chaotic scene and could find no other targets. The Marines were tired, too tired to be afraid. They had taken on the enemy with a passion, unleashing all their pent-up frustration. No prisoners were taken. No one asked to be taken prisoner. Shaeffer was already going from one wounded man to the next, carefully laying his gun muzzle against the sides of their heads. Hawk got to his feet.

"Look! Look here, men." Chuck Lasker and Joe Canlon were on the other side of the stream. Lasker was holding something shiny over his head and shouting.

"Get down, stupid," the sergeant shouted back at them. They ignored the rumbling exhortation. The rest of the Marines converged cautiously on Lasker. Hawk finally did the same.

"Look at all this shit!" Canlon cried. Hawk looked around the sandy river bank. It was literally paved with stacks of U.S. supplies: C rations, K rations, ten-in-one, cans of gasoline, crates of guns and ammunition, medical supplies—everything, including rifle grease. Shaeffer kicked a dead body off one of the crates.

"No wonder we been eatin' fish heads and maggots. The goddamn Japs been gettin' all the good stuff," Canlon bellowed. The cans, crates, and boxes stretched endlessly into the forest. They had to have been hand-carried to the spot, and that would have taken weeks.

"And look at this," Lasker added. There in a hand-cart were several bars of what appeared to be gold, shimmering orange in the gloomy light of the jungle. "We got us some rich Japs," Lasker laughed, exposing a jagged row of teeth.

"Rich Marines, now," Canlon corrected him.

"Hey, look, I'm a second lieutenant." A man named Pacht was balancing a gold bar on each shoulder. "What the hell is this doing here, Sergeant Hawk?"

Hawk rocked back his helmet. He couldn't answer that one. The supplies had probably been captured by the Japanese during their counterattack. But, if that were the case, why were the troops they'd encountered on the Little Gopher so grossly underfed? The gold? There was no explanation for that; maybe it was the Japanese payroll. The sergeant offered no theories about any of it. He merely advised the men to beware of booby traps.

After a few minutes, he roared, "Awright, you son of a bitches, let's get goin'."

"What about all this shit?" Canlon asked.

"Leave it. We're movin' up onto that range while we're still in one piece. You goddamn bastards go crazy when you see a can of beans. One grenade could wipe out the whole sorry bunch of you."

Canlon looked up at the low range of hills that

poked just above the treetops. "You, too, Hawk," he mumbled. The men grabbed as many cans of rations as they could carry. Hawk gathered all the gold bars together and replaced them in the handcart. He sat on the little wheelbarrow, preventing anyone from succumbing to any further temptations. He was concerned that the skirmish might bring more of the enemy down on the platoon.

He led the men up to the high ground and had them safely dug in by nightfall. Communications men from battalion came up the hill after dark, stringing wire. Telephones were hooked up to the battalion CP. Hawk found that he was far beyond the other Marine units. Later that night, other platoons from his company occupied the hills on each side of him.

Throughout the night, the word "gold" rose above the sweating trenches like a recurring asthmatic cough. Hawk turned the ingots over to a lieutenant in the company and the officer had them brought up onto the range.

It was also learned that night that General Kravanart was very unhappy about the Marine attack. The maneuver had been a complete success and Liloila was no more than three miles away. But Kravanart was more than unhappy; he was outraged. That wasn't Hawk's problem, for now, anyway. He glared at the steaming black swamps below him. His only problem was staying alive.

4

A RIFLE COMPANY IS WHERE THE DIRTIER ASPECTS OF A war are actually fought. When men join up to fight a war, or when they finally run out of places to hide and are drafted, they try to get into any other available outfit. This gives them a self-respect of having served their country, and it also prolongs their life span. The wretchedness of warfare will most assuredly come in shorter and less lethal doses in any other job category. The foolhardy who intentionally request placement in a rifle platoon—and there is always room for them— usually regret their choice within the first few seconds in the field, and all their efforts then turn to the problem of getting out of it.

Sergeant Hawk loved it. He had the backbone, the nervous system, the temperament, and the hormones for the job. He had nothing against lesser men who couldn't do it; he felt obligated to do it for them.

So it was that he volunteered to head up the perimeter that was to guard the base of Hill 309 that night. The company was thrust miles ahead of their own lines, and this perimeter would be thrust far ahead of the company. The remaining majority of Dog Company stayed up on the summit of 309, on one of the adjoining hills, or on 309's reverse slope, where there were sheltering caves.

The night was hideous. Its survivors would dream about it for the next twenty years. Infiltration was heavy. The sly Japanese slithered about the Marine positions, almost at will. The men on the summit could hear gunfire below. In the pale muzzle flashes they could see the thrashing silhouettes in hand-to-hand combat. They could hear the screams of souls being squeezed out of throats. The men below took on a supernatural quality: the demons, and the gods fighting them. Only a supernatural creature could stay down there. Occasional infiltrators made it to the summit, but how much more horrid must it have been down there in the perimeter?

At dawn, Canlon saw Hawk and his three remaining men climb up the slope. Two of the riflemen were badly wounded. Leathery trails hung from Hawk's eyes to his cheekbones. He was covered with dried blood.

"Rough night," he said to Canlon.

* * *

GENERAL KRAVANART CALLED two majors in to help him move his desk. It was beneath the air conditioner and the cold air was giving him a pain in the neck. A lieutenant colonel came in with a message that would give him an even larger pain.

"Marine units have crossed the Little Gopher Line and established positions on Hills 309, 274, and 237, sir," the colonel informed him. Major Clements, the General's balding chief aide, winced in horror. He could only imagine the extent of the tirade that was to come. But Kravanart sat down behind his newly transplanted desk. His face turned a sickly white. He didn't say anything to the colonel except ,"Carry on."

"They've violated direct orders." Major Clements broke the strange silence in the two-room shack. He wanted it known that he had passed the order along— it wasn't *his* fault. "I'll bet Colonel Heller is at the bottom of this, sir." Kravanart continued to stare at the far wall without blinking. His air conditioner hummed in the background. He drew himself up with a deep breath.

"I want to know precisely which units are on that range, Major Clements—and, to the extent possible, which men. I want no other units, Marine or otherwise, to enter the area. There will be no evacuation of any wounded. See if you can make telephone or radio contact with those criminals."

Within a quarter of an hour, Clements had all the answers for him. Companies D and F had attacked the Little Gopher Line. Company F had been virtually destroyed and assimilated by Company D. Company D had proceeded beyond the line, where they contacted the enemy.

"Contacted the enemy?" Kravanart interrupted.

"Yes, sir. They overran several enemy units near the Hazard River." Clements continued, "First Platoon, under a Sergeant Hawk, is on 309; Second Platoon, under Lieutenant Rutledge, is on 274; and Third Platoon, under Lieutenant Williams, is on 237." Clements looked up from his report. "They're requesting relief, sir."

"I'll just bet they are," Kravanart spat out. "There won't be any, though."

The general was younger than Clements. The major didn't approve of much of what Kravanart did, and Kravanart knew it, but the general seemed to enjoy this unpleasant relationship. Clements never voiced his opinions and Kravanart never asked for them. The general sat glaring triumphantly at Clements, his black hair and moustache shining under the bright office light. Outside, it was dark.

"They can just die out there," Kravanart replied to Clements' unspoken thoughts.

"We have Lieutenant Williams on the phone, sir. Would you care to speak with him? The Japs will probably cut the lines tonight. It may be your last opportunity, sir."

"Very well."

Clements handed him the phone. The general's questions were fast and furious, the answers weary and clipped. Who gave the order to attack? The skipper. Where is the skipper? Dead. Exactly what sort of resistance did you meet in the territory between the Little Gopher and your present position? Light. Has *anyone* been in contact with Colonel Heller? No. You did this thing on your own, then; you went against orders? Yes. You don't expect us to bail you out, do you? Yes.

"Well, we're not going to. You're on your own, Lieutenant, just like when you attacked the Little Gopher Line!" Kravanart shouted into the telephone. A few moments of silence followed.

"Sergeant Hawk found a cache of Jap supplies, sir." The lieutenant's wavering voice crackled over the wire.

"Hawk?" Kravanart wrote the name down.

"Yeah, Hawk. They were really *our* supplies. I guess the Japs captured them."

"That's yes, *sir,* and captured them, *sir,*" Kravanart roared into the phone with all of the anger of his authority.

"Yeah. And we found some shit that looks like it might be gold," said the lieutenant. Kravanart sat there staring at his desk top. Clements watched his face; it seemed to change somehow.

"Oh, really?"

"Yeah. Hawk found it."

"What's that man's full name?"

"Uh...James Hawk, five-striper, I think. He's leading First Platoon now."

"On 309?"

"Yeah."

Kravanart handed the phone back to Clements. The general stood and paced back and forth between the two rooms.

"Tomorrow I want air reconnaissance to see what those boys on 309 are up against," Kravanart said at last.

Clements reminded him that there were Marines stretched out along the entire range of hills, not just 309.

"Check the whole area, of course, Major. Do I have to spell it all out for you?" the general sneered.

At 0530 he had the report. Heavy concentrations of Japanese were in the swamps below the range of hills, including armor and heavy artillery. There were no fixed lines established as of yet. The recurring word in the report was "heavy".

"It would be easy for the Japs to overrun those Marine boys, Major," Kravanart said after reading the report.

"It's a certainty, General."

"Well, I won't have it. Not after all they've been through. Let's get some artillery trained on those swamps. We'll give those Nips something to think about."

Clements smiled. The cavalry to the rescue. "Yes, sir." He saluted and went outside and over to the staff tent, greatly relieved. Overnight, Kravanart had had a change of heart. They might even be able to salvage the beleaguered company. He called Lieutenant Williams and asked him to appoint a forward artillery observer.

Williams' gratitude at the unexpected relief was evident in his voice. He reeled off a few range-finding coordinates himself, and ended with, "I appreciate this. I'll never forget it." And he didn't—he died that very day.

The sky thundered with the American barrage. Dog Company watched the shelling from the safe haven of 309. From the summit they could see huge black fists crush the delicate palm trees. After each hit, white smoke filtered up through the wreckage of their trunks and leaves. Balloons of flaming orange rose over the explosions like ascending spirits. They hung in the air for a moment and disappeared into wisps of black smoke. The mortars of the Marine weapons platoon lent their support to the holocaust.

The general ordered the fire to be walked in toward 309, lest the enemy be driven upon the Marines. The closer to 309 it fell the less danger the Marines had of being overrun. The enemy would have to go through the center of the barrage to get to them.

Hawk clenched his teeth as the earth-crunching explosions fell within a thousand yards. The massive

155-millimeter shells sucked tunnels of air behind themselves as they soared overhead. Lieutenant Rutledge sent a runner over to 309. He was becoming concerned about the proximity of the friendly fire.

"The lieutenant says he's consolidatin' second and third platoon into a weapons platoon. They're both gettin' together with Lieutenant Williams over on 274," the runner explained to Hawk. "You're supposed to take your men down on the other side of 309 into the caves. You can wait out the barrage there. He's afraid a short round might clean us out. Second and third are gonna maintain their mortar barrage, and we'll watch for any attack. You guys can lay low for a while."

"We'll be blind down there on the reverse slope," said Hawk.

"Yeah, but I wouldn't argue about it. You'll be safer than we are," the messenger smiled. He was a buck sergeant in his late thirties. Hawk put greater store in his advice because of his age. He didn't like the idea, but he couldn't tell Rutledge. There were enough breaches of discipline already.

"Don't worry, Sarge," said the messenger, "we'll save you a few. We'll let you know if they come up the hill. Leave a man up there if you want." Hawk left a lookout.

Pidge Shaeffer stayed behind. Canlon led First Platoon off the hilltop, far down the safe side of the slope and into the shallow caves. The entrances to the caverns were covered by woody brush. The ground was not rocky this far down, and the loose soil made the interiors of the caves appear to be unsafe.

The shrieking artillery shells were barely clearing the hilltop. They ultimately convinced Hawk that going below wasn't such a bad idea. First Platoon lounged about the fringe-covered mouths of the caves. Morale was higher than it had been since the landing. The Marines had been saved from imminent Japanese encirclement. The enemy was undergoing total annihilation in the swamps on the other side of the range. Hawk felt pretty good himself. The artillery was clearing the way to Liloila. He would soon discover the Jenningses' fate and, with another slight breach of authority, possibly even rescue them. Canlon sat beside Hawk, stretched out in the grass several feet from a cave.

"Pretty noisy," said the corporal. "How'd you like to be on the other end of that?"

"I don't even like this end of it." Hawk had to raise his voice above the annoying assortment of vibrating noises.

"Yeah. Pretty noisy. Look," Canlon's helmet slid to the back of his head as he tilted it back, "that's them egg-crate rockets. They're really layin' it on 'em." He squinted through the treetops. Black streamers hung in the air following the trajectory of each rocket. There were so many of the black tubes arching over the hilltop that they soon began to mesh and darken the whole sky. The rockets pressed heavy layers of stinking smoke downward into the close jungle, where they billowed and spread and refused to evaporate. The egg crates were terrible weapons that fired rockets like a machine gun.

"I mean, they are really pourin' it on them bastards." Canlon shook his head.

Hawk pulled his lower lip between his teeth. "Yeah," he said. The rockets did not have a good range. They had to be launched from somewhere nearby.

"What are we gonna do with all that gold?" Canlon

suddenly asked. He had already decided he was going to live through all of this. "They put it in that cave over there. We oughta grab a few bars for ourselves. I bet there's a few missin' by now."

"Don't lose no sleep over that shit," Hawk advised him. He took off his helmet and turned around to look at the hilltop. It was his barometer of how close the barrage was falling. The black tubes were arching steadily lower and the summit was buried in a choking cloud of smoke. "Something must be goin' on. They're droppin' their fire."

"Nah," Canlon assured him. "I'll get the walkie-talkie for you." Hawk took the receiver and pressed the hot bakelite to his ear. He spoke briefly with Lieutenant Williams.

"Well?" Canlon asked.

"No attack yet," Hawk answered. "Williams says the general is fixin' to drop some fire behind the hills in case the Japs try to circle us."

"Well, goddamn! We're *behind* the goddamn hills." Canlon's interest in the barrage was suddenly renewed.

"No, we ain't. We're *on* the hill. They're gonna shell *behind* it."

"Well we're on the back slope." Canlon stood. "I hope them crazy bastards know what they're doin'. I'm gettin' the men into the caves."

"Awright."

A few minutes later Shaeffer came stumbling down the hillside, his face blackened by smoke. "Shit," he said, "they nearly took my head off."

Rockets began falling behind as well as in front of 309. The men watched solemnly from their caves. It should have been a comforting sight, but being in the center of a barrage is not comforting. There is none of the tranquility there that is reportedly found in the eye of a hurricane. Reason may tell you that those are *your* shells falling, but your ears don't like them any better. Hawk considered the whole maneuver dangerous and more than slightly foolish.

The once-solid earth lost its reliability. It seemed to have springs under it and it bounced with nauseating constancy. The rhythmic regularity of the bouncing was interrupted only by the falling of still larger and closer rounds. He knew it couldn't be true, but it looked to Hawk as if the Army was walking the artillery toward 309. He retreated into a cave.

Smoke gushed through the cave entrance. The men hugged the ground, but it jerked and tore away from them. Explosions flashed outside the narrow cave opening as if a child were flicking an electric light switch on and off.

* * *

"GENERAL, we're running low on 155's. They're bringing in more—there's very few left on the beach," Clements calmly reported.

"Yes, Major, but it's going well. No Japs will get behind those boys."

"No, sir, they won't," Clements laughed. "It's a smart maneuver, that's for sure—but I'll bet you're giving those leathernecks a good scare, too."

Kravanart laughed along with him, enjoying that thought perhaps a little too much. "Probably. But they'll forget all about it when we get them back here and feed them some hot chow."

Clements laughed again—what a great job they were doing.

"Major, I believe we've just about done the trick. Here, take these instructions with these coordinates. Give it everything we've got, everything we can get hold of. That should do the job."

"Yes, sir." He took the piece of paper and walked toward the door. He glanced down at the paper, chuckled to himself, turned around, and returned to the general's desk. "Sir, there's a little mistake here. You almost gave those Marines a *really* good scare. These coordinates *include* Hills 274 and 309."

"What?"

"Yes, sir. See—7-8-0-9-3..."

"Give me that, Clements. That's nonsense!" Kravanart looked at the paper. "Utter nonsense! It may come near the base of the hills, but it most definitely does not include the hills proper. They're safe on 274. The order is correct, Major. Carry on, please." Kravanart shook his head. "I've got so much to do..."

"But...uh...sir, if you'll take a quick look at the overlays..."

"Major Clements, do you realize that, while you dawdle here, you are jeopardizing the lives of every one of those Marines?"

"You're quite right, sir. But let me explain—"

"Do *not* correct me again, Major," said Kravanart, glaring at him.

"No, sir." Clements saluted and went briskly to the door, opened it, and left. His pace slowed on the other side of the door. Why was Kravanart doing this? Did he really think those coordinates were correct? Was he doing it because he didn't like being corrected? And the big question: Would he try to shove responsibility for the mistake off on Clements? Kravanart must know something Clements did not. He must have received further intelligence reports. That was the answer to why he was doing this—and, if it wasn't, Clements *thought* that it was—and that was enough to clear him. He strode cheerfully across the sand. My, but it was a hot day.

* * *

HAWK's first hint that the barrage had walked in a little too close was when the mouth of the cave disappeared in an avalanche of soft, sandy dirt. In the darkness, the men looked at one another, their eyes solid white with fear. Adrenalin had contracted their pupils to pinpoints. Hawk knew that the barrage had walked over him when the roof of the hole fell in. His legs were pinned under a ton of debris.

Like all things, the barrage finally came to an end. Lasker and Shaeffer managed to dig the sergeant out. Dazed, deafened, and with his eyes out of focus, he stumbled out across the smoldering hillside and fell onto the grass. Rivers of sweat cut through the layers of grime on his face. He rolled over on his stomach and lifted his head. The jungle behind 309 was now a flat, smoking desert. Canlon sat him up and handed him a canteen. He could hardly recognize the shattered terrain as being the same he had left an hour before. Canlon was saying something but he couldn't make it out. The corporal pointed to the hilltop.

The conical peak of 309 had been sheared off. The summit was gone, and only a flat table of seething smoke remained. The upper quarter of the hill had been blasted into oblivion. Hawk set the canteen down and stared, dumbfounded, at the spectacle.

"And that's where we was," Canlon shouted. Hawk heard him this time.

"How's 274?" he shouted back.

"There ain't no 274, or 237 either," the corporal answered. "They just plain laid it on us like we was a bunch of goddamn Japs or something. Them guys up there never had a chance."

* * *

"MAJOR CLEMENTS," Kravanart said after the barrage had been lifted, "when those Marines radio in, I want to talk to them personally."

Since Kravanart had said that, Clements couldn't figure out why he seemed so surprised when told that Sergeant Hawk on 309 wanted to talk to him.

Kravanart listened patiently to the stream of obscenities from the Marine non-com. For all Clements could tell from that end of the conversation, Hawk was gratefully thanking Kravanart for the murderous barrage.

"You get back on the summit of 309, Sergeant, and I'll have a relief column on the way. We'll get this thing straightened out." Kravanart signed off.

Hawk did as he was told. Minutes after his conversation with the general, the artillery barrage unexpectedly began again. The shells fell behind 309. The eyes of the Marines opened wider and wider as the shells fell closer and closer. The explosions were climbing the reverse slope of 309 like an angry, hungry giant.

"What the goddamn hell is goin' on?" Canlon asked.

Hawk didn't wait to find out. He led the men at double time over the hill and down the forward slope, past the perimeter of the night before. Swollen bodies still lay around the trenches of the perimeter, some still clutching at the throats of their dead foes. There seemed to be no way out of the trap. The Japanese were in front of them and American artillery was chasing them from behind. But a Marine always has one way out. Hawk led them off 309 and into the swamplands below. He was headed for Liloila.

To his credit, the sergeant tried to do the right thing. .He waited till he was two miles north of 309, in the heart of enemy territory, before he radioed HQ. He was getting gun-shy by that time. He didn't know why, but he had the strangest feeling the Army was trying to exterminate him.

With these suspicions in mind, he reported his position as being half a mile farther south than it really was. Any other right-thinking soldier would assume that two consecutive mistakes had been made by the boys in artillery. But staying alive had become a habit with Hawk; he didn't put much stock in consecutive mistakes. So he was not surprised when, minutes after he radioed in his position, batteries of vicious 7.2-inch rockets lashed and sprouted across the swamp seven hundred yards to the south of the Marines.

"I think they're tryin' to kill us," Canlon mourned.

Hawk ordered complete radio silence. On either side of him, according to the radioman's monitors, were roving bands of disorganized Japanese. He was more concerned about the men firing those rockets finding him than he was about the enemy. He led them northward, hopelessly deeper into Japanese territory. He moved steadily toward Liloila. The swamplands ended and they entered a rocky terrain covered with dense forests.

The men forced themselves to lift one heavy boot over the other. They were well supplied with captured rations but they suffered from the exhaustion of terror. They moved in a widely spaced single file, their faces twisted into the fearful expressions of tortured coyotes.

At the front of the line marched Sergeant Hawk. His expression was that of a betrayed wolf. Somebody would answer for this. Somebody had killed two platoons of American Marines. And it looked intentional. But first, he had business in Liloila. It wouldn't take long.

At some point during this agonizing march, Hawk's brain fell back into place. The shelling had tilted it off its underpinnings. He could see the right half of his body, but his brain kept telling him it wasn't there. His right hand was out there doing things but couldn't control it. Gradually this was wearing off. It took several seconds for his brain to tell his right hand what to do, and it reacted awkwardly for a while, but, eventually, the peculiar affliction went away. To celebrate his recovery he called a break and sat down to think. Shaeffer and Canlon came and sat with him.

"Nothing up ahead," Shaeffer reported. He took off his helmet and fastened its strap to his belt. "It's hotter'n fresh dog shit out there."

Hawk ran his fingers through his sandy hair and sighed. "Scout all the way up to Liloila. We'll be goin' in."

"That's kinda risky, ain't it?" Canlon grunted. "The

Japs are bound to try and hold a damn shittin' town like that. There's plenty of 'em fartin' around out here."

That was when they realized their situation. Hawk said the words the others really should have known already. That didn't make it sound any better.

"There's nowhere else to go."

5

A COUPLE OF THE MEN IN FIRST PLATOON HAD AN IDEA OF a better place to go than Liloila. Private Pacht, a short, thin, lantern-jawed man, wanted to go back for the gold. A direct hit by a 155 had buried it in one of the caves on Hill 309. Pacht, a little bit of a schemer, had just about talked another man, Owens, into going back with him. That was before the rocket barrage. As they moved north, they were again considering it.

"That's deserting," Owens complained every time Pacht came near to persuading him.

"We been disobeying orders ever since we landed on Lamare!" Pacht would always answer. "We might as well get something out of this—besides dead. You'd have to desert anyway to get away with the stuff." Pacht never worked up enough enthusiasm in Owens to get him to go back, and he didn't yet have the nerve to go back all by himself. He didn't mention the gold or his plans to Sergeant Hawk. The sergeant wasn't interested in gold. Pacht often sat, shaking his head, staring back at 309, and muttering to himself, "Goddamn gold's probably up to forty or fifty dollars an ounce."

Sergeant Hawk was more interested in learning why he had been chosen as a bull's eye for U.S. artillery. As he neared Liloila he began to worry about Amelia Jennings. Would she be there, and, if she was, in what condition? If she wasn't, where was she—and was it possible to rescue her?

Gold held no interest for him. Money had lost all meaning once he became embroiled in the war. There was nowhere to spend it, and nothing that it could buy would keep you alive for one second longer. Hoarding money seemed like a silly pastime, from his perspective. He subscribed to the philosophy of Pidge Shaeffer. Whenever anyone mentioned the gold, Shaeffer said, "If you can't eat it, shit on it." Not everyone felt this way, though. Many men had died trying to pick up their few dollars during crap games that had been disturbed by air raids. There were a million ugly ways to die out here, and a million things that could kill you—but money wouldn't be the one that got Sergeant Hawk.

Marisette, the radioman, listened with dread fascination to the ubiquitous Japanese broadcasts being bounced through the forest. He thumbed through his Japanese dictionary but he couldn't get the slightest indication of what they were talking about. Lasker crouched beside him, trying to relieve the mounting tension by talking over the crackling static. Marisette was afraid.

"Listen to them bastards," said Lasker. "They sound like a bunch of parrots. They must be everywhere."

Marisette was shaking. "It's like being in another world. I wish he would let me try to raise headquarters again. We've got to explain things to them. We just can't keep going deeper into Jap country."

"He tried," said Lasker. "Don't worry, Hawk knows his business. Canlon said we might try to get to the ocean and then come up behind our lines. The Army won't let us walk through them, that's for sure."

"You've got to make it clear to them," Marisette insisted. "I think he just wanted a crack at the Japs. The guy's a maniac, I tell you." Marisette looked up. "Planes!" he said. "They've come for us!" He jumped to his feet.

Two Avengers and a Warhawk slid rumbling over the treetops. Everyone scrambled for the forest. Marisette waved and shouted at the banking planes.

"Get outa the trail!" Hawk shouted. "Cut that shit out, you dumb bastard!"

Marisette didn't stop until Hawk grabbed his shoulder and pushed him down. The planes did not return.

"They were our own planes!" Marisette raged at him from his place on the muddy trail. He was crying.

"Them was our own rockets that cooked second and third platoon," Hawk raged back at him.

"So what do we do—join the goddamn Japs?" Marisette jumped angrily to his feet. "You can count me out. You haven't got any right to order us any further. You haven't even got the right to be here."

"I got the right to do whatever I goddamn well please with a piece of shit like you." Hawk took a step toward him and he took two steps back. "Tell me what else you ain't gonna do," he challenged the cowering radioman. He took off his helmet and tossed it into the trail. Marisette continued to back away.

"You're violating orders," Marisette whimpered.

"I'm what? I didn't hear you. I'm what?"

"Nothing. I didn't say anything."

The men looked on solemnly, fearing for Marisette. The sergeant wheeled to face them. "Let me tell you men something. I didn't start this war. I done what I was told when I attacked the Jap lines. Them that told me to do it is dead. If I'd a-stayed on 309 like I was told, I'd be dead." Hawk took a deep breath and lowered his voice. "I don't know what's goin' on. The Army's out to get us for some reason. Maybe the artillery don't know there's Americans out here. We've got to find another way back to our lines, that's all. In the meantime, don't go wavin' your skirts at no kind of goddamn planes."

The forest was quiet. Lookouts faced away from the men at the point, the rear, and the flanks. They ignored the outburst and studied the threatening underbrush. The other men stood still and watched Hawk pick up his helmet and slam it on his head. Marisette sighed.

Marisette couldn't conceive of Americans trying to kill Americans. Hawk didn't try to understand things; he took them at face value and dealt with them. He adapted quickly. Marisette took longer.

* * *

AIR RECONNAISSANCE REPORTED SIGHTING the Marines on the trail leading to Liloila. General Kravanart took the news stoically. In a tone devoid of all emotion, he discussed the matter with Clements. The Marines had violated direct orders and were continuing to do so. Colonel Heller had had nothing to do with it; there were no mitigating circumstances. Sergeant Hawk must be dealt with quickly and severely. Kravanart called for a dozen of the best long-range recon patrollers in the division. He spoke privately with the ranking NCO among them, Staff Sergeant Malcolm Gill.

Kravanart sat across his desk from Gill, pretending to study the file spread out before him. The general was acutely aware of the NCO's presence. His shoulders cast a shadow across the entire back wall of the HQ building. Clements had told the general all about Gill, lest any of Kravanart's precious time be wasted in reading service records. Gill was in his early thirties, a lifer, a recipient of the Bronze Star in New Guinea, divisional boxing champion in 1939, and generally known as a mean bastard. He had been tried and acquitted of the summary execution of twenty natives on New Guinea who had refused to help in a work project.

"Sergeant Gill, I suppose you've heard of the cowardly desertion of two full companies of Marines this week?"

"No, sir."

"Yes. They just decided that they didn't like the way I was doing things and went over the hill. The Japs accounted for most of them—" Kravanart broke into a wide grin—"but air recon reports a platoon of them still on the loose out near Liloila."

"That's pretty far behind Jap lines, sir."

"Yes, isn't it? They're very resourceful, these Marines. Much more resourceful as outlaws than they were as fighting men. They've been sitting in front of Liloila for a month now and they couldn't take an inch of ground. I can't understand how they ever got a reputation as fighting men."

Gill didn't say anything. He was stupid, but he knew

that Marines *were* fighting men. He might hate them and brawl with them but he was willing to give the devil his due.

"There's a traitorous cutthroat in charge of them now, named...uh...James Hawk. He's killed two platoons of his own men by continuing to move forward. He can't come back because he knows what I'll do to him. His men must stay with him because they're afraid of him. I consider them just as guilty as he is." Kravanart shuffled his file. He was actually reading it now; he had never opened it before and it piqued his curiosity. "We don't know what he has up his sleeve. I've received two rumors...or theories...thus far.

One is that he has a woman up in Liloila, and that's why he went over the hill; the other is that he ran across a cache of Japanese gold and decided that a few bucks meant more to him than a clean service record. I don't know why he's out there," said Kravanart, as if Gill had asked him, "or what he hopes to accomplish. I just want you to find him. And I think you're just the man to do it."

"Yessir. What do I do with him?" Gill asked, as if he could just reach outside the door and drag Hawk onto the carpet. "What if he puts up a struggle?"

Kravanart smiled. "Let me say this. Let's understand one another. The Articles of War requires us to bring him back and try him. I prefer him out there dead and rotting in the sun. In other words..." He chuckled. "If you must defend yourself, do it vigorously. And defend yourself at the slightest provocation. You see, if you bring Hawk back, the goddamn Marine Corps is going to take up his side. They won't care what he's done, they'll do anything to thwart me. If you don't bring him back...well... You see, Sergeant, I can really build this thing up and make the Marines look bad. I'm a very powerful man. I can make *you* look good, for example."

"I see. I think I get your drift, sir."

"Good." If Gill didn't get the drift, his twelve men must have gotten it from somewhere. The drift: kill Hawk and anybody with him. The chosen recon patrollers were an odd assortment of alcoholic criminals quite accustomed to grueling treks behind enemy lines. Scarcely a man among them had ever brought back a Japanese prisoner alive.

Kravanart dismissed Gill and called Clements in.

"Major Clements, are there any Marine units still in action?"

"There are no Marine units at all, sir, other than First Platoon, Dog Company."

"Good. I don't want the lives of any innocent men jeopardized. Sergeant Gill has just given me some alarming information. The Japs have taken to wearing Marine fatigues. Pass the word: shoot first, ask questions later."

"Yes, sir. But what about First Platoon?"

"We won't concern ourselves with those criminals. The safety of my men is more important than the safety of murderers."

Clements saluted and left the office. His conscience was bothering him. Kravanart was acting like a man who had taken leave of his senses. Fortunately, he only acted that way in dealing with First Platoon. He was handling the rest of the campaign quite well. Clements knew the whole story. He had pieced it all together. He knew why Hawk didn't come back; he couldn't. Hawk might have disobeyed orders in attacking the Little

Gopher Line but, after that, he had merely been trying to stay alive. And he was doing just that, in spite of the efforts of two of the world's most powerful warring nations. Major Clements knew that Kravanart wanted to be free of Marine interference, but he couldn't bring himself to believe that the general had intentionally shelled 309 or that he wanted any harm to come to First Platoon.

Clements didn't know about Gill's patrol.

* * *

PIDGE SHAEFFER PRONOUNCED LILOILA DESERTED. Unable to believe in such good fortune, Hawk approached the village cautiously and took a preliminary look at it himself. It looked quiet enough—so quiet that a few hundred Japanese might be holding their breath in the nearby forest. The platoon was split into two halves, and these circled the town. They made no contact with the enemy. Evidence indicated that the Japanese had

been there as recently as a couple of hours ago. It looked as if they might have migrated toward the American lines. Lasker was sent into the town first.

He ran down the main street, fell to his knees, and then pitched forward on his elbows. He aimed his BAR at the silent shops in front of him. A flock of tiny birds swirled over him and alighted nearby. They began busily to inspect some horse droppings in the street. He stood and ran forward a few more yards. The birds dispersed and flew off, jabbering disgruntled complaints.

Hawk sent three more men in. They went from hut

to hut. Half of the platoon was sent into the hamlet and still no contact resulted. Men ran from the stilted huts to the shops to the frame houses, pushing their jostling helmets from in front of their eyes, stopping at doorways, and holding their rifle muzzles under their chins as they edged by windows. The running was the only sound to be heard. The forest remained quiet. The men finally crouched against walls and peered anxiously up and down the street. They knew that being wounded out here was as good as being killed.

Hawk unslung his Thompson and walked down the center of the street. His mildewed shirt was unbuttoned, his rotted pants legs were tucked into his boots. It was a bold maneuver, one sure to draw fire if there was any to draw. His eyes shifted quickly back and forth beneath the brim of his helmet.

"Joe," he barked, and pointed at the large row of shops at the end of the street. He kept his right hand securely on the trigger and pistol grip of his submachine gun. Joe Canlon galloped toward the indicated building, a general store and the largest structure in town. It had a loft for storage above the main floor and would be a likely place for any hangers-on to nest. The corporal stopped at the door, put his back to the wall, and peeked gingerly through the door. Hawk's boots crunched steadily down the street. His chin muscle contracted, forcing his lips tightly shut.

Canlon slid the spoon of a grenade from behind his belt. He looked back at Hawk. The sergeant shook his head negatively and continued walking, straight for the door.

"I hope the crazy bastard gets killed," Marisette

whispered to Pacht. They crouched quietly under a toppled-over hut.

Canlon stood aside. Hawk eyed the narrow window on the second floor. He stepped up onto the sidewalk and, without breaking his stride, walked inside. "Joe!" his voice came from the dark interior. Canlon ducked inside and knelt in the doorway. "Cover them stairs," the sergeant ordered. He walked across the room and checked the back door. Locked. He walked toward the stairs, thinking of what an excellent way this was to get killed. He took one step at a time until he could see into the loft. Slipping a grenade from his jacket pocket without pulling its pin, he lobbed it onto the upper floor. It was thrown high into the air so that it might land with a loud crash. When the grenade stopped rolling about and there still was no sign of life, he went all the way up. Soon he stepped rapidly back down the stairs. "Looks clean."

Canlon exhaled tensely and stood up. He looked around the room. Long tables were carefully arranged in the store to serve as counters. They were stacked with merchandise, goods that hadn't been there when the Americans took the town the first time.

"Great gobs of goat shit," Canlon grunted, "look at all this crap." Canlon went to a table blanketed with Japanese and American brands of cigarettes. He began shoveling the American brands into his pockets.

"Shit! Watch it, man," Hawk admonished. His caution disappeared when he saw a pile of cigar boxes.

He squinted at the door, smiled to himself, and went over to the cigars. They had a Spanish or possibly Italian label. He dipped double handfuls of them into his pockets and tucked a couple of boxes under his arm.

He went from these to the chewing tobacco. "Damn," he mumbled, "what else we got here?"

"This," Canlon answered. He ripped open a bottle of scotch and poured the golden liquid down his throat.

"Must have lifted that from American officers' supplies."

"Yeah," said Canlon. "No man would drink it."

"Get what you want and then let them other vultures come and get what they want. They come in two at a time. Marisette and Pacht come in last." This order nearly set off another incident.

But Hawk couldn't concern himself with jerks and bastards at this time. He brushed past the crowd of men and went over to the frame house with the porch swing. The house was empty. After a quick search, he stood on the porch, looked down at the swing, and sighed. His eye caught a scintillating sliver of sunlight.

"Well, goddamn. Ain't that cute?" he grumbled. A thin trip wire was attached to the bottom of the swing. It ran through the floorboards of the porch. He looked under the house. The wire ran to a wooden box filled with explosives which sat in a hole, hidden from sight. Hawk pushed back his helmet with a thumb and snorted, "Dirty son of a bitches." It was the only booby trap in the entire town.

"Hey, Marisette, come stick your ass in this swing," he called to the crowd of men. They gathered around the awesome trap. Shaeffer suggested blowing it before a strong gust of wind did it.

Hawk looked around the front of the old house. It still smelled of smoke. "Leave it," he finally decided.

"Somebody'll get hurt," said Chuck Lasker.

"Reckon?" Hawk slung his Thompson and moved

the men to the northern end of the barrio. He slid a cigar between his lips and lit it. There was no evidence of what had happened to the Jenningses or Calvert. He had looked all through the house for a note of some sort, including under the mattresses.

"I guess we better get to moving on before the Army flattens this place," he said. Canlon nodded, but, as the men filed onto the trail leading north from Liloila, he pulled Hawk aside.

"Hey, Hawk, you gonna let the Army chase us to Tokyo or something? I mean, what's the plan? We can't keep running from them."

Hawk shrugged. "I don't know. They ain't gonna kill me, though." The sergeant turned and took up a position in the middle of the single file of men.

"You better forget about that woman. She's long gone," said Canlon.

"You and Pidge guard the rear," he answered.

Joe nodded and stared at Hawk's retreating back. Mule-headed bastard, Canlon thought. Joe was the only man left in the town. Thirty feet away, Shaeffer stood at the jungle's edge, cradling his Reising submachine gun.

Far down the street at its southern end, a short, stocky figure rounded the corner of a frame house and began walking energetically northward. He took off his bullet-shaped helmet and dried his brow with his sleeve. It was hot. An Arisaka rifle was slung across his back. Every stitch in the man's grey uniform appeared distinct to Joe.

"Baby Jesus!" he gasped prayerfully. Canlon's brain let go of his bladder and hot liquid squirted down the front of his dungarees. "Pi-idge!"

Shaeffer turned around. Two more of the enemy

rounded the corner. They were all looking at the ground, as if absolutely sure they were the only ones here.

"God—*damnit!*" Pidge whispered. "Run, stupid!"

Canlon backed slowly toward him. "Nothin' sudden, Pidge," Canlon urged. He wasn't sure if he could run. He had almost made it to the forest when they spotted him. They hastily fought their rifles from their backs. Canlon turned and found out that he could run quite well.

Shaeffer was a few yards into the jungle, on the ground behind a double trunked tree. His Reising rested patiently in its crotch. Canlon ran past him.

"Where you goin'?" Shaeffer caught his pants leg.

"Where the hell do you think? Buffalo, New York— if I can make it."

"We're the rear guard," Shaeffer said calmly. "Get down here and help me."

"Get down, shit! You get *up* and run! They're comin'." Joe was a corporal and Shaeffer was still technically only a private, so Joe's excited words were really an order. Nonetheless, Shaeffer stood his ground. Fighting every instinct in him, Canlon finally threw himself down on the other side of the trail. He wouldn't leave Shaeffer.

The Reising bowled three of them over as they tried to enter the forest. Warned by the reception, the others did not try to follow. They avoided the trail. Canlon and Shaeffer heard them crunching and barging their way through the underbrush on either side.

"Baby Jesus," Joe choked, trying to look in a thousand directions at once. Everywhere, his guts screamed; they're everywhere. The Reising rattled off half a dozen rounds. Pidge sounded serious. His clip only held twelve rounds.

Warned by the shots, Hawk ordered a sweep to the left through the forest. He intended to come through the jungle into the barrio and, it was to be hoped, behind the Japanese. As he put this plan into execution, the firing intensified, and he realized that he could lose his rear guard—and two of his best men.

The platoon broke through the woods and scrambled through the random arrangement of huts that lay off the main street. "Set fire to them haystacks!" Pacht shouted. The village huts were purposelessly lit and consumed within minutes. The Marines ran and crawled to the southern end of the town and spread out along the street opposite the frame houses. Hawk and Lasker lay along the edge of the sidewalk that ran in front of the general store and shops. The sergeant saw what looked like a squad of Japanese running in, out, and between the frame houses. On the edge of the forest another three or four men were firing at Canlon and Shaeffer.

Hawk pulled a half-used clip from his submachine gun and stuck a new one in. He snapped it back against the trigger guard. His eyes flicked from the forest to the street as his mind searched for a solution. For the sake of the rear guard, it had to be a quick one. He pushed his safety forward with his thumbnail. Under a nearby hut, Owens and Pacht were feverishly trying to set up a Browning thirty-caliber machine gun. They were not machine gunners. Owens plopped the tripod down and Pacht dropped the gun on it and began fiddling with the latch and pintle. Owens stuck a hand in and twisted on the elevation wheel. Marisette was hovering behind them, the fabric belt of ammo wound around his arm, occasionally trying to jam the brass end tag into the chamber. Hawk couldn't wait any longer.

He snapped off several three-round bursts before the enemy spotted him. The other Marines opened up. Several of the surprised Imperial soldiers dodged for cover among the frame houses. Others lay dead or wounded in the muddy street. After securing cover, the Japanese returned the fire. Decorative corbels were splattered from the overhanging awning on the sidewalk. Pieces of wood rained down on Hawk's helmet and he ducked behind the corner of the building.

"That wasn't worth a goddamn," he growled, letting his helmet fall back against the wooden siding. The enemy's attention had been diverted away from the rear guard, but little else had been accomplished.

"Shoot that porch swing," Lasker suggested.

"Nah, it'd blow the whole town to shit."

"Somebody's gonna do it anyway. The place is on fire now."

"Yeah." Hawk edged the gas compensator of his muzzle around the corner of the building and squeezed off a single shot. He had taken a particular dislike to a soldier crouching in the window of the Jenningses' home. After each shot he fired he could see the large black holes spew into the wounded lumber under the window. He couldn't help but think that he would have to repair those holes before they rotted the whole house down. Things rotted easily in this climate.

His opponents were not similarly concerned. They replied with a vicious outburst of rifle and pistol fire that chewed up and down the sidewalk, burning the wood with white perforations and showering the Americans with splinters.

"God damn!" Lasker held his helmet down as he cringed against Hawk.

"What's wrong with them son of a bitches on the machine gun?" the sergeant asked, casually sliding a cigar between his lips. Something had to be done—a quick victory or a quick withdrawal. The shooting was sure to attract a limitless number of Japanese in the vicinity. A withdrawal would have been easy, but Sergeant Hawk wanted to kill, and this was his opportunity.

He slung his Thompson with the muzzle pointing at the ground. He stood, jumped, and latched onto the roof. Putting a boot on a windowsill, and the other on the naked bolts of the shattered awning supports, he pulled himself up. His leg went over the eaves and he rolled out of sight.

The line of stores were merely the partitioned rooms of one long building. They had a common roof. An ornate stucco facade decorated the front of the building and hid the roof from the sight of men below. Hawk ran, bent at the waist, behind this facade. He heard the raging gunfire beneath his feet as he raced from the American side of Liloila to the Japanese side. He peered through a drainage slot in the facade.

It wasn't going well. The marines had been through a lot but, for some reason, they were still bashful about trading shots with their courageous foes. On the Japanese side of the street, over which Hawk crouched, the enemy was not so bashful. They dashed to and fro in open view the way fatalistic, hardened combat veterans do. They fired more frequently and from better positions.

Two limp Japanese dead lay in the middle of the street. Large red lakes floated on their baggy uniform shirts. Their overturned helmets were nearby. Three more were scattered between them, engaged in their last death throes. They were on the American side of the street, slinging blood hither and yon in a frightful manner. Two other less severely injured men were crawling toward the Japanese side of the street. One of these had been hit in the leg, the other in the back.

Hawk thrust his gun through the drainage slot and squeezed the trigger. The blazing neon of the muzzle flash streaked from the roof to the ground. The head of the man with the leg wound jerked back, then his face rammed forward into the mud. He lay still. Hawk turned his sights to the man with the back wound. He stitched a line of shells up his back and into his head. They lifted, shook, and dropped the screaming victim back to the ground. Wisps of smoke danced over his smoldering clothing. Hawk picked off two more of the enemy as they dashed from house to house before they discovered him. Shots began to pepper the facade.

Hawk sat against the facade and blew the sweat off the tip of his nose. He hated to waste a grenade, but he slipped one from his jacket. The Japanese were too spread out to get more than one or two of them, unless he hit the porch swing. The swing was attached to some newly developed American explosives, stuff that made TNT look tame.

The grenade's cotter key, attached to the ring pull, was bent so that it would not accidently slip out of the bomb while it was being carried. He slid his long black-bladed hunting knife from its sheath and straightened the pin. If he blew the porch swing, the Jenningses' home would be utterly destroyed.

"Tough shit," he grumbled under his breath. He ripped the pin out and held his thumb on the safety lever. As he judged the distance he would have to throw, shots rang in an ugly pattern around the drainage slot. "Houses are easy to build," he grunted, edging close against the facade and drawing a leg up under himself. He hesitated, studying the serrated cast-iron sections of the little pineapple's body. It had meaningless little things stamped on it, including a number 20, a plus sign, and a diamond. What did those things mean, he wondered. "Everything don't have to mean something," he said. His thumb slid off the safety lever and it sprang across the roof. Smoke spewed from the grenade as the spring-loaded striker smacked home. He stood and threw it overhanded and hard, right onto the porch swing.

The Jenningses' house, three houses to the north of it, and two to the south were knocked over like matchboxes, with the little matches trickling down like confetti. Three other homes collapsed under the concussion. After the smoke and debris cleared, a crater appeared, stretching halfway across the street. Hawk vaulted over the facade and landed lightly on the ground. Holding his machine pistol before him, he walked through the swirling smoke past the vaporized homes and proceeded toward the southern end of the street. A Japanese soldier staggered drunkenly from one of the doorways. Hawk lashed him mercilessly up and down with forty-five-caliber bursts. The man catapulted himself through a charred wall.

The sergeant could hear desultory knocking about on the floor of a neighboring house. It sounded as if there were several men inside, possibly dazed or wounded. He fired through the wall. A screeching cry came from within and, shortly thereafter, a white flag shot out of the window. Hawk held his Thompson in one hand. The clip was dry.

Four groggy, terrified men stepped sheepishly out onto the porch. Hawk held his empty gun on them. Their hands were held high. One carried the white flag.

"Not shoot, American son of a bitch," one of the little prisoners said. Hawk tapped the top of his helmet with one hand. They complied with his pantomimed order by interlacing the fingers of both hands over their heads. "Not shoot, American son of a bitch," the same man repeated.

"Who you callin' a son of a bitch, you son of a bitch?" Hawk gestured toward the shops at the end of the street with his gun. The prisoners ignored his angry question and filed by him. They stepped over a dead comrade and proceeded toward the general store. Hawk followed them. It was the first time he had noticed the corpse. He had mentally dismissed it as an inanimate object the first time he stepped over it—which, indeed, it was. Strips of burning flesh hung on the remaining part of the skeleton.

Canlon and Shaeffer came out of the northern forest together with a lone prisoner. This one was wounded in the shoulder. He was herded together with the other prisoner once they had all reached the general store. Hawk indicated that the Japanese should lie on the ground near the sidewalk. They did so, face up. They were allowed to remain that way as Lasker quickly checked them over for weapons. The other Marines came out of their hiding places to have a look at the catch.

"Not shoot, American son of a bitch," their spokesman said. He smiled a friendly smile as he said it. When Shaeffer heard this, he cocked his Reising by flicking the finger catch on the bottom of the stock.

"Let me kill 'em?" Pidge asked politely. Hawk shook his head. He asked the prisoners if any of them spoke English. The one man repeated the same sentence. He evidently didn't know what it meant. Shaeffer insisted that he did. It was entirely possible that he did; the Japanese were an extremely brave people. Shaeffer leered over the prone spokesman and jammed the barrel of his submachine gun into his face. "Blowee brains out?" he asked.

"Not shoot, American son of a bitch."

"We gotta kill 'em," said Shaeffer. "We damn sure can't take 'em with us."

Hawk stared down at the pitiful specimens. He felt like executing the emaciated little fellows. It certainly would make things easier. But he decided that killing them would be sort of chicken shit. Shaeffer pretended to be taking aim at the head of one of them.

"Take it easy," said Canlon, "you're gonna lose your grip if you keep acting that way."

The corporal stole a glance at Hawk. He knew Hawk well. He was hoping the sergeant didn't plan on shooting them. But Hawk was a rabid killer of Japanese, and these didn't speak English. They were useless; they could tell him nothing about the Jenningses. "Let's get some sulfa on that wounded one," Canlon said to a boy standing next to him.

"Skip the horseshit," Hawk growled.

"It'll get infected, sergeant," the boy said.

"Yeah, what a dirty rotten disgrace." The boy put the envelope back into his belt. He accidently dropped a wound tablet, and didn't pick it up. The boy's name was Collins.

Hawk noticed this, but he didn't say anything. He knew what had to be done. He reached down and grabbed the talkative prisoner by the ankle. He dragged him forward and dropped his foot up on the sidewalk. It was about two feet from the ground. Hawk brought the heel of his boot down on the man's knee. The leg snapped like a dry stick. Canlon turned away with a curse. Shaeffer snickered. Everyone else was silent—everyone but the man with the broken leg.

The prisoners began to talk among themselves. Hawk latched onto the ankle of the second prisoner and dropped it on the sidewalk. The Japanese conversation increased in volume and speed. The second man was not going to be as cooperative as the first. He took his foot off the walk and tried to get up and run. Four Marines held him down while Hawk broke his leg. The others did not have to be held. They lay there with resigned patience.

"They can still tell the others which way we went," Shaeffer said after the grim ordeal was over. He still wanted to kill them. The leg-breaking was just for fun; now it was time to get serious.

"What do you want me to do? Cut their tongues out and poke out all their eyeballs?" Hawk asked angrily.

"Naw, just kill 'em," said Shaeffer.

"There's plenty that got away. They know where we're goin'. These boys are out of this campaign; that's all I care about," said Hawk. He was wishing that he was out of this campaign. He had three dead boys of his own to bury. The Marines hurried the task. Some still had entrenching tools.

The men stood solemnly around the shallow graves.

"Sergeant Hawk! I think I hear something. Maybe armor or something," Lasker called from his lookout post at the edge of town. Something was coming from the South. The men remained standing there, looking down.

Hawk put on his helmet and looked around at the line of tired, hurt, mad, scared faces. "Awright, then," he said quietly, "let's get outta here."

6

Sergeant Gill crossed over the remains of Hill 309. His point man, Sergeant Jack Calicote, led the recon patrol into the swamps below the blasted range of hills. They threaded and cursed their way through the heavily shelled marshes, once a major gathering place for the Japanese. Hundreds of enemy corpses were displaying various stages of decomposition. The Army squad passed these grim reminders of what fate had in store for them and wondered why one man had been here or a dozen had been there. A few disabled tanks and shattered big guns were the most cheerful decorations found.

Calicote was a shrewd woodsman. He followed the Marines' nearly nonexistent trail quite accurately. It was slow work. Calicote was a tall, skinny, ugly Kentuckian who'd have looked at home under a coonskin cap. One afternoon, he found a group of starving Japanese in a spooky swamp grove.

Gill encircled them, captured them, and searched them, even though he had less than half as many men as they had. None of them spoke English. Gill lined them up. They knew what he had in mind. They pushed their colonel to the back of the doomed formation. Neither riot nor protest followed. In fact, not a sound was to be heard other than the shuffling of the captured men's feet.

Gill raised his heavy BAR. He put the selector on the maximum rate of fire. "I just wished to hell this was Sergeant Hawk," he said to Calicote. Then he started cutting them down. The callous, brutal recon patrols turned away in disgust. Amidst the smoke and men falling over one another, the Japanese colonel disappeared in a patch of ferns and crawled away. No one had seen his escape. He didn't run far. He was sick and suffering from malnutrition. He lay panting in the grass and watching as the Americans stepped over his dead men and went on their way.

"Sergeant Hawk," the colonel whispered. He would forget neither the name nor the atrocity.

* * *

SGT. HAWK KEPT to his northerly course. He found little evidence of the passage of the Japanese. His unspoken plan was to overtake the party that held the Jenningses and Calvert, but it began to look like a futile hope. The danger of being discovered by the Japanese lessened as the Marines marched deeper into a trackless wilderness. Unfortunately, the chances of Amelia Jennings' being discovered also lessened. The sergeant had all but decided to return to Liloila and await his fate—either at the hands of the Army or of the enemy—when Shaeffer ran across some Filipino partisans. Most of them spoke some form of English, and one of their leaders had been in the barrio when the Japanese evacuated.

Raymundo Ramos was brought to Hawk. He was tall and shirtless and wore dirty khaki pants. He had a pistol belt over his shoulder and carried a Japanese submachine gun. These were rare items, similar to and about as unreliable as the Reising; both weapons could be easily mistaken for a carbine.

The jolly little-brown-brother demeanor did not accompany Ramos. His black eyes burned with hatred. Hawk suspected Ramos wanted to kill all of the Japanese in the world by himself, without assistance from anyone, especially Americans. This was considered a noble sentiment by the American Marine, though he had long ago learned that there were enough Japanese for everyone.

Hawk sat on the ground with him and offered him a cigar. It was thanklessly accepted. "Did you see what happened to the Americans in Liloila?" Hawk asked.

"Yes." Ramos shook his head slowly. "Many Americans live in Liloila. American women. Jap take American men years ago."

"Yeah. What happened to the women? They're gone now."

"This time Jap take *them*. Take all American women. They say no one can stay in Liloila. They kill one who did not want to leave. Then others are afraid; they go with Jap."

Hawk studied the features of the brooding Filipino. He knew he was getting the truth. "You know some folks named Jennings?"

"Jennings? American women?"

"Yeah."

"No."

"Two women, a young one and her mother. They was with a fella, an American civilian, who was sick or something."

"These people I know. Did not know this name, Jennings. Young lady named Amelia. Very pretty. Very —" Ramos held his hands about three feet away from his chest. "Man's name I forget."

"Yeah. That's the ones. What happened to 'em?"

"Jap take them north."

"North, you say? Reckon where up north they'd be headin'?"

"Young lady, Jap probably take to Porkeet, seaport or northeast coast. Old lady and silly man probably dead somewhere in between."

"Why do you say that?"

"I know Jap."

"I mean, about Porkeet. Why would they take her there?"

"Sell her to Moro pirates. Moro sell her again to Tamara people or sultan in Borneo. Not far. They buy women. Big money for American women. War is on and American can't do anything about it. They not sell Filipino woman. No Christian woman. You bet on that —kill them quick." Ramos seemed to be working himself into a rage. He was proud of the fact that the Moros were afraid to kidnap Filipinos, and it seemed to Hawk that he might be just as proud that they weren't afraid of selling Americans.

"The Japs would do that?"

"Jap do anything," Ramos snarled. "Jap general in Porkeet is crook son of a bitch. He know he losing Lamare. He know he losing war. He steal everything he touch for himself." Ramos rubbed his pocket, indicating that the general put stolen property in his pocket.

"He jump up in tree to tell you a lie when he could stand on the ground and tell you truth."

Hawk maneuvered his cigar from one side of his mouth to the other. "Moro pirates, huh? They operate out of this here Porkeet?" Ramos nodded. "And they're in with the Japs?"

"Pirates in with anyone who pays. Not all pirates are Moros, not all Moros are pirates—we call them that. Not believe in Jesus. Moros no good son of a bitch—" Ramos ran his finger across his throat "—they kill you to laugh." Hawk knew that the Moros lived in the south of Mindanao. They were an entire race of people. It wasn't much of a lead.

"And these Tamaras, where are they?"

"They on island in Samar Sea, or maybe Jintotolo Channel. Not sure. You bet Moro pirate know where."

"Yeah, I bet. What's the Tamaras' angle in this setup? Do they believe in Jesus?"

"Tamara *not* believe in Jesus. Moro man not believe in Jesus because he's bad. Tamara man not believe in Jesus because he's stupid. Tamara is not a civilized man like you, me."

Hawk nodded. They were probably some tribe running around in their drawers. Ramos considered the Moros "bad" because they were Moslems. The sultan in Borneo was a Moslem, too. The Tamara were either Moslems or wild men with witch doctors.

"What a crocka shit," Hawk growled. "How would a man go about gettin' to this Tamara?"

"Man get boat in Porkeet. Get fishman to take him to

island. If man is you—American GI—or me—man forgets whole thing. Many, *many* Jap in Porkeet."

Hawk looked over his shoulder. No one was listening to the conversation. "Well, Ramos, I tell you, that don't mean shit to me. I can't remember when I *wasn't* surrounded by the bastards. I'm gonna try and get that woman back before something really nasty happens to her."

Ramos squinted at him. He imitated the American, looking over his shoulder to see if anyone was listening. His lips slithered into a smile. "You crazy man." He and Hawk laughed. "I go with you then. I crazy, too. No more hide in jungle and run, see Jap and run. I go with you and we kill many Jap." Ramos chopped his right hand into his left.

"Yeah," Hawk answered.

That night they camped in the forest. The somber camp consisted of three groups of men. Two of the groups talked among themselves in low tones. The Filipinos made up one group, the Marines made up another, and the third consisted of Sergeant Hawk. Canlon left the Marines and came over and sat with Hawk.

"Some of the men don't much like what you got planned," Canlon said.

"Yeah? Who's that?"

"They figure we oughta go back and get straightened out with the Army and all. If we could get back to Colonel Heller..."

"Kravanart tells Heller when to shit and what color."

Canlon ignored the interruption. "Heller might be able to help us straighten this out. We done a good job in that attack; he oughta help us out. We can just explain to him that we had to head for the hills on account of some mistake the guys in artillery made." Joe lit a cigarette. "The men figure you're just headin' deeper into Jap country. We're already so deep we probably can't get back. They figure it's on account of that babe in Liloila."

"What do you figure?"

"Oh, I figure I'll stick with you. Most of us want to stick with you. One way or the other, I figure you got a better chance of pullin' us outta this alive. That goddamn artillery scared the piss outta me. I ain't in no hurry to go through that shit again."

"Who's the ringleaders in this shit?"

"Now, don't go gettin' all hot about it. Pacht and Owens and Marisette, they're the only ones. Maybe a couple of others."

"Them three shitbags ain't worth a goddamn for nothin' anyway."

"No," Canlon agreed. "But they're your men."

Hawk aimed a fiery glance at Joe's downcast helmet. He stood and walked over to the group of Marines. They stared self-consciously at the ground as he spoke to them. "The ones of you that want to go back can do it. Pacht's goin' back for the gold and to get hisself killed. Marisette's yella. Owens is stupid." He sighed and took off his helmet. "I plan to catch a boat somewheres. With a boat we can circle back behind our lines and get back to the landing beach, or else the Navy will pick us up. We run the risk of gettin' picked up by the Japs, but that's better than gettin' blasted by the goddamn shellin'. On the way back I plan to pick up them Americans the Japs took outta Liloila. I might even make a detour if I think I can find 'em." He shrugged. "That's the way it is. You can think it over tonight."

They thought it over. Marisette, Pacht, and Owens left in the morning. The others who wanted to go back wanted to go back with Hawk—but not without him. Pacht was in a good mood when he left. He told everyone that he'd save a bar of gold for them. Hawk let them take the machine gun.

Ramos suggested that the rest make their way to the east coast and try to catch a friendly fishing vessel up to Porkeet. Without fully developing a plan, or even considering the danger, Hawk agreed.

Two days later, Jack Calicote, Gill's second in command, found Owens in the jungle near Liloila. Owens had become separated from Pacht and Marisette. He was lost and frightened. He became ecstatic when he spotted Calicote far ahead of him. Calicote immediately recognized him as a Marine. He raised his trusty rifle and shot him through the head.

Marisette's death was not so merciful. Hawk and the platoon found him in a marsh near the eastern coast. He was naked and tied by one leg to a tree limb. A wooden board was nailed to his back. The words on the board were written in blood. Strips of flesh had been sliced from Marisette's hip and down his thigh. The sign on him read:

For Sgt. Hawk—Bon Appetit! We saved some of this rotten meat for you. *You* will be our next meal!

It was signed by a Japanese colonel, the same colonel Gill had accidently spared in his cowardly massacre. Hawk didn't know about any of that. Lasker tore the sign off the body. The cruel sight struck the Marines shamefully dumb. They linked it with the leg-breaking in Liloila. It looked as if the enemy knew their identity.

"Do you think they really *ate* him?" Canlon asked.

"Jap do anything," Ramos said.

"They made it look like they did," Hawk said quietly. "Lasker, Shaeffer, scout around for the other two jokers...and, uh...take a shovel."

"What's bon appetit?" Canlon asked, holding the bloody sign.

"I don't know." Hawk stared at the ground. "Some kind of Jap shit, I guess. Ain't no excuse for this kinda shit..." He didn't know the enemy colonel had reason to think otherwise.

"We get to beach plenty fast or we be same way," Ramos warned.

"Yeah," Hawk answered softly.

They never found Owens. Pacht had already sneaked around Gill's patrol and crossed 309. He was digging up the gold in the bombed-out cave there as First Platoon resumed the march to the beach. They never heard from him again. He didn't keep his promise to save them each a bar of gold.

* * *

WHEN THE JAPANESE counterattack overwhelmed Liloila, the Jenningses and a full company of soldiers were surprised in their sleep. A determined squad of American Army troops took Amelia and Mrs. Jennings into the forest in an attempt to hide them. In the excitement, Calvert was left behind, moaning in his bed. The

Japanese found him and, after two or three light kicks in the stomach, he told his captors where to find the escaping Americans. The Japanese captured the women and took them and Calvert north to General Kirijo in Porkeet. No one told Mrs. Jennings how the Japanese had been able to find her, but she knew.

* * *

GENERAL KRAVANART WAS ALL ATWITTER. General MacArthur was coming to visit him. The Supreme Commander had heard what an excellent job was being done on Lamare. Kravanart immediately ordered a new Quonset hut HQ constructed, upon hearing the news. It was to have three spacious rooms and six air conditioners. He personally chose the site for the building. It was no closer to the front than the old HQ.

The news jolted Major Clements. He recalled the situation around Liloila to Kravanart. The front had moved halfway across the island, yet the Japanese were gathered in strength a mere seven miles away. Clements felt that this would look bad. There might be droves of reporters. You could actually *hear* the fighting from the beach.

"Quite right." Surprisingly, Kravanart agreed with the major. "But you know, Major, those renegade Marines are prowling around out in that sector. It would be extremely dangerous to move men in there."

"Dangerous? There's only a handful, sir. Begging your pardon, General, but there were twenty-seven thousand Japanese here when we landed."

"That's true, Clements. But American soldiers aren't up to killing fellow Americans. Japs are one thing. Now, you take that incident the other day...what was that Marine's name?"

"Owens, sir."

"Yes, that Owens Marine. He comes running out of the bush and attacks our boys. It's a good thing I had the right outfit up there to deal with that sort of affair. I see we have Calicote up for a bronze star for killing that nut. It takes a lot of mental presence and courage to do something like that, Major."

"Yes, sir. I was surprised by that attack."

"Ah, Clements," Kravanart grimaced, "you have to expect those things. Those Marines are all nuts, anyway. They make them that way; leave 'em out in the sun too long, and it cooks their brains. But there's more to this than meets the eye. My theory is that this Sergeant Hawk has stolen government property. He's up to something. You don't disobey orders and mount your own attack, killing two platoons of your own men, and then refuse to even be rescued just because you're a *little* nutty. No, he's a shrewd fellow, all right. A despicable..." Kravanart shook his head and gave up trying to find the proper word.

"Yes, sir. Do we have proof he did all of those things, sir? I mean, the attack was ordered by a Major Breeding, as far as I've been able to discern. Hawk was actually following the orders of his own company commander who, in turn, took the order from Breeding."

"Is that supposed to be some sort of excuse? You sound like a Nazi, Clements. Do we so easily excuse ourselves from responsible behavior? I think not. Hawk is holding up the entire eastern flank of our front. I suspect this is no accident."

"No, sir," Clements agreed. He knew it was no accident. The line officers were actually begging to attack, but Kravanart had forbidden the front to move an inch. It was no accident.

"I suspect..." Kravanart looked pensively at a map behind him. "This Hawk must be in league with the Japanese. He's gone over to them and stalled the whole damn front."

The idea was presented so suddenly and was so ridiculous that Clements couldn't think coherently. What you think and what you say must be carefully coordinated when speaking to a general. Finally, Clements managed to say, "But, sir, couldn't we press the front if we wanted to?"

"My God, Clements." Kravanart smiled and shook his head. "You still don't have a grasp of the situation, do you?" Clements didn't, and now they both knew it. "That's why some men are born to be generals and some are born to be majors. Anyway, I can't have any more of this. I've sketched out a little flyer here; something you can embellish. It should go something like this..."

Kravanart read rapidly from the paper in front of him, skipping lines and modulating his voice appropriately. "At the top we put 'Renegades!' and then, 'Sergeant James Hawk, U.S.M.C, approximately six feet tall, blond hair, blue eyes, one-eighty to one-ninety pounds, service number 6247347 rumored to be tattooed on right upper arm. Wanted dead or alive. Charged with violating direct orders, disobeying orders under fire, desertion under fire, murder and mass murder, treason, collaborating with the Japanese, and theft of government property. Accompanied by entire First Platoon, Dog Company, U.S.M.C, among whom is L/Corporal

Joseph P. Canlon, five feet nine inches tall, brown hair, brown eyes, one-sixty to one-seventy pounds. All of these men should be considered extremely dangerous, as they have attacked U.S.A. troopers. It is recommended that they be shot on sight to prevent further loss of life." It was signed, General Leslie R. Kravanart, U.S.A.

"Uh—can you *do* something like that, sir?" Clements stood holding his hands in front of himself.

"Damn right I can! This is an emergency. Now you can add to this and make it more dramatic, if you like."

"It's pretty dramatic already, sir."

"Yes." Kravanart laughed. "There's a war on, and strong measures are needed. We'll drop these over all our positions and over every town on the island. We'll get that criminal."

"Yes, sir."

"Pretty clever about the tattoo, wasn't it? I found someone who used to serve with Hawk. Oh, yes, I wanted to put in there that he talks like a Negro. Try to work that in."

"A negro, sir?"

"Yes, a heavy Southern accent."

Clements took the paper and bobbed his head as he read over it. It was no joke; it was all there, just as Kravanart had read it. The credibility of the information was unimpeachable. It was so outlandish, it had to be taken as gospel. And yet Clements had seen the entire episode created right off the top of Kravanart's head. Why? Clements finally adapted to the situation. Perhaps the phenomenon of the Big Lie finally hypnotized him.

"Shouldn't we put a reward in here, sir?" Clements asked.

* * *

WHY? Sergeant Hawk asked himself as he read the incredible leaflet. The folded flyers were strewn all along the beach when First Platoon came out of the jungle. There were enough of them for everyone to pick one up and read.

"God damn," Joe Canlon mumbled as he pored over it, "they stuck my goddamn ass in it. What's it all about?"

Hawk gave a quizzical laugh. "Hell, I don't know. I guess they're talking about that attack on the Little Gopher Line. The theft might be those supplies we found. Treason—I ain't real sure what that is; I think they can tack that on to just about anything you do. Collaborating with Japs—maybe that's because I didn't kill them four at Liloila?"

"Nah, that ain't collaborating. You ain't supposed to kill prisoners." Joe scratched his head. "I don't think." Hawk crumped the leaflet and threw it down. "What about this murder and mass murder?" Joe asked.

"I don't know," said Hawk, pushing back his helmet, "pure horseshit."

Pidge Shaeffer overheard. "Maybe them Japs we killed was Filipinos or something?" Pidge offered.

"No," Hawk drawled thoughtfully, "I expect this has got something to do with them tryin' to shell us."

"Yeah." Canlon crumped his leaflet. "They're pissed off because we wouldn't sit up there on that mountain and eat rockets."

"I bet that's it," Shaeffer agreed. "I betcha somebody made a mistake about that—and now he's trying to cover his ugly ass."

Hawk nodded. "Yeah, there's something funny goin' on."

But standing on an open beach several miles behind Japanese lines was no place to ponder over it. Ramos recommended that they walk north along the shore in the hope of spotting a passing boat. Hawk followed this advice, taking the men a few yards into the forest in case the first boat seen turned out to be unfriendly.

The men trudged wearily behind Ramos and Hawk. Occasionally they would cast mournful looks out across the spongy, apricot-colored beach. Palm trees grew in the sand, some within inches of the lapping waves. They were tall, with their only foliage high in their tops. The blustering wind blew them always to one side; their long leaves looked like the hair of young girls blown forward across their faces. The sea breathed heavily in and out.

The men were shocked, completely disoriented by the leaflet. They were wanted by their own country. They had always been wanted by Japan. Sergeant Hawk was the only authority, the only law they had. The whole affair was obviously a gross misunderstanding, but getting it cleared up was going to be a rather delicate task. It was possible that someone was using them as scapegoats, to absolve himself of responsibility. This was merely a vague suspicion, but it did serve to make them think of Hawk as something of a martyr.

Sergeant Hawk was no saint, by any stretch of the imagination. He was no one's ideal of our All-American-Boys Fighting Overseas. He had a mean streak as wide as his back and a temper like a trip wire. He was no perfectionist when it came to rules and regulations. He was merely an experience-toughened man with an uncanny ability for staying alive. But the injustice made him look like a martyr.

Hawk sensed the feeling the men had for him, and he was not above playing the role they cast him for. He wasn't entirely sure that he was completely innocent.

Maybe he had been a little too anxious to get to Liloila and find Amelia Jennings. Maybe he shouldn't have run from 309. If he had spent as much effort worrying about getting to the landing beach as he had about getting to Liloila, he would have been there by now. But they needed a martyr to keep them going, so he became one. He was subtle, and sometimes he forgot that he was acting, but sometimes he didn't. It was a simple case of an honest, unassuming personality charming an entire platoon.

And what kept Hawk going? Not much. He didn't need much, it was a force of habit. He got into situations and then got out. He operated largely on animal instinct.

He had grown up in the Delta during the Depression. His childhood was a series of rusty roofs that let in the cold in the winter and the mosquitoes in the summer. He stole to eat and worked at hard labor from the time he first learned to pull himself up on his own hind legs. He learned to survive alone because that's the only way anyone can survive. Times were when a blackbird killed by a slingshot was a good meal for him. The United States Marine Corps, even at war, had looked pretty good to him. It was luxury, in fact; not many could say that. He repaid it with unflinching loyalty. If he couldn't abide by all of its rules, he could still fight for it, and that made up for everything else. He wasn't angry with the Corps or the United States, or even with the Army. He had no bitterness for the injustice done to him. They probably thought they had a legitimate grievance. He would straighten them out. But first he had to find Amelia Jennings.

Her situation was worse than his own or that of his men. They were in the Marine Corps to fight. They had written themselves off as dead long ago. He would give his life for any one of them if he had to; but they had to fight, and for as good a cause as any. A little rescue operation, and then they would all go back to the beach—and get killed somewhere else.

He thought about Amelia all the time now. She had seemed attracted to him, yet there was her strange relationship with Calvert. He was naturally attracted to her in return, but he had remained standoffish during the brief time they'd had together. He was a loner, a man of strong drives, unaccustomed to flirtation and lovers' games. He didn't know how to take her. He couldn't understand any of it. Being apart from her made him forget all that. She was a beautiful and vulnerable girl, caught up in the raging holocaust that engulfed the Philippines and the world. He kept his distance from her when he was in her world; there he was the fragile one. But now she was in his world, and he was the only one who could help her. Perhaps, to him, she was all that is good and pure, what men go off to war and think they fight for. Sergeant Hawk was a bit unsophisticated when it came to the opposite sex.

Joe Canlon took out the leaflet again and unfolded it. though he had read it a dozen times, his lips still moved as he scanned it.

7

STAFF SERGEANT GILL WAS TRAPPED. A MILE SOUTH OF Liloila, with a tenacious Japanese patrol on his tail, he called a halt. In front of the town the enemy was reforming their lines. He was caught between the hammer and the anvil. He faced annihilation if he didn't move somewhere.

"Let's see if a plane can pick us up," Calicote suggested.

"No, we're moving out," the surly leader announced.

"Where?"

"Forward. Just like that goddamn Hawk did."

"But, Sarge, you're talking about going straight through the Jap lines."

"Then we will."

And they did. The lines were thin and the little attack was sudden, and Gill got through. He suffered two men killed and two captured—and had to run through the jungle like a striped-assed ape for three days—but he got through.

* * *

THE TREK along the eastern shore of Lamare proved to be long and fruitless. The Pacific waters off the island were too hot, in a manner of speaking, for normal fishing activities. Anyone in a boat along that coast was suspected of being a combatant. All of the vessels seen by Hawk's patrol flew the bloody-wound flag of the Japanese Navy. They were mostly small boats policing the shoreline; only once did they spot a cruiser far out to sea. No one saw the slightest indication of any American presence.

Up in exotic Porkeet, the rotund Tausag pirate, Garrotero, had finally convinced the Japanese general Kirijo to sell the American woman to the wild Tamara. Garrotero had been a pirate for thirty-five years; he knew the best markets and how to milk them. General Kirijo was easily persuaded. He had never tried to sell an American woman before. He had been considering selling her to the sultan in Borneo. The general knew the sultan could afford the price. Garrotero explained that Borneo was too far, over too much open water, what with the American invasion in full swing.

In his most convincing tone, the pirate told Kirijo that the Tamara were in possession of an ancient Spanish treasure, hidden somewhere on their island, and that they spent it on nothing but women. They were the best bet. Only a fool or a man obsessed by avarice would have believed such a story. But Kirijo had double-checked his sources. The Tamara did in fact live on an isolated island where a four-hundred-year-old Spanish castle stood. They were reputed to be the descendants of Japanese colonists. When Garrotero told the general that the tribe was not known for its trading ability and that he might be able to get an even higher price than from the sultan, Kirijo was swayed. Of course there was an added element of danger; the Tamara were fond of their isolation and were not always friendly to strangers. This meant that Garrotero's commission had to be higher, too. It was all agreeable.

Amelia Jennings, her mother, and Calvert were loaded onto the pirate's motor launch, like so much cargo. He used the launch when operating in settled areas. They were reloaded onto a larger boat in the open sea and left the northern shore of Lamare behind.

Hawk continued on his northerly journey, hiding in the jungle that fringed the beach; it became obvious that he was not going to find a fishing boat. By the time the men became discouraged about this they were getting near Porkeet. Hawk was then able to encourage them with the knowledge that their destination was close.

As Porkeet neared, the barrios became denser in concentration. Hawk avoided the little towns. He was too far behind enemy lines to risk the wagging of civilian tongues. He called a halt on a hill above the bustling port city. It was now easier to appreciate the magnitude of the problem faced. Porkeet was liberally decorated with bright Japanese flags.

The town seemed to lean and snuggle over the ocean, as if everybody and everything in it wanted to draw near the water. The residential quarters were mainly bamboo houses set up on stilts. The more substantial structures of wood and tin were near the harbor, and in the harbor were hundreds of houseboats teeming with life.

You could tell at a glance that there was a war going on and that Porkeet was playing a part in it. Every structure had the thatched roof of the traditional Filipino. Many cars and trucks were parked about the town. Three small tanks pointed menacingly toward the hinterlands on the road that led to the town. Hearing the tramp of feet, Hawk looked down at the foot of the hill below him. A column of snappy enemy soldiers were marching back into town along a jungle road, looking secure in the knowledge that the front lines were far behind them. Hawk scanned the scene with field glasses, then turned to his Filipino guide.

"Ever been here?" Hawk asked Ramos.

"Been everywhere."

"Got any buddies here?"

"Buddies everywhere."

"This don't look so goddamn easy. I see sandbags and bobwire all over the place." Hawk lowered the glasses and handed them to Ramos. "Where's the general's headquarters?"

"Division headquarters—see tin building along waterfront?"

"Yeah. I could take that place if I had a couple hundred tanks." Hawk slid a cigar between his lips. "Do you know anybody on the inside of the general's operation?"

"No. Know a lot of people who know a lot about him. But no one work in headquarters. Jap not trust Filipino here."

"Yeah. I figured that. Well...shit." Hawk scratched a thumbnail over the head of a match and lifted the red bud of flame to the tip of his cigar. "Somebody down on the docks mighta seen something. Can you get down there and mix without gettin' killed?"

"Can do."

"I ain't askin' you to risk your ass or nothin'. Just see if anybody saw anything'...and...find out where the general lives, if you can, and any place that he might keep records."

"No risk. Can do. Just ask questions. No killing, no risks."

Hawk nodded. "Awright. We'll be waitin' here."

Ramos left his weapons and walked brazenly down the road that led into the town. A checkpoint, consisting of a guardhouse and two sleepy soldiers, was at the place where the road entered the town. No one stepped out of the sandbag-flanked shack as Ramos walked by.

Two hours later he came back, swinging his arms and grinning to himself, as any innocent civilian would do. Again, no one stopped him. He climbed the side of the hill that faced away from Porkeet and reported to Hawk.

"Tausag pirates take your woman in pamboat, maybe four days ago. Old woman, silly man go with her."

"Good news." Hawk allowed a rare smile to flash across his somber mouth. He looked at the faces of his men, huddled around him. None of them smiled. "We can bump off those pirates a hell of a lot easier than some shittin' Japs."

Joe Canlon ventured a cautious nod of his head. He didn't especially want to bump off anyone—or, more accurately, he didn't want to *get* bumped off. But if they were going to tangle with someone, he would rather it wasn't the Japanese.

"Where'd they take her?" Hawk looked back to Ramos.

"Not know."

One minor detail.

"What are these Tausag pirates? Where they come from?"

"South. Sulu Sea, Celebes Sea. They sail everywhere —Borneo, New Guinea. They some Tausags, some Bajaus, they a mixed bunch; live on water."

Canlon looked down and hid his face under his helmet. New Guinea, he thought; wonderful.

"I gotta know where them son of a bitches went," Hawk growled. "Didn't you hear anything about the Tamara?" Ramos shook his head. "Where else did you say they could go?"

"Sheik in Borneo. Not know. Not know much about sea."

"How about the general? Where's he stay? Where's his records?"

"He stay on boat, with Filipino servants. Keeps no records where he stay—all records in division head-quarters."

Hawk rubbed the bristly blond beard along his jaw-line. "Listen, I'm gonna bust into the division headquarters tonight and see if I can dig up any record of what happened to her."

"Very dangerous." Ramos looked sullenly at the ground. It sounded as if this American madman had finally gone too far. Ramos wanted to fight, but suicide was against his religion.

"That's a long shot, Hawk. There probably ain't no record; and you ain't gonna know what to look for. I bet there's a lot of paper down there," Canlon pleaded.

"Yeah, but it's gotta be done. I'll go by myself. I just need Ramos here to get me a few tools. I ain't gonna find out anything sittin' out here. If this don't work, I'm gonna nab the general himself and beat the information out of him."

After he said that, no one tried to dissuade the sergeant. He was determined to go. The Marines' only hope was that Ramos could get them a boat after Hawk got himself killed. They breathed a sigh of relief, however, when he left that night. At least for tonight he wouldn't be leading them into anything.

He ran down the hillside in a crouch. Avoiding the road, he entered the city through a clump of huts on its outskirts. A dim half-moon ducked in and out behind heavy clouds. Hawk removed his shirt and blackened his skin with mud and ashes. He moved brazenly through the little knots of villagers gathered around their cookfires. He hoped that, by acting unsuspiciously, he would not attract their attention.

He became more cautious as he neared the center of town. The streets were mostly dark, some lighted by swaying lanterns hung on porch steps. Enemy soldiers patrolled the avenues at every turn. But they were garrison troops and they were not expecting anyone with the skills of Sergeant Hawk. He slipped among them, hiding in the shadows and letting them pass. He wanted no confrontations. He carried no firearms. It would do no good to fight here.

From house to house he darted like the disembodied monster the war had made of him. He reached the perimeter of the Japanese base. Several aprons of barbed wire and chainlink fence separated the camp from the rest of the town. There was no way through it.

Watch-towers peered over the thorny mesh at fifty-yard intervals. Unlit searchlights perched on the tops of the towers. He backed away from this challenge and circling around the camp, slinked through the town and toward the waterfront.

Pressing himself against the wall of a boathouse, he edged along a pier that ran out into the harbor. When he reached the end of it, he lowered himself into the murky, lapping sea. He felt an icy chill when he realized that the ocean had no bottom. Hanging onto the pilings, he came back down the other side of the pier and to the edge of the wharf itself. The divisional headquarters were only a few feet from the wharf.

The water was cold. It slapped at him constantly, though it was calm everywhere else. It was as if the sea were angry at him alone. It smelled of sewage, and a film of oil and gasoline clung to him. In the moonlight, the film made little rainbows of color on the surface. Unseen creatures nibbled at his legs. As he latched onto the wharf, however, he felt bottom.

A Japanese patrol boat was moored directly in front of the tin structure that served as the general's head-quarters. It bobbed gently against the dock, throwing bright yellow patterns of light from its deck and port-holes. Hawk lowered himself until only his eyes peered above the filthy brine.

No one manned the patrol boat's crow's nest. Crew members occasionally plodded along the deck, blotting out the glaring boat lights. Hawk edged into the narrow space between the patrol boat and the wharf. He pulled himself up and looked over the splintered beam that formed the top and brink of the wharf. His back scraped the overhanging hull of the patrol boat.

"Goddamn son of a bitch," he muttered at the pain, ignoring the two dozen enemy sailors inches above him. The HQ was dark. Two guards marched in front of the building. They met in front of the only visible door as he watched. He lowered himself. The next time he looked they were gone. They were evidently marching around the entire circumference.

He noticed a group of yew and banana trees at one corner of the structure. If he could make it to this concealment before the guards reappeared, he would be momentarily safe. A more prudent individual would have timed the guards, waiting for them to reappear from their trip around the building, and then scheduled a dash for cover when they were known to be on the far side. Hawk didn't see them, and that was enough for him. He lifted himself, sloshing, out of the water, and scurried across the open space to the clump of vegetation. He crawled through the slick-feeling protective leaves and, breathing heavily, pressed his face against the corrugated metal wall of the building. The sailors on the patrol boat hadn't seen him. This might have been due to the suddenness and stealth of his approach, but was probably due to pure luck. He always expected a great deal of luck.

The boots of the guards went crunching by his hiding place. The corner of the building was dark and the leaves were dense. He lay there quietly for a moment, enjoying the comparative safety of the spot. Relative safety in the midst of danger was a pleasure he had always relished.

Finally he took a waterproof bag from his belt and opened it. He removed a large screwdriver and a pair of metal cutters.

His fingers ran along the galvanized sheet metal and found a place where two of the sheets overlapped. He worked the screwdriver between the edges, just above a bolt. When he had wriggled a lip into the metal, he jammed the cutters between the sheets. He cut a neat little square from around the bolt and it fell free. The procedure was repeated on the next bolt, a yard above the first.

A glassy sheet of perspiration encased his body. He slumped against the wall to rest. A guard stomped by. He looked out through the banana leaves to make sure nothing unusual was going on. The crew of the patrol boat appeared to be playing Chinese checkers in the wheelhouse. He took note of the evil-looking Hotchkiss air-cooled machine gun mounted in the stern of the boat. Reflections from the boat lights played along the series of cooling rings that ran the length of the barrel. The barrel was pointed at the clump of banana leaves. Was there a crewman behind the gun?

His gut constricted. He pulled back into the darkness and every muscle in his body tensed. The expected shots never came. He looked out again. No one was manning the gun. The light was playing tricks on his eyes. With a ragged sigh of what could hardly be called relief, he turned back to the loosened sheet metal.

He forced his fingers under the knife-sharp edge of the pale blue metal and slowly folded it back. A guard walked by. Hawk stopped and waited, then started folding it again. Sweat flowed down his face and onto the metal. He feared that the tin would creak and screech as he bent it. He reached the point where his hands could bent it no more. Lying down, he jammed a shoulder under it and forced it a bit higher. The opening was finally big enough. He thrust a hand inside.

It hit something solid. There was an inner wall behind the outer layer of tin; probably of sheetrock or plywood.

"Goddamn Jap bastards," he whispered vehemently, and ducked under the sharp fold of tin to have a look. It was too dark to see. His fingertips caressed the inner wall. It felt like little upright cylinders. The inner wall was of bamboo, or something similar. He slid his jungle knife from its scabbard and inserted it between two of the bamboo poles. Within a few minutes, he had hewn and bullied a hole through the inner wall. Sticking a hand through the hole, he discovered nothing but thin air blocking his path. Without pausing to congratulate himself or to take another look outside of the banana leaves, he ducked into the hole.

Grey columns of light, visible around the window blinds, were the only relief of the complete darkness. The tomblike atmosphere was in stark contrast to a bustling, brightly lit, open-all-night American head-quarters. He crawled along the floor, feeling his way around the legs of desks and chairs. As he neared the center of the building he saw his first signs of life. A dim light shone from a closet-sized office near the door that faced the harbor. A guard had to be in that office.

The guard had to go. It never occurred to Hawk, as he pulled his knife from his sheath, that he himself might be the one to go. He saw the breaking into and entering of the headquarters as a complete act and the murdering of the guard as only a small part of it. He crawled on his hands and knees toward the glowing shaft of white light. Paper rustled in the little office.

Rustling paper had never sounded louder. The smell of unswept dust filled his nostrils as he stopped at the door.

He peered in from the ground level. A reading lamp was on a bench and, in front of it, a lone soldier sat in a swivel chair, thumbing through a magazine. The cover of the magazine depicted a Japanese soldier trampling on an American flag. Hawk stood.

He wadded up the waterproof bag and stepped confidently into the office, as if he did this every day of his life. The sentry looked up, unstartled, because the movement of his visitor was so casual and unhurried. The marine stuck the bag into his mouth with one hand and slashed his throat with the other. The man tumbled from the chair, falling heavily to the ground and taking the lamp with him. Hawk caught it before it hit the floor and replaced it on the bench. The dying man moaned and twisted about in a serpentine manner, squirting and smearing blood over the entire floor of the office.

"Bastard," Hawk growled angrily, and fell on him in a burst of temper, viciously chopping him with the black-bladed knife.

He took the bag from the mouth of the dead man and shook the last of the articles from it: a carbide lantern and matches. He lit the tiny lamp and a bluish-white flame hissed from its concave reflector. As he worked, drops of blood pitter-pattered from Hawk's hands onto the floor.

He took a deep breath and walked around the room that evidently housed the general's staff. The desks were neat and uncluttered. A dozen filing cabinets were stuffed with papers. He opened one and lifted out a sheaf of documents. It looked like chicken scratches to him. He pulled his lower lip in and looked around the room.

"Twelve cabinets of this Jap shit," he muttered under his breath. A door to another room caught his eye. He reasoned that, if a general was doing something underhanded for his own profit, he would keep the records as close to himself as possible. He strode across the room, his little lantern hissing, and tried the door. It was locked. He forced it with his knife.

The room behind the door belonged to the general's secretaries. Two small desks were in the office, and beside each of them stood a filing cabinet. He took an armload of papers from one of these cabinets and thumbed quickly through it. It was impossible. American intelligence could have had a field day with the material, but it was all useless to James Hawk. One last door led from the secretaries' office. It had to lead to the general's chamber. Again, the door was locked.

He forced the latch from the striking plate with his knife and swung the door open. Definitely a general's office. A huge teak desk took up most of the room. In the corner stood a large cage with a cockatoo in it. The bird raised the feathers atop his head and said something to the intruder.

"Shut up, buzzard," Hawk snapped, and tossed a cloth over the cage. Someone had forgotten to cover the parrot. Unless someone was coming back. Hawk narrowed his eyes and looked over his shoulder through the two forced doors. The main room was quiet, the sentry's lamp burning contentedly.

The general's quarters did not have the benefit of any filing cabinets. The desk drawers were locked. He tried the knife blade on the top center drawer, but it gave and complained as if it might break. He tore the drawer open with the screwdriver, careless of the desk's fine finish. The opening of this drawer unlocked all of the other drawers. Three manila files lay in the center drawer. He leafed through the first one and noticed something unusual—a piece of paper smaller than the rest. He pulled it out. It was two small pieces of paper stapled together. The paper on the bottom was printed in English and he had seen it before. It was Kravanart's leaflet. The other leaflet seemed to be a Japanese copy of the American edition. He guessed at this by the arrangement of the words. It was obvious that the Japanese had copied Kravanart's leaflet and that they wanted the outlaw band of Marines, too. Why the enemy would so trouble themselves was a mystery to Hawk. He didn't know of Gill's atrocity and of the Japanese colonel's mistaking him for Gill. The world seemed to be a very lonely place to Hawk as he put the flyer back into the file. He would take this file with him.

He opened the second folder. A stack of multicolored currency fell out: bills with "Japanese Government" printed on them in English, in varying denominations of pesos. This file looked interesting, too. On general principle, he decided also to take along the third file. He tore through the contents of the other drawers.

He found no other files and no papers other than stacks of blank forms. Hawk hoped that the three files

he held were the General's personal under-the-table transaction records. Finding a leather attaché case near the desk, he stuffed the files into it. Before he closed the flap, he carried the case into the secretaries' office. He might as well nab some militarily significant information while he was here. After all, there was a war on; Sergeant Hawk was never one to forget that. Only one file drawer in the entire office was locked. That one had to be the top-secret information. He pried it open. It all looked like nonsense except for a few photos and maps, but he stuffed it all into the briefcase.

It was time to go—or try to go. The sergeant felt an urge to do something dramatic; something worthy of a "renegade" wanted by both sides of the war. He returned to the general's office and carved his name into the desktop. Taking an ashtray from the desk, he went back to the dead sentry. He put his boot on the dead man's neck and forced some blood into the ashtray. He poured the blood into the carved-out letters on the general's desk. He looked up from admiring the originality of this work of art to see a framed certificate hanging on the wall. It drew his attention, because it was written in English. Among other things it said: "University of California at Los Angeles...Yasuro Kirijo...1919."

Hawk looked at the lopsided diploma for a moment and then shrugged. Everything didn't have to mean something. He had to get out.

He stepped into the sentry's office once more to relieve him of his pistol. He put the pistol into his waterproof bag and tied it onto his belt. On his way out, he opened all the filing cabinets and threw their contents across the floor and desks.

The attaché case came sliding silently out of the hole in the corner of the building, followed by Sergeant Hawk. He lit a handful of crumpled papers and threw them into the room behind him. He kept the flame within the hole that no one would see the flash. A guard tramped by, then another. He stuck his head through the shiny foliage that hid the corner of the headquarters. It was clear. He scampered to the boardwalk and lowered himself into the harbor. Holding the case above the water, he made his way slowly back to the pier; the return trip was far more dangerous than his approach because, for the most part, his back was to the patrol boat. But escape was his only thought, and once he had quit the water, he fairly flew through the town and back up the hillside to the waiting Marines. They sat anxiously watching the fire in the headquarters building below. Alarms were reverberating from one end of the town to the next.

8

After the infiltration of the Japanese headquarters in Porkeet, the Marines thought it best to retreat deeper into the wooded north country of Lamare. The pickings were good for information, food, and supplies in the densely populated vicinity of Porkeet, but the Japanese presence was prohibitive. The Americans expected heavy patrols to begin scouring the hills for the saboteurs of Kirijo's HQ.

General Kirijo did nothing of the kind. He was a very sly man. He was not so naive as to believe that Sergeant Hawk had actually broken into *his* headquarters. He knew that Sergeant Hawk was nothing more than an ignorant, brutal, half-starved outlaw, stumbling around in the jungles of the far south, near Liloila. No, this sabotage was something far more sinister and threatening. Whoever broke into the general's office knew exactly what they were after. They had taken his personal files and all of the top-secret files dealing with the campaign. An educated man could tell that it was the work of an insider. It had probably been one of the three top members of the general's staff. They were all selfless, patriotic fools, jealous of any man who knew how to turn a quick profit.

The fire was merely a ploy to cover their tracks. Kirijo would not take their bait, however. He sent no patrols on wild-goose chases up and down the hills. He didn't even play cat-and-mouse with them; he simply ordered all three executed. They honorably killed themselves before the appointed time came.

Thus ended any notion that the three staff members might have had of extorting anything from him in return for the files. He had reacted so hastily, however, that it didn't occur to him that he would now never know what had happened to the files. At first this didn't bother him. He knew that the staff members' deaths would drive any hope of extortion from the hearts of anyone in league with them. But, later on, he began to have nagging fears that one of the staff might have mailed the file, or a part of it, to his influential family in Japan. He ordered all mail stopped. But he might have been too late; it might have already gone out. He stopped sleeping at night. He began feeling dizzy and having terrible chest pains.

* * *

GENERAL KIRIJO WAS MISTAKEN. Sergeant Hawk had the files, and the executions would not keep him silent. No amount of mere death and misery would ever impress him. Hawk discovered that, although Ramos spoke Japanese, he was unable to read it. Speaking and reading the language were two separate arts due to the difference in English letters and Japanese characters.

Hawk led the men through the rain-drenched, snake-infested backwoods to a barrio where there reportedly lived a man fluent in several languages. The platoon nearly stumbled into an enemy patrol boat as they crossed a swollen river. The sailors might have spotted them, but evidently they did not recognize them as Americans. They might also have thought it best not to engage whoever the ragged band was, in the tangled undergrowth. In a few days, in the barrio of San Miguel, they found the man called Bival who could read Japanese.

The jovial, hefty mayor of San Miguel had straw mats brought and spread on the plaza around the town's fountain. Hawk emptied the briefcase and Bival sifted through the papers. Bival was an elderly gentleman with a scholarly demeanor.

The Filipino closed one of the files and set it aside. "This one is a copy of this one," he told Hawk. In effect, therefore, Hawk had captured only two files from Kirijo's drawer. The third was merely a copy of one of the others. This seemed to be a setback.

"What's this?" Hawk picked out the leaflet stapled to Kravanart's flyer.

"That is a copy, more or less, of the English paper attached to it. It says: 'Renegades...'"

"Okay. So the Japs made a copy of this and passed it out to their army, too?" Hawk rubbed his beard.

"Yes, indeed. I myself have seen copies of this same leaflet, written in Spanish. It says on the Japanese leaflet that this man, Sergeant Hawk, executed thirty prisoners and tortured four others near Liloila. He is a man without a country; a man gone berserk."

"Yeah, I've heard of him. He's a real bastard, all

right," said Hawk. "You see anything anywhere in there about a deal with some king of Tausag pirates? The sale of an American woman, maybe?"

"There are notes concerning many negotiations. There are contracts and orders for goods. A certain sea bandit is mentioned often, man named Garrotero. I do not know whether he is a Tausag." Bival put down the papers and rubbed his eyes with a thumb and forefinger. His white hair was combed straight back. He slapped his hand over it. "It is a terrible man who would trade with the Japanese. There are even those who fight for them."

"This Garrotero—he is Tausag," said Ramos, as if he had been thinking about it. "Read more about this Garrotero."

"Yeah, we gotta know where they hauled this woman off to," said Hawk.

"Hey," Canlon interrupted, "is there Filipinos fightin' for the Japs around here?"

Bival smiled and shook his head no. He picked up one of the papers that mentioned Garrotero. "This document," the old man said slowly, "refers to an American woman." Bival continued reading without showing any emotion. Hawk smiled.

"Yeah? What's it say?" the sergeant asked, leaning forward.

"They talked of taking her to Borneo. Garrotero refused to do it. But now she is sold. As a courtesy, the woman's mother and—I think her brother—were included in the agreement. "There was no charge for these two."

"That's them," said Hawk. "Where's she at?"

"They were to be delivered to the Daimo of Tamara," Bival answered, "and this is dated five days ago."

"That's about right. That jives with what we figured. This Tamara is an island down to the south?" Hawk asked.

Bival did not know where Tamara was located, but he knew a little about it. The Tamara were a mixture of Japanese, Spanish, and native islanders. They lived in an abandoned castle adjacent to an ancient temple. Travelers usually avoided them because of their isolation and their reputation for hostility.

"Is this a big place, this Tamara?" Hawk asked.

"It is not big. It is not important."

"Good. I'll find her, then. Mr. Bival, we'd like for you to throw in with us. We could use a man that talks Jap."

Bival did not like this idea. It was an extremely dangerous adventure. He wanted to help his country and the Americans, but he couldn't see how this would help either. Ramos intervened. He explained that the Marine before him was none other than Sergeant Hawk. Ramos stretched the truth a bit, and told the old man that the leaflets were all full of lies about Hawk, that the sergeant was working on an important intelligence operation. Then he veered back toward the truth and reported how the Marine had broken into Kirijo's HQ to get these documents and that he intended to return them to the south of Lamare after rescuing Amelia Jennings. The Americans understood none of the conversation. Bival swallowed the story. It sounded close enough to the truth. The men gathered around him looked like fighting men on an important mission. He changed his mind. He would help them if he could.

"Then," Bival said thoughtfully, "we will go to the coast of Naravey, in the north. I have a friend who operates a kumpit along that shore. There is some Japanese activity between here and there, and there will be much for you to observe before we take to the sea." Bival inclined his forehead toward Hawk as he spoke. He helped the sergeant pick up the captured documents and replace them in the briefcase. Hawk nodded silently.

They were all primed for an early start. The Marines did not relish the idea of staying too long in one place. Since Porkeet, imaginary enemy patrols marched up and down their fitful dreams. Though this was not the case, the enemy was definitely present in the region. Major roads, minor roads, villages and rivers were all teeming with Imperial soldiers on the lookout for Filipino partisans. Reconnaissance planes occasionally buzzed the mountainsides and the jungle treetops. And the rumor was that tiny San Miguel was due to be visited by a Japanese garrison within the week. This was enough to make anyone want to leave.

Possibly because of this threat, the town was holding a fiesta. It began the morning the Marines left. The men had no time for fraternizing with the local girls, but they did pick up a few bottles of native liquor. The villagers were going in one direction in a loud procession from the church as the Marines filed solemnly by in the other direction. Hawk noticed some ornate candleholders decorating the walk leading up to the church's door.

Sergeant Hawk's eye was trained for one purpose—killing. When he looked at a tree, it was to measure its thickness and its bullet-stopping capabilities. Rolling landscape was not a thing to admire but a puzzle from which he picked out the high and low ground, the good places to seek cover, and the bad places to force the enemy. Sharp objects were made to stab with, fire was to incinerate Japanese, rope was to choke them, water was to drown them. His mind operated that way. So it was not unusual that, when he saw the little votive-light holders in front of the church, he immediately recognized a way to use them for killing. They were stuck far into the ground on long metal shafts. He pulled one of them up and took the glass candle holder out of the metal prongs that gripped it. Throwing the vigil light on the ground, he slipped a grenade from his pocket and jammed it into the holder. It fit tightly and perfectly. Calling for Canlon's M1, he slid the long shaft of metal down the thirty-caliber barrel. Again, a perfect fit.

"You riggin' up a way to kill yourself?" Canlon asked.

"It might take two good men to make it work, but I think these'll make pretty fair rifle grenades."

"Looks like a hand grenade on a stick to me. I hope you ain't plannin' on me bein' one of the good men."

Ignoring such skepticism, the sergeant took a rifle bullet and made a blank out of it. He took the hand grenade out of the candle holder and fired the blank cartridge. The rifle threw the holder onto the roof of the church.

"That thing'll go two hundred yards," Hawk judged as the holder came rolling off the roof.

"It'll be heavier with a grenade," said Canlon.

"Okay, man—a hundred yards."

"And you gotta pull the pin and shoot the rifle both."

"Shit, yeah, you gotta pull the pin. Why don't you just admit it? It's a damn good idea."

Canlon shook his head. He had to admit it. "Yeah, it'll be like havin' a mortar."

Hawk ordered Lasker and Shaeffer to pull up all the decorative candle holders. An excited priest interrupted their rather thoughtless appropriation.

"What are you doing?" the little Father cried in outrage. "These are not gold. They are only gold-plated. Do not steal these." Shaeffer ignored him. "You thieving jackals!" the priest raved.

"Hello, Padre," Hawk greeted him, unperturbed. "We ain't after no gold. I'll sign a receipt for you, for the little gadgets. We're makin' weapons out of 'em."

"Weapons, hah! You are as evil as General Kirijo. He has already taken all the gold from the church—from *every* church on Lamare—and melted down all of the priceless treasures, for himself."

"Like I say, I can sign a receipt, see, and the U.S. government will reimburse..."

"Beware American thief. The Kempeitai investigated General Kirijo some time past. They forced him to mend his ways. All gold is the property of the Japanese Empire. They confiscated all that he had." The priest shook a finger at Hawk. The Kempeitai was the Japanese version of the Gestapo.

"Yessir. Well, he'll get by, I reckon—but, like I say..."

"Oh, yes, he still steals our gold; but he must change it into currency very quickly now. The devil always has another path around virtue." The priest turned away from Hawk and shouted at the none-too-virtuous Pidge Shaeffer. "I know very influential men in the Kempeitai. Replace those candles at once or you will deal with them."

"No, Padre; see, to tell you the truth, them ain't the

kind of boys we'd like to mess with. Uh—Mr. Bival, maybe you could talk to the man, here..." Hawk leaned over the old Filipino. "Make him happy, but make sure we get them candle things."

After a good deal of Spanish conversation, which ultimately involved Ramos, things were smoothed over. They placed on the priest's patriotic sympathies and his hatred of Kirijo. They managed to get both the candle holders and an assurance that the priest wouldn't inform the secret police of the Marines' presence.

The procession of Marines finally managed to leave San Miguel and headed northward toward the coast. They moved slower now, living off the wilds. This way of life had taken its toll. Weight losses were universal. In spite of this, physically, the men maintained a lean hardness. Their energy and morale continued to be drained by the breathless, mind-scattering heat. They conserved their strength in any way possible, so the news of a possible confrontation was poorly received.

A small native barrio lay between San Miguel and the coast of Naravey. It was little more than a collection of mud and grass huts. Because it was the nearest township to the coast, the Japanese had stationed about twenty men there as a garrison. The garrison was replenished with men and supplies every two weeks. The enemy troops had little to do, other than getting drunk and bullying the locals. The inhabitants of the hamlet were primitive tribesmen. Before the war, Bival had befriended them, bringing them gifts on Christmas and trying unsuccessfully to convert them from their animism to Christianity. He was irritated by the treatment given them by the Japanese, and asked Hawk to intervene. There was no question but that he would.

The little village served no strategic purpose. The Marines could have bypassed it in good conscience, with the world being only slightly the worse for it. Nevertheless, Sergeant Hawk saw his purpose in life as to kill Japanese, and he would always go out of his way to do that. He would risk his life unnecessarily to do it. Perhaps he thought this was his duty, but it was more likely that he enjoyed it. The little barrio drew him like a magnet. Those of tender sensibilities might have considered him an agent of purposeless evil, but it was the unprovoked oppression of the Japanese that ultimately attracted him. He just happened to be the stronger of the two evils. Bival recognized this and put it to good use, as the U.S. government had done before him.

The Marines crawled through the wet jungle. Steam rose from the damp earth like smoke. They formed a semi-circle south of the barrio. They lay sweating and melting in the midday heat for what seemed like hours.

From the thick, itchy greenery they observed the drunken enemy soldiers. The Japanese, for the most part, lounged in the cool interiors of huts built upon the ground. An occasional bark of an order could be heard from within the primitive huts. The tribesmen milled about, performing their usual tasks and waiting upon their captors. Three men in G-strings hung onto a railing in the middle of the town, threshing grain with their feet. Hawk chewed placidly on his tobacco as he watched them. He waited for the slightest polarization between the innocents and the enemy. It appeared that this might never occur; the two groups were hopelessly mixed. They occasionally stopped to speak to or at one another.

Then came the mess call. The soldiers grouped together in a knot around a table with a bucket of rice at its center. Hawk spat out a stream of black tobacco juice. His eyes showed no emotion.

"The grenade launcher," he said in a low voice to Canlon. Canlon passed the word down to Shaeffer, who was carrying most of the candle holders.

Pidge wasn't sure if he himself was supposed to fire into the enemy or if he was to pass a holder up to Hawk. Since he had gone to the trouble of marking a few blanks just for this occasion, he decided to do it himself. Shaeffer came the closest to sharing Hawk's thrill of excitement at the prospect of combat. The others looked on in hypnotized terror, wondering if they were to live or die, tightly squeezing their legs together to keep from urinating and defecating all over themselves. Those possessing more grace under pressure than the others watched the situation, and themselves in it, as something detached, something happening elsewhere to someone else. Shaeffer and Hawk actually enjoyed it. They were somehow convinced that, no matter what happened today in this, smelly hole in the jungle, they would survive.

Relying on his young lightning reflexes, Shaeffer pulled both the pin of the grenade and the trigger of the Ml himself. The fuse of the grenade was approximately four or five seconds. He pulled the pin and hurriedly adjusted the rifle. It would have to be called "adjusting" rather than "aiming," since it was done in such a haphazard manner. But he managed to do it without blowing himself up. And, as it turned out, the grenade was well placed.

The blank cartridge snapped and the candle holder

dropped into the middle of the huts. It hit a man standing in the chow line and knocked him down. By then the fuse had exhausted itself, and the dozen or so men in the chow line were blasted in all directions. For a moment the village was paralyzed as a wavering column of smoke blew about the point of the grenade's impact. Then the tribesmen gathered their wits and ran for the jungle. Some of them ran toward the Americans and stepped over them in their aimless flight. The Japanese who survived could do little more than stumble about in dazed circles. The wounded set up a chorus of cries that froze the marrow in the bones of the listeners.

Hawk stood, released his safety, and walked into the village. The breechblock of his Thompson shuddered frantically to and fro as he turned the deadly muzzle from one confused man to the next. The other Marines followed him in. It was a quick mop-up, with no American casualties.

As Hawk neared the site of the grenade explosion, a wounded man lying on his belly looked up and cried out to him. His chest was horribly mangled and he held a red hand over it. His voice rose and lowered in pitch as he begged the sergeant to help him. Like a whip, a flash crackled from the muzzle of the Thompson. The barrage was loosed across the face of the Japanese, bursting his head like a balloon. Where another man might have seen another human being, injured and deserving compassion, Hawk saw only a snake hungry for his own life. And this time he had been right.

The sergeant turned the body over with his boot. The man held a small corncob grenade within the ragged edges of his brutal chest wound. Hawk spat down onto it.

The villagers didn't return. Neither did an estimated three or four fleeing Japanese, and for good reason. Nothing in the poor hovels was worth looting. No order was given but, as was often the way in those situations, the huts began to sprout red spires of flame. To his discredit, Hawk gave no order to extinguish the fires. He only ordered the men to keep moving.

MILES TO THE SOUTHEAST, SERGEANT GILL'S RED-RIMMED
eyes watched the sea at his right. He wondered, as he
struggled closer to Porkeet, if the Marines had boarded
a boat. He called one of the patrol's frequent halts. Gill
was getting low on stamina. Hawk could run wherever
he wanted and Gill had to follow. Hawk was living off of
the land like any other lower form of animal. Two of
Gill's men had fallen under a hundred pounds. They
were unhealthy and starving. They ate only berries and
roots and they were half afraid to eat those, thinking
that the wild food might be the cause of the endless
dysentery that plagued them.

Gill had no intention of giving up. He hoarded
rations to keep up his strength. His weight had fallen to
around two hundred but he remained fit. He was
exhausted twenty-four hours a day, yet every night he
got down on the ground and did six hundred sit-ups.
His dwindling patrol considered him rather crazy. They
sweated, excreted, and evaporated flesh from their
parched bones while Gill did childish exercises.

The men were nearly spent—but Jack Calicote was the exception. Calicote seldom ate, seldom slept, seldom spoke. If Hawk was an animal and Gill a madman, Calicote was a machine. The dirty beanpole had no physical reason for still being on his feet. Yet the more he did without, the more he thrived.

Gill couldn't especially do without. He required nourishment and rest, and saw to it that he got more of both than any of the others. Justification for this came from his athletic background. He deserved pampering because he was better than other men. He could whip any two of them at once. Gill had never really grown up. Athletics, contests, were a part of his psyche. He had joined the Army to demonstrate to the world that he was tough—not that the world knew or cared. And he participated in every contest to win. What he didn't realize, however, was that chasing Sergeant Hawk was no game. Hawk didn't play games. You couldn't back away and try again tomorrow in Hawk's world. Calicote might have understood this, and understood this weakness in Gill. But Calicote never spoke.

Gill found out from an old Filipino that Hawk had cut overland to San Miguel. The Marines were an awesome number of miles behind enemy lines. Gill was determined to pursue them. His dying band of recon patrollers followed him.

* * *

HAWK WAS a long way from Sergeant Gill—not that he was aware of that fact, nor would he have cared if he had been. The Marines broke through the brush along the coast of Naravey. The vast ocean turned to a deep purple in the distance. The broad, wide-open expanse was cheering after so many days in the close woodlands. Naravey was not the name of a village nor of a body of water. It was the term applied to a stretch of shore on the northern coast. Fishermen found good hunting there and often congregated off the wild beaches. Poor traders were drawn to the region in the hopes of selling their wares to the isolated men of the sea. They operated strictly from their kumpits and seldom put ashore. The fishermen and traders drew pirates. The ruthless bandits of the ocean were probably the reason villages hadn't grown up in such an attractive area.

Bival, shading his eyes with one hand, searched the fleet of craft bobbing on the horizon for his friend. He assured Hawk that in good time the friend would show up and that, if he didn't, a similarly trustworthy means of travel would arrive. They should make themselves comfortable and wait. Hawk was a Southerner, not given to pointless hurrying about trying to look efficient. When given a choice, which was very seldom, he walked slow and he talked slow, and he still managed to get everything done that needed to be done. He understood the tropical lack of concern for the importance of time. But this was one of those times when something had to be done. He flagged the nearest boat in to the beach.

The captain of the little vessel would have nothing to do with the Marine. Bival asked about his friend, a captain named Cesar Alonso, but the man hadn't heard from him of late.

"You American GI, go this way on beach." The captain smiled at Hawk and pointed toward the east. As he smiled, there was something unfriendly in the way the flesh on his face rose over his high cheekbones. "Something for *you* there."

"Yeah? What?" Hawk squinted up at him from the knee-deep surf. "Japs?"

"Maybe. You see. 'Round those trees." The captain turned away and ordered his men to shove off. He didn't look at the Americans again. He seemed to be in a hurry. Hawk considered cutting his throat and stealing his boat. He dug deep and scraped up enough moral fiber to overcome the urge. As the boat pulled away, demonstrating its prowess against the barrier of water, Hawk tightly gripped the trigger of the gun at his side. He lit a cigar and sent Shaeffer scouting in the direction the captain had indicated.

Pidge was back in less than half an hour. He breathed heavily through his parted red lips. His large eyes darted anxiously along the jungle fringing the beach.

"Supplies, Hawk. Army stuff, just like we found at Liloila. A bunch of them. There's a coupla Jap Marines guarding them. I saw a wagon with two horses hitched to it, too." Pidge unsnapped his canteen and took a long drink. Hawk looked at the tantalizing fishing boats weaving in and out on the gentle sea. He dragged thoughtfully on his cigar.

"How are them Japs gettin' American shit way up here? There ain't been no counterattack in this area. It's solid Jap. Why would it be up here? Ain't nothin' up here."

"It got here on a goddamn boat," said Canlon.

"Yeah," Hawk agreed. "It's probably goin' out the same way. Horses can't get through this shit. There's something funny about it, awright." He snapped the cigar from his mouth. "How many Japs you reckon they got staked out over there?"

"Like I say," Pidge answered, "I only seen two. I crawled around 'em. Only two."

"Makes a man feel obligated to bump 'em off, don't it?" said Hawk, putting the cigar back into his mouth. And he would have if Cesar Alonso hadn't sailed around the western bend in the shoreline. Bival interrupted the sergeant's preparations for an attack with the news that Alonso had arrived. Feeling more cautious now, Hawk withdrew the Marines into the forest and allowed Ramos and Bival to signal the boat. The two Filipinos waded out into the brownish-green part of the surf and spoke with an open-shirted man on the boat. The conversation sounded like mere noise-in-the-wind from the Marines' vantage point. The salty air and the panoramic view made the place seem somehow fresh and safe. After a minute or two, Bival waved his arm. Hawk led the men brazenly back onto the beach. In another quarter of an hour, as a result of negotiations the Americans didn't understand, they were all on board Alonso's kumpit.

Hawk studied the craft with a trained eye. It was a big, ugly thing with an outrigger on each side. These helped the ungainly boat keep her balance on the high seas. Alonso used her for fishing, cargo hauling, passenger carrying, or whatever he had to do to keep body and soul together in an honest manner. A tin-roofed shed shaded most of her deck, and there appeared to be a substantial hold beneath the ancient but well-cared-for deck. The boat had the speed of a wounded turtle and could withstand little more than a broadside of peashooters. Hawk naturally noticed this, but he dismissed the uncomfortable thought of a confrontation at sea. They would simply lose, and pay with their lives, in such an eventuality.

The drab, dirty-looking kumpit had a look of utility about it that was often lacking among the other lively, colorful boats that roamed the coast of Naravey. As Hawk slowly pulled himself to his feet with the aid of his Thompson, he noticed one outlandishly colorful vessel in particular. A boat that resembled a Chinese junk was making its swift way toward the shore, where the American supplies were reportedly stacked and ready for shipment. Judging by the speed of the gaudy craft, it was motorized, although it had a huge, Chinese-lantern-shaped sail. The sides of the junk were covered with bright emblems of red and gold, Oriental writings and artwork, and various other designs indistinguishable in the distance. It disappeared around the bend in the shoreline.

"I got a sneakin' feelin' we ought not let that ship see us," Hawk told Canlon. He had disliked bright colors ever since he had been bitten by a coral snake as a child.

The men were ordered to keep below the gunwales till they reached the open sea. Bival was told to ask Alonso to sail past the junk on his way out. As the kumpit cruised by the stern of the junk, Hawk saw two enemy Marines and several crewmen loading her with American supplies. All their heads were industriously bowed.

"Let's sink it," Shaeffer suggested.

"Naw," Hawk whispered. He was thinking more along the lines of following her. That would have solved a minor mystery, perhaps; the mystery of how the Japanese managed to have such free access to American goods. But there was a rescue to execute. He had to let it go. Amelia Jennings was calling him. So much time had passed, and there was so much danger. The kumpit rocked close by the stern of the junk. The Japanese Marines looked disinterestedly at the shabby Filipino boat. Stenciled on the side of the junk in large Gothic lettering was the word "Garrotero." The idling engine of the junk thudded in Hawk's ears and caused the deck of the kumpit to vibrate.

* * *

IN THE FAR-OFF SULU SEA, on the lost island of Tamara, Amelia Jennings stood upon the roof of a crumbling keep in the heart of a Spanish castle. In the prison cell below her, Calvert tossed and turned with delirious malaria. The man's ailing inspired nothing but hatred in the breast of Mrs. Jennings. The hapless fellow had made the mistake of asking Garrotero to leave him at a port of call and take only the women to the wild island. This was a wise course of action to attempt; the mistake was in letting Mrs. Jennings overhear his plea. Amelia had to tend to him alone, covering him with blankets and pouring water into him.

It was a pretty day on Tamara and the wind blew through Amelia's hair. Her mother sat distraught beside her, sobbing quietly to herself.

"So far from anything," said Mrs. Jennings. "How I miss everyone so. Such a tragic way to end our lives. Oh, Amelia, if only you weren't here—I would gladly stay in your place."

"Oh, Mother, it's me they want, for God's sake. Let's not make things worse by continuously crying about them." She held her mother's head against her knee. "Don't worry, now; I have the oddest feeling that someone will find us."

"Oh, you poor dear. No one could ever find us here. Decent people never come here. No one could save us even if they knew we were here. Even if there were no war, I doubt that anyone could do anything."

Amelia had a specific individual in mind, and no one had ever accused that particular man of being decent.

* * *

THROUGH THE NEXT FEW DAYS, the word stenciled on the side of the pirate ship haunted Sergeant Hawk. Amelia Jennings might still have been on board. No one knew for certain if she had ever reached Tamara. If she was still with the pirate, Hawk might have lost her forever. She could have been destined for any port anywhere in the South Pacific. He talked it over with Bival and the understanding old gentleman assured him that they could again find Garrotero. The pirate had never been one given to stealth or hiding. Bival thought it best to follow the trail they already had and to go to the mysterious island Alonso told them was in the distant Sulu Sea. Hawk went along with the plan.

He sat in the middle of the deck. As the sun and salt bleached the boards of the deck white, they burned him brown. Almost to a man, the other Americans clung to the gunwales and threw up for two straight days. Recovery from the seasickness was difficult. When they turned around, they saw Hawk spitting black chewing tobacco across the deck, no sight for those with sensitive stomachs. Pidge Shaeffer, green from the neck up, sat quietly in the stern. He never threw up, but he never moved much either.

"I tell ya, I'm dyin'," Canlon finally cried out in exhaustion. "Put me off somewheres. I can't go on no more."

"A little goddamn water and you son of a bitches fall to pieces. There ain't no place to dump your ass or I awready woulda done it. We done passed two Jap cruisers. You wanta end up with *them*?" Hawk roared at the corporal, exhibiting his usual patient, sympathetic, and tender style.

"I volunteered to fight for my country," Canlon groaned, "but no man should have to put up with this. I been sailin' before, but not on a goddamn cork. Gimme to the Japs, I tell you. Hawk, you crazy bastard!"

"Ah, shut up. You're gettin' on the boys' nerves," Hawk answered. The boys were too occupied with themselves for Joe to be getting on their nerves. The Filipino crewmen couldn't understand Canlon, so he wasn't bothering them. The only person whose nerves might have been irritated was Sergeant Hawk, and that presupposed he *had* nerves.

The trip went on for two days. No land was in sight, only green ocean, stretching off into living, rolling, eternal pastures. Behind the nauseated men, in the middle of the churning deck, a pool of black chewing-tobacco spittle grew, coursing here and there, depending on the roll of the deck. Very little gave solace to Sergeant Hawk; he wasn't about to give up his chewing tobacco.

The sergeant ate the nasty fish offered him by the crewmen, but the others fasted for two full days. He crunched the bones between his teeth and cursed the men for needlessly weakening themselves.

Toward the end of the miserable second day, Alonso cried out from the straight-backed chair on the roof of his deck-shed. The chair served as his crow's nest. He had spotted a plane. A hazy thought filtered through Hawk's sunbaked brain. It didn't matter whose plane it was; he had to hide his men. He ordered them into the hold.

Below the deck, in the clammy, pitch-black hold, was the most ungodly, fishy odor ever visited upon a landlubber's nostril. The men slid into the grave of decades of dead sea creatures.

"Goddamn." Canlon grabbed his nose as he skidded along the fleshy walls of the dungeon. "This is exactly what a man needs to settle his goddamn stomach." The hatch fell shut, sealing them into the disgusting pit. The unrestrained vomiting was making Hawk irritable. He began to curse so loud and long that he didn't hear the grinding of the plane overhead. The men made weak threats on his life as they fought to keep their faces from touching the filthy floor or walls. Bival opened the hatch and delivered the welcome news that the plane was gone.

Hawk was the first man out. He snorted to get the odor of fish and vomit out of his nose, but it would remain for several days. "I'd like to know how you bastards can keep pukin' without eatin' nothin'," he complained as he helped the men out. "Whose plane was it?" he asked Ramos.

"Your plane. United States Navy. Circle us and fly off to Lamare."

"Hmm." Hawk grunted and sat down on the deck.

He had been hiding from a Navy plane. That kind of hurt him. It hadn't especially bothered him that the Army was after him. He had the early volunteer's disdain for anything connected with the Army. It was like having the Internal Revenue or a petty county sheriff after you. There was nothing significant to that, nothing anti-American. But the Navy—that hurt. It gave him a dull ache below his chest. His country had abandoned him. It was the same leaden feeling he got when he thought about Amelia Jennings. His fierce blue eyes paled as he stared across the barren sea.

The third day brought rumblings of misgivings from the troops. They recovered enough from their intestinal difficulties to evaluate their predicament. The heat boiled some common sense from deep within their skulls, and the acres of shark fins that surrounded them revived their instincts of self-preservation.

The mutiny never became serious. Hawk had the stronger personalities behind him. One was a man from Arkansas, named Calvin Davis who, although a poor seaman, was a fine combatant in a shoot-out. He had a tendency toward panic when any sort of shelling was involved. In his late twenties, he might have passed for a middle aged transient, so wrinkled and wasted did he look. He liked Hawk merely because he was a fellow Southerner, and "would have followed him anywhere" —which was exactly where they were going.

George Phillips was a quiet, intelligent man, who usually went along with the crowd, even when he knew better. He needed a leader and the sergeant was the only choice. He and Davis were respected by the other men, and their loyalty held great weight. Oddly enough, Davis and Phillips didn't get along well together. They moved in separate circles, which only broadened Hawk's support. Davis didn't like Phillips because he was from California.

Pidge Shaeffer had no friends. Everyone was half afraid of him. In normal life, men are afraid of big or powerful men, but in a war they're afraid of men they should be afraid of. Shaeffer liked to fight and kill, and one had the impression that when he was through with the Japanese he would start on the rest of the world. Shaeffer was drawn to Hawk, the only man who'd ever approved of his grisly nature. No one particularly liked Shaeffer but they all wanted to be on his side.

Joe Canlon would remain loyal also. Even though he wasn't intelligent, he had a folksy, mature sort of wisdom. He supplied Hawk with a conscience and common sense when the sergeant's ran low. Until now, this loose alliance had prevented any mutinies. It was an accidental mixture of personalities that ultimately furthered Hawk's purposes.

There were those, however, who had come close to joining the ill-fated Marisette-Owens-Pacht venture. Since Marisette had ended up a blue-plate special, this group had made no further protests. The man most likely to rekindle the fire of discontent was Merle Stroot. Stroot never opened his mouth unless it was to gripe, and his mouth was usually open. He probably didn't really want to leave; it was just in his nature to be dissatisfied with whatever situation he found himself in.

Stroot began raising the rhetorical question: Now that we have a boat, why can't we go back to the landing beach? This was a dangerous question for Hawk. There was no answer to it, other than that Hawk wanted to rescue the American woman. It shouldn't take long.

That answer was good enough for Canlon or Shaeffer or Davis or Phillips or even good-natured Chuck Lasker, but not for Merle Stroot.

Hawk was solemnly studying the tin roof of the deckhouse. The salty spray had turned it a slick, leaden blue. Stroot approached him with the question, thereby touching off the incident. Hawk gave him an undiplomatic, unsympathetic, and somewhat indecent reply. This forced Stroot to take the question back to the "people." Two or three of the people gathered behind Stroot and they again approached Hawk in search of an answer, or, more accurately, in an effort to bend him to their will. Hawk didn't bend.

The situation wasn't acute. Hawk knew this. Cowardice prompted the question, but it wouldn't get an answer. Tempers flared, angry words were exchanged, and Stroot's followers began to disperse when they saw Hawk's rage growing. They wanted to go to the landing beach, but not without him. The whole thing would have ended in a fizzle, except for Calvin Davis.

Davis immediately assumed that the innocent George Phillips was on the side of the mutineers. After all, he was a Californian, who spoke distinctly, occasionally used big words, and did all the other things right-thinking people consider uppity and unmanly. It was only logical that a Californian would want to turn back. Davis could picture Phillips in his knee-shorts, prowling the decadent beaches of the West Coast. Phillips was accidentally standing next to one of Stroot's backers. Davis decided to end the mutiny after it had already been ended. He pushed Phillips and followed the push with a series of punches. Phillips couldn't ask him what the hell he was doing because it would look like he was backing down. Other than being overwhelmed at first, the quiet Phillips gave a good account of himself.

"Land ho!" Shaeffer gave a joking shout from the crow's nest. The scuffling continued below. No one joined in the fight. The men just watched Davis and Phillips grunting and groaning and were glad to remain still and conserve their energy. Hawk didn't intervene. He knew he had to let Davis get the meanness out of his system; perhaps Phillips could beat some of it out.

"Land ho," Shaeffer repeated. Alonso climbed onto the deckhouse and began shouting instructions to his crew. One or two of the Filipinos responded, but the fight held the rapt attention of the others.

Davis got Phillips down onto the deck and waved a machete over his bloody head. Chuck Lasker decided that the contest had gone far enough and kicked the blade from Davis' hand. Another foot shot past Lasker and caught Davis in the chest, knocking him onto the deck.

"Separate 'em," Hawk ordered. Canlon stepped in and took a few angry elbows from Davis. The two of them went tumbling toward the stern and the rest of the men gathered at the gunwales to see land looming over the horizon. Phillips remained seated on the deck, still somewhat amazed by his role in the erstwhile mutiny.

Bival wriggled through the crowd to stand at Hawk's side. "Alonso says that is Tamara. We have arrived."

"Has the captain ever been here?" Hawk asked.

"Yes, but he has never been ashore. He is too superstitious." Bival looked up at Hawk and smiled. The oldtimer seemed to be enjoying the adventure. Hawk nodded and stared at the shoreline.

"They got a barrio here or something?"

"As we have told you, there are some old fortifications. The natives live in the ruins. There is only the one village, I presume. It is a small island."

The sky behind the low hump of land was as bright as a mirror. As they drew closer, the fingers of palm and tree fern leaves were silhouetted against the mirror. Highlands rose from the middle of the island like slumbering giants. The sharp folds and creases of the mountains leapt out of the blinding looking-glass background. The boat rocked to and fro, closing the distance and causing the mirror to disappear and become a hazy fog that embraced the ridges of the interior. Green like crushed emeralds extended from the trees off the beach and on up the mountainsides. From the ocean, the vegetation looked like little more than a carpet of thick fungus. The hull of the kumpit rose and fell with hissing splashes.

The setting sun painted the surface of the sea bright red. The crimson hue was reflected by the ghostly ground fog that hung over the island. Tamara had a dreamy, eerie presence to her like few of the men had ever seen. They forgot their differences as they watched her draw close.

"Peculiar-lookin' place," Hawk commented. The island had the appearance of a private haven. No welcoming party gathered on the long stretch of salt-white beach. "He goin' in, or does he want a boat put over the side?"

"You are ready to go ashore?" Ramos asked, leaning over Bival.

"I came here ready."

Ramos returned in short order. The captain lowered

a boat over the side. The natives were reputed to be an inhospitable people. Seamen took such scuttlebutt seriously—it was as much a part of their stock in trade as their nets. As the Marines were going over the side, the captain spoke at length to Hawk in the Tagalog language. With one leg on the deck and one dangling over the ocean, the sergeant awaited Bival's translation.

"He wants to know how long you are staying," Bival said. Ramos listened intently to the conversation. He watched Alonso's face.

"He say he *not* staying," Ramos added. "He say he might come back thirty days."

Hawk took the information with a brooding scowl at the shore. "Why can't he wait?"

"Nothing to wait for," Ramos shrugged. "There is big war on. Money to be made. No money on jungle island. No fish here but shark. No boat, no people ever come here. Tamara people might kill all, and if they don't, Jap be along soon. You see?"

"Yeah, I got the picture." Hawk looked down at his men, assembled in three small boats. None of them had heard the conversation. They rose and fell with the swells like mindless, inanimate objects. "Anybody wanta stay on board?" he roared. "This bastard's leavin' us." He could see their lips moving as their heads turned from one agitated face to the next. He couldn't hear them. Stroot wasn't saying anything. Sharks thumped against the sides of the small boats. A young, sick Marine decided to stay on board.

"I want to go," Ramos called from the deck. "But I must stay, make sure this no-good son bitch come back for you GI. Get another boat if you have to. Be back three, four days, maybe." Hawk nodded. That sounded good to him. Hawk held his breath as the sick Marine returned to Alonso's vessel. He feared a general rush for the safety of the deck above.

One of the small boats banged viciously against the hull of the kumpit as the boy climbed aboard. No one else bolted. "Shove off!" Hawk shouted before any more faint-heartedness could take hold. The Filipino crewmen, sent along to bring back the landing boats, poled them away from the kumpit.

"Kinda cold," Canlon observed, as the tiny boats slid inevitably toward the shore. It had been flesh-drying hot out on the ocean. A cool breeze emanated from the island.

"Yeah." Hawk spat over the side into the white-capped waves, "I've noticed that in a couple of landings. Must be a scientific explanation for that." He watched the swaying of the lonely treetops.

"Yeah," Canlon agreed. He turned away from the beach. He didn't want to think about what was to come. He consoled himself with the thought that it couldn't be any worse than landing on a beach infested with Japanese.

Ramos saw them from the deck of the kumpit. They blended into the sheet of red that laminated the front of Tamara. Red helmets bobbed in a blood-red sea of twilight.

10

FIRST PLATOON RAN AGROUND A LITTLE BEFORE DARK. The men went inland but only far enough to get sufficient cover from the openness of the beach. Hawk set up a triangular defense perimeter. Few slept that first night. Most sat up listening to the strange whoops of the nocturnal birds. When morning came, Hawk struck out for the highlands. He intended to wander aimlessly until his path intersected with that of the Tamara. The island was small; it shouldn't take long.

During the night, Merle Stroot disappeared. Whether he succumbed to a stealthy night creature, or whether he tried to return to the ship, was a matter for conjecture. He was just gone. With him went all the opposition to Hawk's leadership.

They wound through the odd fairy jungle, following the course of a narrow animal trail. Whatever animal had cut the trail was a short one. The path was of hardened dirt, and soft leaves hung over it, obscuring the boots of the Marines. Blindly, they waded through the sea of foliage. Little white moths clung like pearls to the stalks of the overhanging leaves, and would rise up in alarm at the passage of the first man, leaving a snowy cloud of insect wings for the others to swallow and slap from around their eyes. The plant life was dense but tolerable; no great effort was required to struggle through it. Large tender leaves of green, pink, and yellow bowed politely as the men passed, and pliable stalks of thick grass bent low beneath their crunching boots. The cool air blew down from the mountains.

Hawk called a halt as they reached the foothills of the mountains. The men picked bananas and sat on the ground, leisurely eating them. Hawk discovered one of his favorite delicacies, a wild pepper plant. He ate them by the handful. Canlon tried one and cursed Hawk for the remainder of the day for allowing him to put the acid-hot vegetable into his mouth.

With these amenities taken care of, the journey resumed. They charged unhesitatingly up the gradual slope of the mountain. The gentle slope caused the men to underestimate the size of the mountain. They had taken a two-dimensional view of the summit, and figured it as being much closer. The climb was easy and no one complained.

They crossed over the top, huddling in their jackets and pulling their collars up around their necks. Some of the men, who had taken to carrying their helmets, replaced them on their heads in an attempt to warm their ears. Davis slit his helmet cover and let it hang down onto his shoulders like the flaps on the backs of the caps of the French Foreign Legionnaires or the Japanese. Others pulled their lengthening hair down over their ears. The cold didn't last long and it served to invigorate the heat-saturated men. They crossed the summit and plunged down the other side before midday. In the distance, across a slimy bog, they could see the legendary castle. Night was coming on before they quit the mountain. The other slope, by contrast, was a steep one. Hawk felt they had gone far enough for one day. It was senseless to try to go on.

The stone structure stood on the eastern horizon. It was far from beautiful. The ancient Spanish builders had probably constructed it without the aid of architect or artisan. What it lacked as art, it made up for in size, a size that spoke of tremendous strength. It looked like a good place to sit out even a twentieth-century artillery barrage. The monolithic walls were relieved by intermittent towers and battlements. The coloring of the gigantic sun-beiged stones was barely discernible in the sudden twilight. The castle leered at Hawk from across the morass, and he leered back at it.

Behind it were other rambling structures, also of stone. Minarets lanced the grey dusk, lending an incongruous Oriental appearance to the lesser buildings. Judging by their tumbling state of disrepair, they were even older than the castle. It would have been an interesting display to an archaeologist or a student of architecture, but to Sergeant Hawk it was just a pile of rocks.

Both of these groups of structures were set together on a low, flat-topped hill, which could only remind the sergeant of 309. He stopped on the slope to survey the scene. One leg was higher than the other on the steeply inclined slope, and he balanced himself with sheer muscle sense. His arms hung at full length, with the Thompson loosely attached to his dangling fingers.

A golden full moon ascended behind the great walls. Hawk's angle of observation left him at a higher elevation than the castle. He could see the glowing orange bowl of the moon peering through the minarets of the Oriental temple grounds. He watched it until it was level with himself. It bathed him in a fiery amber aura that made him into a bronze statue on the slope. He could have been a monument standing there, but he was only a man in the moonlight.

* * *

THE NEXT DAY they came down from the mountain and entered a strip of forest that bordered the swamp. It was an enchanting place, with vines slanting up to the tops of giant trees like guy wires. Leaves of a thousand different shapes hovered in mid-air, seemingly unconnected to any supporting stalks. Every conceivable shade of green assaulted the eye. The narrow forest land was marred by the total lack of any game or fruit.

What it lacked was soon forgotten as First Platoon stepped off into the marshlands. Every step released sickening odors from the rotted depths of the slime. Phosphorescent fungi padded the dead claws of decaying trees jutting up from the black water. Above the wading men sat the brooding countenance of the castle, passing an untold judgment upon them. Hawk dragged his black, dripping sleeve across his green, dripping forehead. He was in no way intimidated by the fact that he didn't know what lay in store for him or how he would deal with it.

The cumulative effect of the Marines' odyssey began to tell on them. The simmering ooze of the stagnant swamp filled them with an unshakable torpor. They grew less able to withstand the rigors put upon their constitutions. Through superhuman efforts, Hawk made them cross the unearthly bog in a day's time. They were within striking distance of the old fortification by nightfall. Crossing the morass was a thankless accomplishment, however, for they had to spend the night in four feet of thick, muddy, stinking liquid.

They found a hump of mud below the surface of the swamp water and heaped every tumid, rotted piece of wood they could find on it, in an effort to build an island. In the end, the island fell six inches short of becoming dry land. The weight of the men during the night squelched it deeper, so that those who slept that night did so in about a foot of sludge. It was a cold, wet, singularly miserable night, spent in the moon-shadow of the Tamara battlements.

Hawk took a balsa-wood cigar box out of Bival's attaché case. The case was the only dry thing in the entire patrol. He slid one of the long, thin cigars between his mud-spattered lips. Cupping his hand over the flame, he lit it. What to the undiscriminating eye appeared to be another full moon loomed over the castle walls. He puffed gravely on the cigar and considered his predicament. He hadn't come this close to sit in slop. After a few more ritualistic drags, he knocked the fire off the tip of the cigar and jammed it into his shirt pocket.

"What are you thinking of doing?" Canlon asked. He had been watching him, and he knew Hawk.

"I'm goin' in."

"Aw, not tonight, for chrissake." Canton hung his head in abject disgust.

"Alone," Hawk added. "Just to look around."

Canton shook his head for a few seconds as his

blood pressure returned from the limits of anger. Then he said, "Okay, goddamnit, but I'll go, too."

"I'll go," said Shaeffer, trying to assemble his field stripped submachine gun.

"Nah, no need. I'm just gonna look around. I better go by myself."

Canton fell back in the mud and rested on his elbows. He wasn't going to argue. Neither did the blood-thirsty Shaeffer argue. He was an adventurous soul, but he really couldn't go any farther.

"How you gonna get in?" Shaeffer asked quietly. He was finally convinced that Hawk was an even bigger fool than himself.

"I don't know. I imagine I will, though."

"Yeah," Shaeffer said to the mud, "I imagine you will."

The men watched numbly as their sergeant and tormentor slogged on without them.

"Crazy bastard," said Canton.

Hawk splashed dangerously close to the base of the castle walls. He wanted to put his swollen feet on dry land, and he didn't care who he had to awaken to do it. He pulled himself out of the sticky silt at the swamp's edge and began to skirt the bottom of the man-made hill upon which the fortifications rested. The walls rose endlessly above him, seeming to lean out from the hill and over him. He paused to consider this optical illusion and stuffed his jaw with tobacco. The taste comforted him and gave him new enthusiasm. He slung his Thompson, muzzle downward, and marched on, determined to circle the walls until he found some entrance in the colossal barrier. His head bowed, his dauntless shoulders slouching, he spat thoughtfully at appropriate intervals. He had almost circumnavigated three-quarters of the fort when the grim truth hit him— there was no entrance.

Opposite the side of the castle facing the encamped Marines, the series of Oriental temples branched out from one of the walls. The castle and the temples seemed to be connected by arching bridges of brick or square-cut stone. What the bridges actually bridged was hidden by the night. Only their curving tops were visible in the silver illumination of the rising moon. They were overgrown with vegetation and treetops peeked over their sides. In the distance off the hill, stood the temples. Their beehive-shaped towers were glazed with some sort of metal that reflected the pale light of the night. These curious spires, arranged in haphazard ways around pyramids and columned walkways, made up the congested temple grounds below the castle. Riotous undergrowth threatened to take over the grounds at any moment.

Hawk stood at the castle's base and took all of this in. He had reached the brink of aesthetic appreciation when he spat and his contemplation returned to the problem at hand. He could get down into those temples fairly easily—for whatever that would accomplish. They had the appearance of being long abandoned. For all he knew, the castle could be similarly empty. It was certainly no Times Square. But ever since he had heard of Tamara, he had heard of its castle, and it must be investigated. He took up his shrugging gait along the base of the wall until he came to a point where thick vines choked the smooth stones. They grew conveniently upward from the base to the summit of the wall.

It was a way in; a rigorous but stealthy way in that

suited his purpose. A normal man probably would have pictured his strength giving out half way up the perpendicular wall. It would take little additional imagination to picture a fatal fall onto the uncompromising stone bridges below. Hawk lashed his helmet to his belt. It could give him no more protection than his own hard head. He put a boot into the vines and began heaving himself skyward.

For half an hour he toiled, hearing nothing but the rustling of the leafy vines, the scraping of his worn boots on stone, and his own heavy breathing. He paused and leaned back at arm's length, his Thompson dangling from his wrist. He looked down at the earth an incredible distance below him. The tops of the temple minarets were on a level with him. He pulled himself back and hugged the wall; the top was still far above him.

"Shit," he whispered. He forced a forearm behind the tendrils of a hoary vine and let himself hang there, sufficiently supported to permit a short rest. As his breathing subsided, he tried to listen for sounds from within the castle. But it, the forest, the temples, and the swamps were all as silent as the rising moon. He began to climb again, hand over hand.

His thigh muscles began to quiver first. Next, the muscles along the backs of his legs lost their strength and turned into contracting, cramping, leaden pain. Still he continued upward, pulling the dead weight with his shaky thighs. Becoming less careful now, he tore at the tender stalks that held him like a drowning man, leaving a shower of cascading leaves to flutter to the ground. He loosened his heavy helmet and let it fall, watching it turn over and over, exposing now its dark interior, now its domed top, like the facets of a spinning jewel, until it struck the ground below.

The great strength in his coiled triceps began to evaporate. Pinching, stabbing pain lanced his arms. He pulled himself up, using only the power of the grip in his thick hands. It never occurred to him that he might fall. He did grudgingly admit that the climb was becoming difficult.

"Shit," he choked. He took another brief rest. He could make it; he was sure of it. The top was only two or three body lengths above him. It took as long to climb the last few inches as the rest of the ascent had taken. Drenched in sweat, smeared with crushed leaves and the ancient filth of the walls, he groaned through the last foot. He felt pounds dropping off his body, as if his constitution knew that it must lighten itself in order to survive. He threw a paralyzed arm over the battlement and, without caution or caring for what lay on the other side, lunged up onto the parapet.

"God damn," he wheezed, and rolled over onto the rampart beyond the wall. He lay there, breathing heavily and staring at the blue-black sky. By force of will, he moved his arms and kneaded cramped muscles with his fingertips. Bracing himself against the stone and once sliding weakly down it, he managed a drunken rise to his feet.

From the rampart, he could see fires below him in the courtyard of the castle. A few hundred bamboo huts were arranged in neat squares on the castle floor, and each had a fire in front of it. The huts seemed to glow from their own macabre orange light, so uniform were the fires. Dark rows of crops were visible in the shadows along the walls. The distance to the ground was startling. The view was like that from a low-flying plane. As feeling returned to his limbs, caution returned to his brain. He dropped to his hands and knees and crawled along the rampart. It was a ledge, six feet deep, attached to the castle wall, covered with a foot of talcum-fine dust. He searched for a way down, a way of less grueling exertion than his means of ascent.

As he approached a corner of the fortress, the right angle softened by a curve in the stone works, he was presented with a crossroads. He could go down or to the keep. A narrow spiral stairway plunged straight down off the rampart. He barely restrained a dizzying sensation as he considered the drop. If stairs were meant to give people easy access to desired destinations, these seemed to defeat their own purpose. They were crumbling and apparently never used. Only a venturesome rat would try them.

Before him, rising from the middle of the courtyard, was the only stone building within the castle walls. It was a huge keep, rectangular in shape, that towered several stories over the tops of the walls. The giant blank wall of its face was relieved occasionally by tiny windows, which infrequently opened out onto balconies. He saw no sign of the Tamara tribe either on the ground or above it.

Connecting the rampart to the ugly keep was a spider-web of a catwalk. It looked to be mere inches wide, though had it been on solid ground, Hawk's eye would have measured it at three or four feet. Nothing held the span in place in the way of pilings or posts, other than at either end; it was suspended over the distant earth by nothing more than that wonder of architecture and science known as the arch. Had Hawk known how complicated the principle of the arch was, and how many centuries ago the bridge had been built, he would not have been as quick to choose this path. It held itself in place there, which is not to say it would hold anything else.

Across the dissolving catwalk of stone, on the highest floor of the massive dungeon, barred windows glinted in the moonlight. Realizing that he would have more in common with prisoners of the Tamara than he would with the Tamara themselves, he chose these windows for his first point of investigation. The catwalk ended in a tiny little balcony on the topmost floor of the dungeon, upon which a door to the interior of the keep opened. If one were to stand on the portico that served as an awning over this door, one could look into one of the barred openings. All of this presupposed that the walkway, the balcony, and the portico did not turn to dust upon contact with any sort of weight.

If the Jennings women were prisoners here, the keep would be the logical place to lodge them. Its proximity made it the attractive destination. It would take only nerve and not strength to reach it. Hawk put one foot on the span, and finding that it held, eased the other one beside it. Gently, he advanced. No wind blew, but the height made it seem as if great cushions of black air were angrily pushing him from this side and that.

"Son of a bitch," he cursed the bridge, halfway across. The span had the same layer of dust as the rampart. It had obviously not been used before in Hawk's lifetime. The view of the ground beneath the catwalk was too fascinating to ignore. He saw shadows moving among the huts, but none could be identified as human beings. Three-quarters of the way across, the full moon hit his back like a spotlight. He had come from under the shadow of the wall and could be easily seen from the ground. Carefully, he went down on all fours and completed the crossing.

Scampering with relief to the balcony, he never stopped until he had mounted the flaking roof of the portico. He latched onto the iron bars in the window above and pulled himself up. The toes of his boots dug desperately at the dungeon wall. He could see nothing within the opening; all was quiet. As he lowered himself, quavering with strain, back to the roof, he heard the murmur of subdued voices. He held his breath and listened: they might be the voices of women, but the words were unclear. They could be coming from only one direction—above him. Now he heard the scraping of gravel. There were people on the roof of the dungeon. Hawk pulled himself back up to the barred window for another look.

After staring into it for as long as his arms would allow, his eyes became accustomed to the choking darkness of the interior. He could see faint light on the far side of the chamber, moonlight. In the light, a narrow corridor of steps could be seen, leading aloft. Doubtlessly, they led to the roof. A moan came from somewhere in the room and he lowered his head a bit.

Sergeant Hawk's burning, half closed eyes searched the cell for the source of the moan. He found it at the foot of the stairs. There lay a heap of rustling blankets, evidently covering a troubled inmate.

"Water. Water, I say." The moaning evolved into English words. It was Calvert.

After resting a bit, he pulled up again and hung onto a bar by one hand. He slid his wooden-handled knife from its sheath and began chipping at the base of one of the ancient bars. The dry old stone surrendered easily to his determined effort. Within minutes, Hawk lifted the freed bottom of one of the bars and clambered awkwardly through the tight space. Once within the cell, in a daze of advanced exhaustion, he replaced the bar.

He sheathed his knife and unslung the Thompson. He felt little need for caution when he held the mighty weapon tightly in his grasp. Kneeling silently under the moon-lit window, he looked about the room. The only way out of the room, other than the stairway, was through a heavy, forbidding door in the wall at his left. He ran in a crouch to Calvert's side, and finding a bowl beside him, inspected its contents. Water. He poured it offhandedly at where he judged the American's mouth to be.

"Thank you. Thank you."

Hawk grunted, reached into his shirt pocket, and pulled out his atabrine pills. For whatever they were worth, he left them at Calvert's side. He slapped the ailing man's shoulder and looked to the stairs. The voices above were louder and more distinct. He sat on the last stair step. The voices stopped. The room was silent, the door was still. All awaited his next move. The room smelled of cedar, for some reason, and it inexplicably reminded him of his childhood. He took a drink of the water; it tasted of quinine.

One of the voices said something. Sweat shot down Hawk's nose. The voice was much closer this time. It was Mrs. Jennings. He took the steps slowly, one at a time, looking above himself at each rise, so that he might see the roof at the first opportunity. Then he saw her in the pale illumination—Amelia. His stomach fell and he moved quickly. She gasped in alarm when she saw the rapidly gliding apparition from below. She jumped away from the stairs, grabbed her mother's arm and spun her away from the sudden danger.

Hawk pounced on the rooftop, fell to one knee and turned the submachine gun in every conceivable direction. The lunar glow made the scene look like it was under water. The two women were alone on the vacant, gravel strewn rooftop. Behind them stretched a view of Tamara at night. They stood together, beholding him in stark terror for a moment, before the younger one recognized him. He stood, with a childish, triumphant smile on his face. Amelia ran to him.

"James! I knew it was you! I knew you would come!" she cried, embracing him tightly and burying her face against his chest. She rubbed her trembling hand hard against the side of his face, until he thought she might tear out his unkempt beard.

"Yeah," he said quietly, winking at Mrs. Jennings. "How are y'all doin'?"

"Dreadfully..." Mrs. Jennings blurted.

"We couldn't be better," Amelia said, "now that you're here." She continued to hold onto him and breathe a barely audible whimper.

"How's old Mr. Calvert down there?"

"Don't concern yourself with that dirty thing, Sergeant Hawk," Mrs. Jennings snapped. She would not let the joyful reunion dampen her hatred of Mr. Calvert.

"Mother, not now," Amelia interrupted her and looked up at Hawk. "I told them that you would come. I knew that you could do it. It's so good to see you!"

"That's for certain," Mrs. Jennings added, clasping her hands in front of herself.

"We never thought anyone would be able to find us," said Amelia, lowering her head, and shaking it in disbelief that he was actually there.

"Well, you was pretty well out of the way, that's for sure," Hawk answered softly. He sensed that she was on the verge of tears. "Is there any guards around here?"

"No," her mother answered for her. "It's such a long climb, you can hear them coming for hours." She stepped closer and lowered her voice. "If they find Amelia and me in the room downstairs, they won't come up here. You can hide on the roof, if we're caught by surprise."

"Good." Hawk smiled at her. He flushed with embarrassment as the girl continued to hold him. He put an arm around her and patted her back consolingly. "We ain't exactly outta this yet, you know," he told her. She looked up and smiled, her eyes brimming with tears, as if to say that now that he was here, escape was a foregone conclusion. The happy, shining, moonlit eyes struck deep into the hardened heart of Sergeant Hawk, perhaps deeper than he should have let them. "But we'll make it," he assured her. He would search a hundred more castles and fight his way around a thousand General Kravanarts for her, if need be. The women took his gentle assurance as fact.

"How shall we leave?" Mrs. Jennings asked. Her tone left the impression that she must pack her bags well in advance of the existing scheduled train departures. Hawk didn't answer at first. With an arm around Amelia's waist, he steered her to the edge of the roof. A little wall encircled its outer edge, to prevent any clumsy fatalities. He still carried his tommy gun in his free hand.

"Now, that'll take some thinkin'." He nodded to himself and looked out over the decaying temple grounds far below them. He knew that they could not retrace his route of entry into the castle. One in ten thousand able bodied men, in the best of spirits and condition, would be capable of that—had they the nerve. "Have y'all seen any gates leadin' outa this here fort?"

"There is a gate hidden in the masonry. It leads toward those shrines out there. It should be right under us," said Amelia.

"I went all around the damn place and I couldn't find no way in."

"Have you ever been to Europe?" Amelia asked.

Hawk shook his head. "Europe?"

"They sometimes disguise less important entrances to castles and stairways by constructing decoration along the walls. They did that here, only there is no main gate at all, only a small hidden one. Evidently, they didn't need a larger one for commercial purposes, and so there is little more than a large door going through the walls."

"You know where it is?"

"Yes."

"Awright. Well, that's handy to know. I don't know if it'll do us any good. That's a pretty good ways from here. I tell you what, though," Hawk yawned, "I'm gettin' a little drowsy. How often do these folks pay y'all a visit?"

"Nothing regular," Mrs. Jennings responded. "I shouldn't think that they'd be back before morning's breakfast."

"That's good to know, I think I might rest a bit here, tonight." He disengaged his arm from the girl and slung his gun.

"Are you hungry?" Amelia asked.

"Yeah. Kinda."

"All we have..." Mrs. Jennings said. "Well, I'll get it, and you can judge for yourself."

"Don't go to no trouble," he said, as Mrs. Jennings left for the chamber below.

"I should warn you about the food," Amelia began, but the food arrived before the warning. Hawk was handed a basket of warm eggs. He looked at them innocently. "Those aren't hard-boiled, James," she said. His square-tipped fingers were gently picking the shell from the egg. A baby bird crouched inside. He frowned at the little dead creature and rolled him around in his hand.

"It's edible," Mrs. Jennings informed him. He stuffed it, whole, into his mouth and munched contentedly on it.

"That's good enough for me, I guess," he said.

"But we simply can't eat them," Amelia added as he swallowed it. "That's why we still have so many of them. They are considered a delicacy in the Philippines, you know?"

"Yeah? Well, they ain't too delicate," he said, peeling another one, "but neither am I." Amelia reached out and put a white hand over his. He winked at her and fell to peeling a third egg. "What's these people on this island like?"

"The Tamara? *Very* strange," said Amelia, looking over her shoulder at her mother for support.

"Very," came the confirmation.

"They are Eurasian in appearance," Amelia continued, "and they seem to follow Japanese customs to a degree."

"Yes, they dress like medieval Japanese," said Mrs. Jennings, holding out her brightly colored Japanese robe.

"Oh, Mother, Japs dress that way nowadays," Amelia contradicted her. Hawk took it all in.

"How are they equipped?" he asked.

"Equipped?"

"Weapons. Machine guns? Field pieces? Grenades?"

"Oh," Amelia smiled, "they're a little out of the mainstream, you see. They have...what do you call them...flintlock rifles, and pistols...and swords, of course."

"Medieval," Mrs. Jennings interjected.

"Well—" Amelia shook her head "—lots of backward people still use that sort of rifle—and Jap officers carry swords."

"I beg your pardon, Sergeant Hawk." Mrs. Jennings was becoming offended by these contradictions. Her nerves were stretched to the limit. "I shouldn't have said Medieval, I should have said that they date from the French Revolution. What difference does it make— they're primitive, aren't they?"

Hawk nodded pensively and continued eating. He figured the French Revolution had to be some time before the First World War; it was pretty old stuff. "In that, case," he said, "we can probably shoot our way outta here, if we got to. I'd rather try to sneak out, but I don't see how we can."

Mrs. Jennings preferred sneaking out, too. The casual reference to shooting a way out frightened her.

"We should go out the same way that you came in," she said.

He explained how he had managed to get in. They both looked incredulously at him.

"You can see that won't work," said Hawk, "especially with a sick fella down there and all."

"Sergeant Hawk, you can just forget *that* particular sick fellow." Mrs. Jennings' temper rose. "He'll continue pretending he's sick until you hire bearers to escort him to Boston."

"Mother...not now...damn."

"*Now,* Amelia. Do you know what he did, Sergeant Hawk?" She looked accusingly at the Marine, as if he might have heard of such notorious goings-on.

"Uh—no, ma'am."

"Turned us over to the Japs, big as you please! And then, when we were on that filthy pirate's ship, Mr. Calvert suggests that they put *him* ashore—since *he* is of no value to them—and just proceed to do whatever they want with us. Now! Can you *imagine—a—man—*doing that?"

"Mother, he was ill."

"His brain is ill."

"Mother, for God's sake, here we are..."

"God's sake, indeed."

Hawk decided to interrupt the exchange. It was not going to resolve itself. "I reckon we'll take him back, whatever he's done." He placed his cigar between his lips. "Won't be of no great extra trouble, ma'am." He lit the dead cigar, a look of strain in his forehead and around his mouth. Bickering irritated him. "What in the hell, if you don't mind me askin', do these folks here plan on doin' with y'all?"

Amelia began to laugh. Mrs. Jennings recovered from her outrage and began to giggle. "They have arranged a wedding for me," Amelia said.

"To a gentleman with fifty wives," Mrs. Jennings added. "It's funny now, but it wasn't before you came."

Hawk smiled.

"Yes, he's a halfwit they call the Daimo," Amelia said, holding her hand two feet from the ground. "He's about this tall."

"Positively retarded. The whole tribe is insane. Inter-breeding, you know. They're devil worshipers," said Mrs. Jennings.

"Well, we don't know that," said Amelia. Hawk waited patiently for another argument to begin.

"I have eyes. They practice voodoo of some sort. That's devil worshipping," she retorted. "Are you a Christian, Mr. Hawk?"

"Uh—yes, ma'am."

"Then I know how you must feel about devil worship. I mean to say, I can understand ignorance, but that is simply revolting. I can understand one being a Moslem, or...say, a Buddhist...but, my goodness...well, it's revolting. These people seem to have been influenced by the Moslem religion, I don't know how they got off the track and became so degenerate. Their temples are Buddhist, or Hindu or something...but I think the temples were here before the people were.

They just moved into them, like a cuckoo takes over a nest. Revolting."

"Yeah." Hawk looked down. "That's interestin'," he said,, his tone indicating that it wasn't. He had heard of native devil cults since the campaigns in the Solomon Islands. He couldn't get very outraged over silly business like that. "I tell you what: I'm gonna rest up some and go back for my men. Sounds like we can handle these yokels without a whole lot of trouble. We're probably gonna have to cross paths with 'em, if we ever wanta get y'all out."

Mrs. Jennings looked at Amelia and then she said to Hawk, "You sleep on it, and we'll all consider the possibilities. Perhaps we should avoid a direct conflict with the nasty things? Well, we'll decide later." She fixed him a pallet on a corner of the roof. Amelia stood near the stairs and saw him fall exhaustedly onto it. "This is what comes from marrying a soldier, Sergeant Hawk," said Mrs. Jennings to the ravaged heap on the pallet. "Never marry a soldier."

Hawk assured her that he wouldn't, and closed his eyes.

* * *

WHEN HE WOKE UP, it was still dark. He hadn't slept for very long. He felt refreshed, and that was enough. The quiet moon was entering its setting phase. Raising himself up, he saw that Amelia was on the roof with him. She stood at its edge, leaning on the little wall that surrounded it. Her eyes were cast down at the jumble of pagodas below. The wind was strong at that height, pulling her auburn hair back more often than letting it rest upon her shoulders. Hawk got to his feet and walked slowly over to her.

"Hi, kid."

"Has anyone ever told you that you snore?"

"No. I don't."

She looked away from him and back at the ground

so far below them. "Any ideas yet?" she asked. Her mood was distant.

"Oh, I guess we oughta wait till they get you down on the ground somewhere. It would be too hard to start from up here."

"Yes," she agreed. Something seemed to have quieted the enthusiasm that he had left her with. "What with Daniel, and all."

"Yeah."

"We had a visitor while you slept."

"Who's that?"

"There's only one of them that ever visits us. He speaks Spanish, the rest speak Japanese. He brings us news and our meals. I think he likes us, but I certainly wouldn't trust him."

"I don't trust nobody. What news?"

"We're going over to the shrines today. To watch some sort of ceremony. We've been before. They do these vulgar dances and pull chickens apart. Very entertaining."

"Yeah? Them shrines are a hell of a lot easier to get at than this place."

"I know. That occurred to me. Something has to be done," she whispered. "Tomorrow they hold the marriage ceremony. That idea frightens me a little."

Hawk nodded his head sleepily. He took a half burned cigar from his pocket and lit it. "I guess we better move fast, or Mr. Calvert'll be marryin' a divorced woman." Hawk studied his cigar intently as he lit it. He glanced up at her quickly. She was looking the other way.

"Yes," she said at last. "I know you've come through a great deal to get here, James. I don't know how you managed to get out of the campaign long enough to waste your time looking for us..."

"I had a little help on that," he said. He explained the differences between himself and the Army, and how he had been left with no choice but to run. He told her of General Kravanart's leaflet, not without some pride in the dark reputation the general had given him.

"Why would General Kravanart do such a thing to you?"

"I don't know, to tell you the truth. I never met the man. At first, I figured it for some kind of mix-up. But I guess I didn't go exactly by the book and that ticked him off. You know them West Point fellas—they get their skirts blowed up pretty easy."

"Mmm. Oh, General Kravanart isn't a West Point man. My great-aunt knows him. She lives in California; she was always writing to us and telling us about General Kravanart, but we never got around to meeting him. He isn't a West Point man, though, and he's rather ashamed of it. He's a proud man, I think."

Hawk listened interestedly to this information about his tormentor. It made the general seem more like a human being and less like a distant prime mover. "I just figured he was a West Pointer," Hawk said, mainly to fill the silence in the conversation. And it did.

"No, no," she answered quickly, "he went to school with my aunt. To U.C.L.A."

"Do tell?" Hawk snorted. College was college to him. He looked up slowly. "U.C.L.A.?"

"Yes. Back when it first opened, I believe."

"Yeah? I wonder when that was?"

"Oh, God knows. My aunt would be in her late

forties, so it would be quite some time ago. Just think—she graduated from college before we were even born..."

Hawk thought it best not to comment on that statement.

"...and here I am," Amelia continued, "throwing year after year away. All because my father was in the wrong place at the wrong time."

"Yeah, that's a hell of a thing," Hawk answered thoughtfully. He heard her talking for a while about the various accomplishments of various relatives at various ages. He had stopped listening.

"...and Mother, at my age, had been married..." She stopped short there. The words formed a complete sentence, but it was an awkward one. Hawk felt that it was originally intended to be longer.

"Well, you're gettin' married tomorrow," he said with mock seriousness.

"Yes." She smiled bravely. "I had forgotten. Won't my friends be jealous? I'm marrying royalty."

"Sure. Quite a catch. Reckon you'd wanta throw him over for a broken-down old sergeant?"

"And give up my throne? Surely you jest?" They laughed for a minute, but Hawk was ill-at-ease. He couldn't say exactly why. He sighed and looked over his shoulder at the setting moon.

"I reckon my men are wondering what happened to me. I'll go get 'em tonight and come back tomorrow. When y'all are on the ground, we'll try to deal with these native folks, real businesslike, but if that don't work, we'll have to get serious."

She nodded and pursed her full lips. She had been wanting to say something. "About Daniel," her voice was barely able to be heard above the rising dawn wind, "he is in a terrible state, and he can't be blamed for what he did. We don't know for certain that he turned us over to the Japs."

"No."

"Mother makes it sound worse than it truly was. She's not very fond of him."

"I noticed that."

Mrs. Jennings might have disputed this charge. She knew that the American soldiers Calvert turned over to the enemy would dispute it.

The sunrise beat the setting of the moon by several minutes. Along the eastern curve of the earth, an orange band was etched in the sky, as if by a straight edge. Above it, the bottoms of the clouds were illuminated a satin-white.

"But I feel so sorry for him," said Amelia. "He brings that out in a person. He's so out of his element, so helpless. You can understand that?"

"Sure enough," said Hawk in his thick Delta accent.

"I just...wouldn't want anything to happen to him—in the scuffling, I mean."

"It won't. Don't worry."

Mrs. Jennings came from downstairs. The Tamara were climbing up to the cell. The two women readied themselves for the day's festivities. Hawk remained there on the roof, surveying the countryside and thinking his lonely thoughts.

11

SGT. GILL HAD MADE HIS WAY TO SAN MIGUEL ON THE embattled island of Lamare. Fortunately for him, the Japanese garrison scheduled for the little barrio never arrived. They were needed in the fighting raging to the south. The United States Army was utterly destroying the defenders. Lamare's days in the Greater East Asia Co-Prosperity Sphere were numbered. General Kirijo had fallen dead of a heart attack when his skills were most sorely needed. Malcolm Gill discovered that the days of his venture were similarly numbered, for the hated Sergeant Hawk had taken to the dangerous sea. Gill made use of a partisan radio, hidden in the hills near the barrio, to tell General Kravanart of this turn of events. The General did *not* see this as an end to the affair. He (not the dog soldiers in the jungles) was winning the most brilliant victory of his career, and he wouldn't have it marred by this incident with the Marine cowards. When Gill informed him that it had been suggested that Hawk had gone off through Japanese waters in search of an island called Tamara,

Kravanart took the news with cool detachment, as if he expected as much. Gill dejectedly reported that he didn't know how he could possibly follow the renegades.

"Pull your socks up, man," Kravanart encouraged him. He told the sergeant to hide along the Coast of Naravey and to be on the lookout for a ship that would pick him up and take him to Tamara. Simple as that. Divine intervention. The ship would resemble a junk and the name "Garrotero" would be stenciled on its side. The captain, a privateer working for the American cause, would go by the same name.

Anyone found in the company of Sergeant Hawk, was to be considered as dangerous as he was and dealt with accordingly. Gill was left with the impression that his mission was to exterminate the entire contaminated population of the desolate isle. Gill signed out and left the humming radio to its keepers. He returned to Calicote and his men in San Miguel. The conversation had cheered him. He was to get Hawk, after all. His men were not so cheered.

They had been turned into starving, terrified beasts. The society of the small barrio had rejuvenated them only slightly. Japanese activity in northern Lamare had increased and they were always hiding from the enemy or the mistrusted locals. Stories of what the Japanese were doing to captured Americans and Filipinos chilled their weakening spines. The Kempeitai were making the rounds in the villages suspected of being disloyal. And all of the villages were disloyal. The patrol made no attempt at sabotage. They were content merely to survive in their deadly environment.

The prospect of being able to inflict major suffering

enabled Gill and Calicote to endure their minor pains. They prepared for the voyage to Tamara. Gill was so excited he did forty-five minutes of sit-ups.

* * *

THE JENNINGSES RETURNED FROM THE "CEREMONIES" late in the day. Their faces looked like those of people who had attended the theater because they had received free tickets and didn't want to offend the donors. The wedding was set for the next day. All of Tamara was agog with excitement, with the possible exception of Joe Canlon and the Marines, who didn't know what was going on. Amelia was one of three brides to be married to the less-than-dashing Daimo.

By nightfall, Hawk had regained enough of his strength to try the trip down the vines. Mrs. Jennings went downstairs with Calvert, leaving her daughter alone with the Marine. Hawk felt this had been prearranged. He doubted the mother was spending her time with Calvert for the pleasure of his company. He walked to the corner of the roof with Amelia and they talked quietly for a few minutes of the day's activities.

She said, "There's no way we could ever repay you for this, or show you how grateful we are."

"No need. It's part of my job."

"We aren't part of your job. You came here on your own, at an unreasonable risk." He didn't tell her that there was nothing reasonable about his job or the risks it involved. "I think we should clear up a few matters before you leave tonight, before this goes any further. So we understand each other and so you can make up your mind about what you want to do for us."

"Yeah? What are we talkin' about?"

"Well, I mean, I don't want you to think that I've led you on or anything." She looked at the rooftop.

"About what?"

She looked into his blazing eyes. They didn't allow a person to look into them for very long, but she tried. "James..." she whispered and put her arms around him. It was a slow and exhausted embrace. "What am I to do?"

"About what?" his heavy voice answered.

"I'm so very fond of you, and yet there's still Daniel."

Hawk didn't say anything.

"He needs me. And it isn't that I don't like him. He's very witty, and he should provide well for me. He's set up well—socially and professionally." Hawk held her loosely now. "I don't really love him, not the way I could love you. But he was first, and he loves me—and I don't really dislike him, or the idea of being well off."

"Yeah, I can see that," he said.

"Mother said never to marry a soldier, and this predicament I find us all in makes me sure she was right."

"Yeah, she is, I guess."

"But..." She pulled back, her velvet-green eyes charged with irresistible appeal. "It hurts me to...want to love you, and to let you go on risking your life for us. It's too complicated for me. I can't sort it all out. I met a man and we're supposed to be married, and that should be the end of it. You should know there's very little chance of our—you know—coming together."

"Oh. Well, that's all right. Don't worry about that. I'm just tryin' to help y'all. All of you. I wasn't thinkin'..."

"Oh, James."

"No, really now, I mean it," he smiled. "It don't matter."

She smiled and leaned forward on her toes to kiss him gently. "I thought that maybe you had fallen for me." She brushed away a tear. He reached out and pulled her to him, holding her close, saying nothing. He could feel her full, soft body beneath the flowing robe. He couldn't help but think it must be uncomfortable for her to be against anything as hard as himself. He held her away from himself and smiled at her and embraced her again.

"It don't matter."

* * *

CANLON BECAME CONCERNED. He had seen no sign of life from the walls of the castle, and no James Hawk. As another night approached, he decided to take the men forward. There could be no objection to this. The prospect of another night in the mud held no attraction for anyone. They marched to the castle wall and searched for an entrance, much as Hawk had done. Finding no way in, they camped there in the shadow of the walls, glad to be on dry land again and in complete disregard for the possibility of there being observers above them. They reasoned that the silent castle had to be abandoned. This was only partially correct. Although the tops of the walls and their ramparts had been vacant for several centuries, the inside of the castle housed an entire race of people. The Tamara continued to live out their peculiar existence only a few yards away, in complete ignorance of the presence of the Americans. No one had ever entered their castle uninvited, and no one was expected to.

* * *

HAWK KISSED HER AGAIN. They held each other for a little while and then he turned to go. They didn't say anything else. He didn't know what to say. Mrs. Jennings came up the stairs.

"After we're out of this, you can rescue my husband, Sergeant Hawk," she said. "Don't you think that would be wonderful, Amelia?"

"Yes," Amelia answered.

"Yeah," said Hawk. "I gotta be gettin' along. You'll see me down in the shrines tomorrow." He slung his gun and went down the stone steps. Mr. Calvert called him over as he passed by. The sergeant knelt over him in response.

"How's it goin'?" Hawk asked.

"I'll outlive you all." Calvert managed to force his nerve-wracking laugh. "Sergeant Hawk," he said, growing serious, "I must tell you that I don't want Amelia subjected to any danger."

"We'll try."

"No, I'm quite sincere about that. I'll prevent you from carrying this matter off if it appears that there is any danger involved."

Hawk ran his index finger up and down his nose. "You get in my way, Mr. Calvert, and you'll be dealt with like any others that do the same." He clapped the man on the shoulder, stood, and went to the window. The moonrise hadn't mounted the walls yet. It was dark out. He took the loosened bar from the casing. "Put this bar back if you get a chance, wouldja?" he called, and the window and the night swallowed him.

Out over the precipitous span, over the wall, and down into the thick vines he scurried, without checking for any spying Tamara. Up to this point, he only knew of their existence by hearsay, and he was willing to keep it that way. The climb to the ground was easier than he had prepared himself for. Aside from the difference in the pull of gravity, he was more rested than he had been during the first ordeal. The old aches in his arms returned before he reached the ground, but they held no dread this time. He could see Canlon and the others at the foot of the column of vines. They saw him, too, and waited with upturned rifle muzzles.

"Damn, where the hell you been?" Canlon greeted him. "Did you find anything?"

"Yeah, I found 'em."

"Now what?"

"Nothin' tonight." Hawk flexed his arm. "Tomorrow we try to make a deal. If that don't work, I figure we can take 'em pretty easy."

"Oh, you do? Are there people livin' here?"

"Yeah, some kind of Japs."

"Japs! Shit!" Joe looked at the walls above him with a new respect.

"Yeah, but they're kinda backwoodsy. I don't think they're interested in the war or anything."

"Then why did you go sneakin' in and come sneakin' out?"

"Just sneaky, I guess," Hawk answered, lighting a cigar. "What kinda food you boys got cookin'?"

"We ain't got none. We gotta get outa this place.

We're gonna be gettin' sicker than shit hanging around this hole."

"I know. Tomorrow."

Canlon nodded. "How'd it go otherwise?" he asked.

"What do you mean?"

"You know," said Canlon. "The girl—was she glad to see you?"

"Goddamn right. Wouldn't you be?"

"Goddamn right. But, I mean...well, what'd she say? Was it...what you expected?"

"No. I don't guess it was."

"That's what I figured." Canlon nodded knowingly. "You went through hell for a pat on the back, didn't you?"

"Yeah. Ain't the first time, though. Every time I been through hell, there wasn't nothing on the other side. It don't matter." Hawk shrugged.

"Son of a bitch," said Canlon, "and here we are still in hell. That's the way it goes, you know. The weak feedin' off the strong and the strong feedin' off the weak and some of the bastards feedin' off both."

"Mmm-hmm." Hawk grunted at this meaningless philosophy. "I did find out something, though. I'm gonna check it out a little, come daylight. I mighta figured out why the whole goddamn world wants me dead."

"You mean about that leaflet and all?"

"Maybe."

The men sat in silent circles without fires. Some were already asleep in an effort to save their ebbing strength. Hawk retrieved his helmet and went and sat among them. The usual small talk ensued, then everyone drifted apart.

The night passed slowly. Hawk felt alone among his shivering comrades. The dull ache of loss in his breast prevented him from thinking. He suffered wordlessly, soundlessly, in his own subhuman way as he cleaned his gun. His emotions were bewitched by a certain hardness of the soul that made it impossible for them to seek relief in crying. He even felt a little sorry for the men who would get in his way tomorrow."

12

At first light, Sergeant Hawk called for Bival. He looked like a Manila businessman, with his briefcase. Hawk slid General Kirijo's personal file from the case and began thumbing through it.

"What are you doin', Hawk? I thought we was gonna get this show on the road," Pidge Shaeffer said.

"Lookin' for somethin'. I got some ugly suspicions." The idle men began to gather around him and he scattered them with a few angry barks. Turning back to the stack of papers like a dog returns to the bone he has defended, he pulled out the American Army leaflet. At the bottom of the page was the flowery signature of General Kravanart. He set this aside and continued to rummage through the unintelligible documents. Column upon column of Japanese writing flashed before his eyes. Then he found *it*. It was written in Japanese, but at the bottom was the same flowery signature that was on the leaflet. The signature could not be read, it was of the type businessmen write when they consider themselves important, the type that is usually deciphered by a typed translation beneath it. This one was not deciphered, but the scrawl was identical on the document and on the leaflet. "Bival," Hawk snarled, "read me this one."

The Filipino read over it for a few minutes. "I do not really know what this pertains to..." Bival muttered confusedly.

"Let me give you a hint," said Hawk, lighting a short cigar. "It reads something like a purchase order or a receipt or maybe even a bill of sale?"

"Yes, possibly. There is almost no explanation. There is a list of goods here—but they are all American military equipment: guns, fuel, ammunition, rations..."

"Yeah, I see. Is that all? Just a list?"

"Above the signature at the bottom there is a clause with the date that says, 'that you may rely on the authenticity of this shipment and know to whom you are indebted, I hereunto set my hand,' then the date and the signature. I can't make out the signature," said Bival.

"I can," said Hawk, scraping up the papers and dumping them back into the brief case. Bival continued reading the document under Hawk's scrutiny. "Don't let this shit outta your sight. It looks like I got a few visits to pay when I get off this island."

"I notice the name 'Garrotero,' Sergeant. It says 'by Garrotero,' or 'through Garrotero' at the top of the page," Bival said, putting the last page back into the case.

"Mmm-hmm," Hawk growled. He handed Bival the case. "Okay, let's move out. We're goin' in after them Americans. I don't want none of 'em hurt. If any of these here Japs get in the way, kill 'em."

The sergeant led the men to the point where the

bridges that ran toward the temples intersected the castle walls. The undergrowth beneath the crumbling bridges was impenetrable. The Marines had to walk on the broken and often disconnected stone crosswalks. The bridges didn't actually span a barrier of any sort other than the jungle.

They walked above the thorny growth on the narrow, purposeless bridges, often having to jump goat like from one age-cracked section to the next. The cross-walks were some twenty feet from the ground, but the plant life grew right up to a level with them, so that they looked like a sidewalk through a lawn. Leafy creepers laced the stonework, making parts of it invisible in the surrounding greenery.

A collective anticipatory twinge rippled through the patrol as they neared a guarded gateway. The bridge sections ended at an opening in the temple's outer wall, and a ramp beyond this opening led to the ground. Several robed figures, bright and alien looking, stood stiffly around this high, ornate entrance to the temples. The robes were embellished with Oriental designs and flapped like flags in the wind, tightening around the bodies of the men wearing them. The Tamara had inter-esting features and coloring, evidence of their confused heritage, but the Marines saw only a group of bizarre Japanese—the enemy.

Hawk didn't waste his perfunctory observations on fashion or racial makeup. He looked for weapons. The entrance guards held pikes and gisarmes, while in their sashes were tucked swords and, as reported, antique firearms. A faint smiled touched Hawk's lips.

The guards became excited when they spotted the advancing Marines. Laden with modern weaponry, horribly unkempt, they did not appear to be friendly visitors. Since neither friendly nor unfriendly visitors had ever been this deep into Tamara, the natives were understandably aghast. Two of the guards stood their ground. The others ran into the labyrinthine recesses of the temples. The two who remained drew their horse pistols and one of them shouted something.

"What'd that son of a bitch say?" Hawk asked Bival. The man spoke in archaic Japanese.

"I can hardly understand him. He wants to know who we are and what our purpose is for being here."

"Tell him to get his ass outta the way or he'll find out."

Bival relayed a reasonable facsimile of this command to the nervous guard. The Marines continued to advance all the while, pausing only to check their steps on the unsteady stone. One of the guards turned and ran, following the path of the others. The last raised his pistol and stood his ground. Hawk flipped the safety of his Thompson and leveled the evil-looking gas compensator at the man's chest. Luckily for his own wellbeing the guard was unnerved by this and left in a flurry of swishing robes and flying heels. He might have only wanted the honor of being the last to retreat.

The Marines stepped from the erosion-eaten bridges and crossed through the macabre gate without incident. Grotesque, carved faces leered at them from endless heights of stone edifices. Hawk stopped at the gate and picked out what he thought to be the main avenue through the temple grounds. Putting a cigar in his mouth, he struck a match on the protruding tongue of a gargoyle that had the audacity to thrust that appendage at him.

"Let's go." His voice was low, but they all heard it. They filed along a dead, dusty lane, lined with rotting columns and tumbling, beehive-shaped towers. The sergeant took the lead, shifting his eyes narrowly from the distant metallic-glazed heights of the pagodas ahead of him to the myriad of nooks and crannies of the ground-level buildings. Thick dust clung to the large pores in the old stone. Low walls running parallel to the close avenue provided excellent cover for an ambush. The entire ant bed of spires was the perfect place of origin for a surprise attack. Hawk left no rear guard at the gate. He continued walking leisurely, in his characteristic swagger, down the petrified street.

The road wound aimlessly through the shrines. Inevitably, the expedition rounded what appeared to be the last unoccupied bend. Ahead of them, carved from a single block of massive rock, was a devilish creature with an open mouth. The road ran through the mouth. Within the demon was gathered a buzzing concourse of rifle-carrying Tamara. They let out a chorus of static-sounding squeals at the sight of the unperturbed Marine leader. Jumping about from one foot to the other, they seemed on the verge of hysteria. Hawk did not try to calm their fears. He continued walking, watching the stone above him more carefully than the men in plain view. He was a firm believer in the maxim that you never see the one that gets you. He saw the men in the gateway but in all the jumble of balconies, walls, and windows that surrounded him, he saw nothing.

The Tamara ceased anguishing over the predicament and fell to aiming their flintlocks at the approaching Americans. Hawk stopped. They shouted at him in high-pitched cries that might have been made by grackles.

"What's all this shit?" Hawk asked Bival. The Filipino could make nothing of it. "Tell 'em to clear out or we'll clear 'em out." Bival relayed the friendly greeting. The squealing stopped long enough for them to hear the message, then began again with even more animation. The gate remained blocked.

"Awright, goddamnit, let's go!" Hawk ordered. He resumed his pace, marching right into the face of the leveled rifles.

One of the Tamara stepped out in front of the others. He signaled to his comrades, possibly in an effort to prevent them from inflicting unnecessary bloodshed. The line of wide black rifle mouths slacked a bit in its tautness. The spokesman then turned and began shouting at the Marines.

Impatiently, Hawk stopped. "Now what the goddamn hell?"

"He asks who you are and what is your purpose," said Bival.

"Tell him we come to see his head guy about an American woman," Hawk snapped angrily, as if he would have preferred shooting it out with the overbearing obstacles. "And don't take no shit off him, either."

Bival translated the message, though he failed to convey the savagery in Hawk's tone. The Tamara may have picked that up on their own. Their spokesman answered. "He says to wait here and the Daimo will send word if he wants to see you."

"I ain't waitin' for nothin'."

"It might be better," Bival counseled. He stood as

close to the poised muzzles as Hawk. "Let them have their pride, Sergeant Hawk. They are frightened. If we push them, they may be goaded into fighting."

A rumbling came from Hawk's chest. He would have liked nothing better. But he said, "Okay. Let 'em put on their show. We ain't waitin' around here all day, though; I'm goin' through that gate pretty goddamn soon."

A messenger was sent to the Daimo. The two groups stared menacingly at each other as they waited. They studied each other's faces, each marveling at how inhuman men can look. The Marines took heart as they surveyed the out-of-date armaments of the tribesmen. The Tamara, for their part, well knew the firepower confronting them. Though they had no modern weapons they had been visited by those who did. Still, the natives stood their ground, growing more courageous as time passed. Hawk noticed this, or rather he sensed it. Under his breath, he passed down an order for Shaeffer to ready a rifle grenade.

Chuck Lasker produced a camera from God-knows-where and began snapping pictures of an intricately carved temple facade. This made the Tamara uneasy but, before they could become too anxious, the messenger returned. The Daimo was willing to grant an audience to the Marines.

The guards stood on either side of the yawning mouth, indicating that the Marines were to pass between them. Hawk led the way through the intently staring natives. The messenger walked ahead of the sergeant, leading him to what appeared to be the main gathering-place of the island. Fearlessly, or perhaps foolhardily, the entire American contingent followed.

The fact that the arena was the main gathering-place did not preserve it from having the state of disrepair of the rest of the grounds. Crumbling steps rose on each side, forming the seats of the amphitheater. Even at the greatest heights, weeds grew in the cracks between the steps. The entire population of Tamara was perched on the uncomfortable benches. They stared down in silence at the field before them.

Hawk marched the Marines onto the field, the mute citizens stacked above him to the left and right. Only a very few of them had firearms, and these were probably the keepers of the peace. In front of the single file of Marines and all the way across the field, the Daimo awaited them on a raised platform. The small number of people and their arrangement was reminiscent of a high-school gymnasium. The total and immediate hush that befell the islanders left the Marines with a cold and creeping fear. They looked to right and left at hundreds of people staring statue-like from above them. Were it not for their colorful robes and for some of them being stripped to the waist, they might have been mistaken for the stone carvings in the outer temple streets.

"Joe, your squad'll take the right side," Hawk said in a voice intended to be heard only by the Marines. The words rumbled and echoed to the tops of the bleachers. The entourage surrounding the Daimo was just as motionless as the others. Hawk crossed three-quarters of the field and, as he did, the last man in the platoon entered the gateway. The last man was the capable Pidge Shaeffer. He knew better than to go any farther from the gate. Hawk called a halt and summoned Bival to his side.

Hawk's eyes slid along the eerie crowd in the aisles around them. His eyes stopped on the Daimo, squinting and tightening the leathery trails beneath them. The Daimo was a peculiar-looking man, under five feet in height. His features were occidental but a pony tail, formed at the very top of his head, made him look Asian when combined with his flowing garb. The lord was speaking in whispers to his advisers. The pony tail flopped from one ear to the other as he spoke. The advisers and religious leaders gathered protectively around him.

"Tell him to hand over the Americans," Hawk told Bival. Bival started to suggest that a few introductory remarks be made, but changed his mind. He was afraid of angering Sergeant Hawk, who appeared to be in no mood for foolishness. Bival made his demand and an advisor answered him.

"There are no Americans, according to this man," Bival said. Hawk ordered the men to train their weapons on the innocent crowd.

"Bring me up a rifle grenade!" he shouted. He stared into the Daimo's faltering eyes. The pounding of a Marine's boots broke the silence. Lasker ran the length of the field with the Ml and candle holder. The Marines looked toward the Daimo, standing amidst his barbarous decorations. The Marines had no way of warning the little lord what he was up against.

Joe Canlon licked his lips and watched in horror as Hawk dropped the candlestick down the Ml barrel. The crowd began to shuffle and talk among themselves. This was the way a flintlock was loaded. Canlon's fatigues were black with sweat. Hawk jammed one of his grenades into the holder and pulled out the pin. Milky smoke spewed from the little bomb.

Canlon knew there was no choice now but to fire the

rifle and that, in less than five seconds, somebody would be dead. Every Marine flinched in shock at the unhesitating maneuver Hawk had made. They clicked their safeties off and waved their expectant muzzles back and forth at the rumbling crowd.

Hawk deftly dropped his hand down to the trigger of the Ml and fired the blank cartridge. The grenade sailed like a long-tailed rocket over the Daimo's head and into the empty rows of stone behind him. The brunt of the blast was borne by the inanimate stone, but enough of the concussion and shrapnel belched over the stage of the Daimo to knock half his retinue to the ground. Of these, half did not get up after the deafening crash.

Hawk dropped the Ml and unslung his Thompson as the sound of the explosion reverberated through the dead halls of Tamara. He stalked forward, leaving the Marines poised facing the awe-struck spectators. Canlon dropped from his knees to his belly; he would have preferred to burrow under the ground.

The crowd was paralyzed by the realization that they might become victims of the bloodthirsty visitors.

Uncompromising, heartless Sergeant Hawk turned the selector of his submachine gun to full automatic. The carrying strap was caught on the top of the weapon and he freed it with a deft jerk of his hands. He rattled off half a dozen bursts into as many men. The flaring quicksilver that leapt from the muzzle blinded and hypnotized the helpless victims. He continued toward the stage, apparently intent on destroying everyone near it. Blood spurted from holes chopped by the point-blank automatic fire. Corpses exploded from the remnants of the platform and onto the ground. Pieces of human anatomy dangled and oozed from the stage and the decorative banners still in place were dotted with dripping red. With the stock of the Thompson, Hawk cracked the skull of a wounded man who was throwing himself desperately about. By the time he reached the stage, only one man that had been on it was still alive: the diminutive lord of the Tamara.

Hawk grabbed the cowering Daimo-by one ankle and pulled him to the ground, exhibiting no regard for the frailty of the human bone structure. He heard the snapping rip of musket balls on the wood of the plat-form nearby. Someone was shooting at him. Then normal hearing was blotted out by the roar of BAR's, M3's, M1's, and a Reising. He ignored this madness and yanked the Daimo to his feet by the uncomfortable use of his ponytail. The firing stopped. He flattened the Daimo's nose with the gas compensator of the Thompson and held it roughly in place. He glared fero-ciously at the standing, shouting throng of Tamara. Their guards clutched their flintlocks with looks of helpless frustration.

The sergeant shouted at Bival. "Let's try it again."

Bival repeated the demand for the Americans. The Daimo began to squeak rapidly in a tone made nasal by the pressing gun muzzle. Bival reported that the Ameri-cans had been sent for. He did not tell Hawk that only two of them had been sent for, for he did not entirely understand the excited command of the Daimo.

Two guards disappeared through a gate opposite the one entered by the Marines. In a matter of seconds they were back with Daniel Calvert and Mrs. Jennings. Hawk did a double-take.

"Where's the girl?" he roared.

"They took her to another temple this morning, farther into this maze," Calvert shouted back to him.

Hawk lifted the Daimo off the ground by the convenient handle of hair. "You goddamn little son of a bitch!" He shook him and bounced him until all manner of squeaking issued from the throat of the terrified leader.

"He says you are too late. She has been consecrated," Bival relayed.

"She better get unconsecrated!" Hawk snarled like a berserk beast at the trembling Daimo. "Get her here, or I'll—" He jammed the muzzle of the Thompson down the man's throat and leaned on it, making the little man gag and struggle until it looked as if he might die in a choking fit. "—pull this out your ass." He threw the Daimo to the ground and kicked him heavily on the side of the head. The leader was dazed and momentarily insensible. Hawk's rage abated somewhat, not out of any compassion, but for fear of destroying his hostage.

"Awright." Hawk rocked back his helmet and ran his sleeve across his sweating forehead. "Bival, get some sense outa this shitbag before I kill him." The Daimo kept his fluttering eyes on Sergeant Hawk as Bival stood over him, firing questions. He was trying to be more accommodating with his answers this time. Around them lay the dead nobility of Tamara. The island's royalty had been forced into extinction within a few terrible seconds. Out on the field, Collins lay very still with a musket ball in his stomach. Collins was the boy who had wanted to help the wounded Japanese prisoner at Liloila. Hawk looked over his shoulder at the wounded, pitiful, small body of the boy stretched out limply on the ground. The dead Tamara were nonexistent for him, but the wounded Marine caused a physical hurting in his chest. Though he had been hurt this way a thousand times before, he could always be hurt again.

"She is in the Temple of Teer, where she is being consecrated to the Daimo for her marriage," Bival reported.

Hawk was still looking at Collins. Lasker was working over him. "Tell him to drop the doubletalk and tell us where she is," Hawk said quietly, not looking at either Bival or the Daimo.

Bival answered for the prisoner. "Teer is a Moslem devil, Sergeant. These people must follow a devil cult. He says the temple is beyond that gate." Bival indicated the rear exit to the arena.

"Joe, Pidge, come with me. Lasker, you keep these bastards covered and kill anybody making a run for the gates. Bival, you're comin' too," Hawk said. He jerked the Daimo to his feet. "And you, buddy."

Hawk led them to the gate opposite the one by which the Marines had entered the arena. As they left the exit, the Tamara seemed to breathe a collective sigh of relief. They returned calmly to their seats. The Marines didn't realize that their recovered serenity was due to a profound conviction that Teer had summoned and was about to devour Sergeant Hawk. The shivering Daimo led the way to the temple of consecration; from his perspective, he was not entirely sure who would devour whom. He continued to squeal at Bival despite the unfriendly cuffs Hawk freely administered to him.

Bival said, "He tells me that no one may enter the temple during the consecration because Teer himself walks the earth at that time."

"Awright," said Hawk, unimpressed.

"He says that Teer will inflict torturous punishment and death upon any violators of the temple, as well as the woman and the Daimo."

"Right."

"He says he will kill himself before he will enter the Temple with us."

"That's a goddamn shame."

The increasingly hysterical Daimo led them down a lane similar to the one that had led the Marines to the arena. He stopped at a particularly old and decrepit structure and announced fearfully that this was the temple. Its entranceway was the open mouth of a huge and hideous snake, whose coiled body made up the exterior of the rest of the Temple.

"This don't look too important to me," said Hawk as he looked over the one-story edifice.

"Me neither," said Canlon. "Let's get the hell away from here."

"The temple is underground," Bival explained.

"Okay," Hawk said skeptically. "I guess I gotta buy this line of shit. But, here—you come here, you little son of a..." Hawk took the muzzle of Joe's carbine and inserted it into the Daimo's mouth. "If I don't come back, blow his head off. And don't go gettin' big-hearted. I want you to kill the little horse's ass."

The Daimo tried to say something. Joe took the muzzle out of his mouth. Bival translated the excited utterances. "He says you will not come back. He has done everything you wanted, but it is you who are trespassing in the hall of Teer. He should not be held responsible for your death."

"Yeah, yeah." Hawk laughed scornfully. "If the goddamn Devil eats me, we won't kill you. Pidge, cover

Joe and fire a warning shot near this here door if any trouble starts up."

"You goin' in by yourself?" Canlon asked.

"Why not? He says nobody's supposed to be in there, don't he?"

Bival nodded. "All of the shamans and conjurers were on the dais with him at the assembly. No one is allowed into the temple at this time."

"Yeah, but do you trust him? And what about this Teer guy—or thing?" Joe asked.

"Come on, man. Did you just fall out of a goddamn tree or something?" Hawk held up his submachine gun. "I got a couple dozen forty-five slugs for Teer if he wants to show me his ugly ass."

He turned away from them and stepped into the evil entranceway. Rock stairs led down into the earth at a steep incline. "How far away is she?" he asked, peering down the winding steps that disappeared into a pitch black nothingness.

Bival reported that she was in a chamber at the bottom of the stairs, bound to a post that the Daimo called an altar, supposedly communing with Teer.

"Okay. *Adios.*"

"Sergeant Hawk?" Bival stopped him. He took a rosary from his pocket and held it out to the Marine. Hawk smiled and refused it. "Please," Bival insisted, "what harm can it do?" He took Hawk's helmet from his head and dropped the beads around his neck. Hawk submitted docilely to the ceremony.

"Well, I reckon I oughta let the Good Lord know whose side I'm on." Hawk winked at Joe Canlon. Joe didn't appear to be enjoying it as much as the sergeant. He only squinted and nodded in agreement. Hawk descended the steps, his Thompson muzzle preceding him. In a few brief seconds, the men on the ground could neither see nor hear anything of him.

* * *

GARROTERO PACED ANGRILY along the poop deck of his pirate ship. He had taken a strong dislike to Sergeant Gill. Gill's men were eating all of his food, drinking all of his liquor, and smoking all of his opium. The sergeant had put on an exhibition boxing match during one of his drunken stupors. He had pounded three of Garrotero's crewmen around the deck mercilessly and offered to take on four more. The pirate chieftain stared through his eyeglass, expectantly searching for Tamara on the horizon. He had just returned from the far-flung little island, and he was irritated about having to go back. If one of his best clients hadn't commissioned this venture he would have refused it. Kravanart was too valuable as a source of revenue to risk alienating. Kravanart had been his friend since the Thirties, when he was in charge of a quartermaster unit in the Celebes. Now that the general had hit the big time, Garrotero must stay in his favor and reap the harvest of success along with him. But Gill was enough to try the patience of a saint, and the pirate was something less than that.

He turned his spyglass to the horizon behind him. There hovered one of those nasty little surprises that often intruded upon the life of a sea entrepreneur. He could see silhouettes of barges in the purple distance. Low in the water, long and narrow, with airplane motors and propellers in their sterns—they could only be Japanese landing craft, sometimes known as scooters, sometimes called airboats. They were following the pirate ship; not especially chasing it, perhaps not even following it, but they were adhering to the same course. The wily old pirate didn't care what they were doing; he meant to avoid them. He avoided all warships unless he had business with them, especially if he carried soldiers hostile to the ships. He preferred unarmed fishing boats and commercial kumpits for his prey.

He had no way of knowing the barges were troop carriers, somewhat off course, evacuating Imperial soldiers from Mindanao and rushing them to the fighting up in Luzon. The Japanese were in no way interested in a native pirate ship until they saw it hit top speed in an effort to run away from them.

Gill's men were sobered as the horizon filled with Japanese. Their breath grew shorter as the gap closed between them and the enemy. They had just managed to regain their strength and spirits and now they were destined for the rigors of imprisonment or a watery grave.

Garrotero watched the approaching fleet with cool detachment. He led them to the shores of Tamara. He planned to deposit his human cargo there and continue running. Gill and the Americans already on the island would serve as enough of a diversion to get the Japanese off his tail.

* * *

THE STIFLING HEAT grew progressively more intense as Hawk descended the clammy steps. He could see nothing in the total darkness; he felt only a vile dampness emanating from the close walls. At the bottom of the flight of steps the temperature soared to blast-furnace level. He gasped and labored for breath. As he walked out upon the mold-padded earthen floor, a gust of wind struck his face.

He froze in his steps and tried to determine the source of the breeze. He could not tell which side of his face it was touching; it seemed to be enveloping him. The lazy flow of air somewhat relieved the incredible heat. Ahead he perceived a dim light. As he moved slowly forward and toward the faint illumination, he had no way of telling how far above him a roof might hang or how far to the sides the walls might stand. He floated onward and inward, aware only of the earth beneath his feet and a light somewhere in front of him.

The light became brighter and, at about the same time, a crippling odor assaulted his nostrils. The smell surged through his nose and grabbed his insides. It was redolent of the nauseating odors of the swamps before the castle, but its intensity was unbelievably magnified. It smelled as if someone had spilled a trainload of rotten eggs in the subterranean chamber. He had no choice but to stifle a curse and breathe the unhealthy air.

As the light grew brighter, an underground cavern became visible. The floor of the cavern was filled with a pool of some kind of liquid. On the surface of the liquid, lapping fires floated and rocked about in buoyant little clumps. In the orange shadows of these fires, he was able to see across the fiery lake. On a ledge on the shore opposite him was a giant post hanging out over the liquid. Tied to the post was Amelia Jennings. Her head and her hair hung down as if she were unconscious—or worse.

The pool extended right up to and possibly under the curving walls of the cavern. There was but one means of approach to the post: A line of glistening, creosoted beams crossing the flaming pond. The beams were ten-by-twelve, supported by log pilings at a height of eight to ten feet above the surface of the oily liquid. Hawk stepped boldly out and onto the first of the slick beams. A fog of steaming miasma clouded his vision and clogged his pores. A memory from his childhood flickered in his brain; he saw clearly the illustration of a horned, winged demon on the page of a long-forgotten picture book. He hadn't recalled that in twenty years. He bellowed out Amelia's name.

She raised her head. "James! You're here!"

"Be still. I'll be there in a second." He carefully negotiated his steps on the sweating beams. The singed bridge had no handrail. His boot slid out a bit and he caught himself. That was when he thought he saw something out of the corner of his eye.

An enormous, lavender face with features grotesque as the carvings outside seemed to appear and disappear over his shoulder and behind him. The features were fluid, stretching and leering until they would completely disappear. He went to one knee, breathing heavily and looking behind himself. There was nothing there.

What was it? "Come on, here. Show me that again," he whispered. The rosary dangled from his neck and rhythmically ticked against the wooden stock of his Thompson. "Come on, sweetheart. Here I am. Come and get a taste of some *real* hell." He looked all around the dark crevices that riddled the cavern walls. Nothing moved but the ghastly steam rising from the pool.

He rose to his feet again. Halfway across the lake he had another glimpse of the fiendish face. It swooped behind him like a giant bird and evaporated into the sulphurous mist that floated over the pond. This time, he didn't stop. "Horseshit," he growled, and continued across.

He stepped onto the ashen soil of the opposite bank, sinking into it for several inches. He hopped up onto the ledge and walked over to the splintered post.

Unsheathing his jungle knife, he came to the girl's side and began severing the scorched ropes that held her. Before he had finished the task, he felt the dead weight of a large human hand in the middle of his back.

"God damn it!" He dropped the knife and wheeled around. Nothing was behind him but the wall of the cave. He snorted angrily, picked up the knife, and slashed the last of the bonds.

"James, James!" she said. "This place is hell. The things I've seen...we'll never get out of here." Hot, dirty ashes smudged her icy-white complexion.

"We'll get out. It ain't nothin' but a carnival spook house. I'll put an end to it as soon as I catch sight of one of them spooks."

"No—it's real. Teer is real. He is the Devil and he's here. He'll never let us leave!" She dug her fingers into his arms.

The stench prevented Hawk from thinking clearly. He angrily shook his head. "Listen, kid, ain't nothin' stoppin' *me* from leavin' here!" He took her arm and tugged her toward the precarious bridge of beams.

"No, no. Don't anger him. Please!" She begged hysterically.

Hawk was not a man to fear angering anyone or

anything. He sneered and dragged her up to the first beam. "Come on, get movin', before we melt in this shit."

"I can't walk across that thing. Don't be foolish. He'll kill us. He wants me!"

"So do I." He picked her up and she kicked violently at the air. She could not tear herself free of his grip. He began the trip across with his gun hand pinned beneath her.

As he tight-roped his way over the bridge, the water under him began to boil. The bubbles popped and gurgled, spitting fiery droplets up at the beams' underside. Before he had taken a dozen steps, he looked down to And that a section of the bridge was missing. It was gone; it had disappeared into thin air. The space left there was too wide to jump across. Hawk growled a stream of obscenities and tested the vacant air with his boot. As he did so, the bridge reappeared and he continued across. She began to scream madly, and struck at him. He ignored the puny blow and those that followed, never setting her down till he reached the solid ground of the far side.

He dragged her by one hand up the stairs. The heat and the odor subsided about halfway up them. He pulled her into the clean daylight and air of the outside. She was exhausted and she fell to her knees. Bival rushed to her side. Hawk smiled at Joe Canlon, who still held the Daimo at the end of his rifle.

"How is she? What's wrong with her?" Canlon asked.

Hawk tossed his helmet to the ground. "She's okay, I guess," he said, drying his sweating hair with his hand. "Funny place down there. I think there's some kind of gas in it, that makes you see things." He pulled a cigar from his pocket. "Either that or there really is a devil down there. Why don't you go check it out, Joe?" Hawk smiled around his cigar.

"Why don't you go to hell?" Canlon leaped off the ground at the suggestion. "You got what you wanted; let's get outta here now." Joe was afraid Hawk might have been serious. Shaeffer voiced no desire to go into the temple either.

Hawk was curious about what he had seen, but he had to get back to his men. In his rage, he had left them in a dangerous situation. Amelia was on her feet now and she staggered over to him.

"You can't get away from him, James. He'll follow you," she said.

"We're goin', right now, and nothin's gonna follow us." He looked regretfully down the stairway.

The Daimo began screeching as soon as Joe removed the rifle from his mouth. He continued to rave all the way back to the arena.

"He says that only a man who is one of the devil's own or the Devil himself could go into the temple during consecration and live," said Bival.

"Tell him he's fulla shit," said Hawk.

13

They returned to the arena. The crowd, lounging in their seats, was amazed at the sight of the recaptured girl. Hawk marched the rescued party and his wounded man's bearers the length of the field as the Marines remained on guard. They withdrew one at a time after Hawk had departed through the far gate. Shaeffer was the last man to leave the field. He had hopes of killing at least one more Tamara, but the hopes were not to be realized.

They set Collins down just outside the arena and Hawk came and stood over him. He was lapsing in and out of consciousness.

"He can't make it," said Calvin Davis. "I've seen them kinda wounds before. He won't make it more'n a day or so." Hawk knelt over Collins. The boy was sweating profusely. The sergeant exhaled harshly and stood up again. "Maybe we oughta finish him off?" Davis said.

Hawk looked up sharply. "What are you talkin' about? That's a Marine layin' there. As long as one of us is standin' we'll carry him along. If he wants to die he can do it in his own good time."

Davis turned and walked away without answering him.

While he was free of the prying eyes of the Tamara, Hawk decided to hide one of General Kirijo's stolen files. The folder containing the copies of Kirijo's personal affairs was removed from the briefcase. This file now had particular significance for Hawk. If he was ever to be a free man, he had to have the file. Because of the powerful men involved in the controversy and plot against him, he knew that he must have clear and convincing evidence of his innocence. He also knew that evidence sometimes disappears.

He decided to hide the copy of the file in a third-story room of one of the pagodas standing outside the arena. If the original should be destroyed during the return trip or misplaced during any court-martial proceedings, he would still have evidence of Kravanart's dealing in contraband. Perhaps it was all unnecessary effort, but not as unnecessary as the end of a rope, or a firing squad, or a life in Portsmouth prison.

While he was in the musty, bird-droppings-caked room, he heard a shot on the ground below. He rushed down to see what had happened. He didn't like what he found. Shaeffer had killed Collins.

"He wouldn't last," said Shaeffer. "You wanted to do it. I did it. We couldn't carry him with us. He was dying anyway."

"You shouldn't have done that, Pidge," said Hawk. The Tamara were coming down from their bleachers now, peeking through the gate at the Marines. Lasker held his BAR on them. Phillips prepared a rifle grenade and handed it to Davis. Canlon got the men to one knee and they aimed their weapons at the gate. The Tamara made no attempt to come through. Hawk and Shaeffer ignored all of this as they stared menacingly into each other's eyes. "You shouldn't have done that. I told y'all not to."

Shaeffer's once handsome eyes had shrunk into his head and were surrounded by purple bags like the eyes of a snake. He hissed at the sergeant.

"It's done. You can't undo it."

"I told you not to."

"We couldn't carry him, Hawk."

"I could carry him."

"You killed him as much as I did. You had *more* to do with it than I did. I just put him out of his misery. You brought him here in one piece and done it to him. It's your fault, Hawk. Don't go tryin' to push it off on me. I was just lookin' out for the ones that are still alive. Don't you think it's about time you did that, too?"

Hawk dropped his Thompson. Shaeffer glanced down at it and up at Hawk.

"That's right, start swingin'," said Shaeffer, unafraid. "That'll solve everything, won't it?"

"I oughta beat your brains in, Pidge. But you ain't got none. You're gonna carry the kid now. We ain't leavin' his body here. You're carryin' it outa here."

"All right, goddamnit, I will. I don't give a goddamn." Shaeffer turned away and stalked off.

Hawk watched him walk away and turned around to see Mrs. Jennings and Calvert in a huddle over Amelia. The girl had collapsed and they were leaning her against the stone wall near the street. He thought at first that they were only resting. His mind was occupied with other thoughts. Then he realized the seriousness of the girl's condition.

"Mother, it was the Devil, and I was in hell!" she cried. "I saw him."

Hawk brushed Mrs. Jennings out of the way and knelt down. He pulled out his canteen and poured water through the girl's dry lips. He held her head across one leg and tried to comfort her,

"Listen, kid, I seen all that shit too. It wasn't nothing but your imagination, though; you see?" He looked over his shoulder at Calvert and Mrs. Jennings. "See, there was a gas burnin' down there. It kinda drugged you and made you see crazy things." He looked down again. "She was in there longer than me. She musta got a pretty strong dose of it." Hawk stood up and summoned Bival. "Ask that little jerk how long these consecration things last. Find out if it makes you permanently...sick," he said in a low voice.

Bival spoke to the Daimo. Brides spent one day in the Temple of Teer, and it generally took another week or two for them to recover from the spells that he cast. Amelia had spent less than half a day down there. Bival whispered all of this to Hawk.

"She's gonna be all right," Hawk announced to Calvert and Mrs. Jennings. "That gas has to wear off. It made her a little sick. Give her a few days."

"James?" Amelia opened her eyes.

"Yeah, it's me."

"He's coming after us right now. Teer is coming."

"No, he ain't, honey. It's all in your head. You'll feel better." He looked up and threw a concerned glance in the direction of the arena. The Tamara were coming to life, running back and forth in front of the gate and shouting at the Americans. He knew he had to move along and take his little crises with him.

"No, James. I saw him, I touched him. He touched me."

"I know. I seen something and I felt something, too. It's all a buncha crap. I've seen worse things swallowin' chewin' tobacco."

"Mother...Mother...James came in there and took me away from him." Amelia began to cry, and she put her arms around his neck. "Now he has to go back there with me." Hawk slowly pulled away from her.

Mrs. Jennings held her daughter's hand. "Sergeant Hawk isn't going anywhere that he doesn't want to go, dear. I can guarantee that. And you aren't either."

"We're going back," said Amelia.

Joe Canlon stood above them and nervously watched the arena gate. He was half convinced that Satan was about to stroll through it, twirling his pitchfork like a baton. Shaeffer watched the gate too. He was more concerned about a musket ball in the head than he was about evil spirits. First Platoon already had plenty of those.

Hawk squared the men away for a forced march. Calvert tried to cheer Amelia.

"Of course, old girl," he said. "Why, if the Devil comes out here, we'll fill him full of lead. You have the full weight of the United States government protecting you here."

"There ain't no devil," Hawk snapped as he walked by and overheard this. "Just breathe deep. I'll take care of the rest."

Amelia was not to be easily cheered. The sergeant gave the order to move out. Enough time had been wasted. The girl would not leave since, as she explained it, she would only have to come back anyway. Tiring of this story, and having no more time to entertain it, Hawk ordered Phillips to carry her. Calvert insisted that he should be the one to carry her. Hawk impatiently approved of this change in orders, failing to comment on Calvert's remarkable recovery from his deathbed of the day before. But Amelia vetoed even the amended plans and required that no one but Hawk touch her. Presumably this was because he was already contaminated and had a den of his own reserved somewhere in the Temple of Teer. Emotionally drained but still physically invincible, Hawk swooped her up and carried her from the temple grounds, over the stone bridges, and beneath the walls of the castle, without a pause.

Before the eventful day had ended they had crossed the swamp. The marshlands had dried out somewhat since they first traversed them. The stagnant mud that was left had the appearance of hot, shiny asphalt, black and hard in the sun.

The appearance was deceiving. The ground was soggy and sponge-like, absorbing legs up to the thighs and disgorging them only after tiresome effort. In spite of this, a great deal of ground was covered and the men reached the beautiful little wood at the edge of the mire by nightfall. They cleared a campground and left a guard to watch for the Tamara. Amelia became more talkative that night.

She was feeling better. She and Calvert entered into a murmuring conversation no one could overhear.

Hawk watched them from across a dancing campfire. They sat close together. Calvert smiled frequently and often laughed aloud. The girl spoke to him just as often as he spoke to her. She never smiled. Her expression told the grim observer beyond the fire nothing. When Calvert laughed, she would look at him with that unnerving, faraway look, and then turn away.

Hawk puffed thoughtfully on a tattered cigar. His back ached from carrying her through the mud.

14

GARROTERO SKILLFULLY MANEUVERED HIS JUNK ALONG the tricky shoals off Tamara. The cruel face of the Tausag showed no emotion when a Japanese destroyer steamed through the fleet of landing craft. It was nothing to him. They would never catch him.

Gill and Jack Calicote were not so detached. Their boat was taking infant steps on the surface of the ocean while the destroyer was taking giant adult steps in her pursuit. As much as they feared death and being wounded, the two bullies feared capture even more. They had both committed a volume of atrocities against the Japanese, and they considered the enemy to be even more cowardly and vicious than their noble selves.

Garrotero had no intention of letting the big ship train its five-inch guns on his tiny wooden boat. He hugged the Tamaran coastline and kept just out of sight of the naval gunners. His breast was filled with more pride than fear as he deftly worked his craft. Probably no man in the world could have taken the junk so close to shore at such a speed, continuously negotiating merging bends and avoiding the very sight of his pursuers. The only way the Japanese would see him again was if he wanted them to do so. And he did.

Gill and Calicote were no seamen. The chase, filled their digestive tracts with freezing, metallic fear. Their hearts thudded up into their constricted throats when the destroyer again loomed angrily into view. Garrotero smiled gently to himself. He loved his little junk; he wouldn't let it be reduced to driftwood.

"We cannot escape this one," Garrotero shouted over the motors to Gill. "I have brought you to Tamara as I promised. You must go ashore, and I will fight the Japs on the open sea."

Gill looked at the pirate chieftain. He had a swashbuckling grin on his face. Gill was so scared he actually believed that the devious old barnacle was offering to defend the Americans. Calicote slapped him across the chest and they fell to gathering their gear together. The frantic soldiers scrambled over the side and splashed into the chest-deep water. They waded ashore, battling the rough waves and climbing onto a little peninsula that was in clear sight of the destroyer. Garrotero sailed around the peninsula and disappeared before they made dry land. He had disappeared for both Gill and the Japanese forever. He was off to ply his trade in friendlier waters.

Disappearing proved more difficult for Gill, Calicote, and their four remaining men. They labored for sixty-second hours in the roaring surf. It drenched and carried and tumbled them about without mercy. They kicked and crouched and crawled until they hit the sandy beach. They clawed at it with their fingernails, fearful that the terrible sea would reclaim them. The destroyer, trying to be helpful, blew the tops out of nearby palm trees with its thundering deck guns. The enemy sailors ingeniously managed to lower their hundred-millimeter anti-aircraft guns to beach level. They played the tree-high bursts up and down the sandy shoreline. Two of the soldiers were cut in two by this savage play, and a falling palm tree crushed the skull of a third, before the survivors could get into the forest. Breathing fire and gall, too frightened even to focus their vision, they lay in the ferns off the beach while the ship shelled the jungle on all sides. Their brains were too addled to realize what use the pirate had put them to. Calicote was beginning to recover his senses and to think that he might somehow live through the shelling when he recalled the innumerable landing craft that were accompanying the destroyer. They were the real fleet. The big ship was merely supplying them anti-aircraft protection. Men made up the bulk of the fleet, tough combat veterans who would soon be ashore.

"Gill—Gill—they're gonna land!" Calicote shouted over the crashing shells. "We gotta get outa here!"

Gill pulled his beefy face out of the powdery soil and nodded stupidly. The three of them got up and ran inland. Several Japanese landing barges puttered past the destroyer like giant insects and slid into the beach. Platoon after platoon of bellowing troopers charged into the undergrowth. The shelling stopped.

* * *

SERGEANT HAWK never took his eyes off Amelia Jennings. She was his. She didn't know it yet, but she was. He wouldn't let Calvert have her—not because

Calvert was a jerk, but because she could only go to one man, and that man was Hawk. Amelia was sitting with the young civilian again and Hawk was alone on the far side of the campfire.

Joe Canlon watched the sergeant through half-closed eyes. After knowing him for so long, he could read Hawk's mind. It was a simple mind to read. Joe was afraid for Calvert.

Amelia left him and went to sit with her mother. Calvert got up, too, apparently in the best of spirits. The men were all bedded down, save for those on guard. They had found a little stream, and the clean drinking water and much-needed baths had refreshed them.

Hawk ran his fingernail up and down the gas compensator of the Thompson leaning across his leg. This clicking and the crackling of the fire were the only sounds to be heard. The clicking stopped and Hawk sat back with a sigh.

He had no claim on her. He had resisted her at first, and successfully. Then they were separated—and absence had made the heart grow fonder. Now they were rejoined. He hadn't really told her anything. She didn't know how he felt about her. He had just expected that his actions would speak for him. Perhaps it was all his fault. That was what he was thinking as he got to his feet.

He walked around the campfire and sat beside Mrs. Jennings, putting her between himself and the girl. He looked across Mrs. Jennings and, clearing his throat, said, "You feelin' any better?"

"Yes."

"That's good."

No one said anything for a while. Then Mrs.

Jennings said, "That was an *experience,* Sergeant Hawk. Let me tell you, it was. It's a frightening thing when you go tampering with a person's mind. Especially a young, impressionable person like Amelia..."

"Yes, ma'am."

"Not that you yourself weren't exposed to the same thing, mind you. Of course, you're a strong young man; you should take it all in your stride."

"Yes, ma'am."

Mrs. Jennings changed her tone to an undisguised snarl. "We all took it rather well, I suppose. Mr. Calvert is certainly doing a lot better, isn't he? Malaria doesn't seem to be a very debilitating illness, does it, Sergeant Hawk?"

"He's gettin' around pretty good," Hawk agreed.

"I don't believe that I have ever loathed anything quite so much as—"

"We all know how you feel, Mother; you've told us often enough."

"Oh...pardon me, Amelia. In that case, I shall lie down for the night. Good night, Sergeant Hawk."

"Night, ma'am."

She got up and there was nothing between him and Amelia. He ran his finger up and down his nose.

"When did the gas wear off?" he asked.

"Gas?"

"I mean...well, are you still afraid of devils and such?"

"Please, let's not talk about that. Yes, I am." She looked down. "At least, now I know that I'm acting hysterically...but I don't think that knowing it will prevent me from acting that way. I still think that what I saw was real."

Hawk nodded and stared into the fire. "Yeah. You're better."

She shifted her legs and came closer to him. "You are a brave man, aren't you? Is there anything you're afraid of?"

Hawk snorted a short laugh. "I could probably find something."

"Why did you do it?"

"What?"

"You know. Come after me."

Hawk rubbed his forehead, his eyes, and his nose.

"I told you there was no way I can ever thank you for it," she said.

"So? Like I told you—no need to."

She looked at the side of his face. The handsome nose, the intelligent eyes, the well-formed chin—all seemed out of place on the savage, earthy creature who sat before the fire.

"Your whole life is made up of violence and challenges, isn't it?"

"Pretty much. Misery would be a better word for it."

"What will you do when the challenges are over—when the war is over?"

"Something else, I guess. Why?"

"Would it be safe to leave the fire so that we could talk privately?"

"I expect so. Sure you're feelin' all right?"

She stood up and took his hand. They walked into the forest, past Pidge Shaeffer, and up onto a boulder perched among the ferns. Calvert saw them leave. He lay beside the fire with his hands behind his head and his eyes open.

Amelia didn't let go of Hawk's hand after they had

stopped walking. She faced him and looked up into his fiery blue eyes. Everything about him was a little frightening; his eyes, his silence, his future. But she wasn't frightened by it now.

"For Gods' sake," she said, "hold me."

For his own sake, Hawk did. He felt her soft body beneath the robe. It melted against him and stayed there. He tried at the last to restrain himself, to save himself from being hurt once more, but he couldn't. He tilted his head and touched her lips against his. He ran his lips back and forth against hers, and tightened his arms around her. At that moment, she wanted to stay there forever.

"Oh, I love you," she said. Tears were in her voice. "The things we get ourselves into," she sobbed softly, and placed her face against his chest.

"You ain't into nothin', kid," he answered. "You don't owe me nothin'. I came after you, because I didn't want you hurt. I still don't. I...know you like that Calvert fella, and I ain't gonna stand in your way."

"You're already in the way."

Hawk held her from him and looked into her long-lashed eyes. "This ain't got nothin' to do with devils and such, has it?" he asked, fearing the answer.

"No," she laughed abruptly, happily. "No, of course not." It was the first time he had seen her laugh since her affliction. There hadn't been much to laugh about.

"What about Calvert?"

"I'll just have to tell him. We've known each other for two years—we can talk things over without any problem. He'll understand. I'll just tell him. If...you want me to." Silence. "Do you?"

"Well...sure."

"Then I will." She smiled.

Hawk looked down at her full lips glistening in the half light. He gave into his overpowering hunger for them. He gave in completely this time. Her head went back under the force of the irresistible embrace. Her copper hair shimmered over the hand he held against her back. She had never been kissed that way by any man—or demon. Her mind was swirled away on a magic whirlwind, to a dark sea-bottom that glittered with desire. And it was a funny thing; though she tried for the rest of her life, she could never forget that moment, or him.

* * *

THE NEXT MORNING, before they set out again, Amelia told Daniel Calvert of her new relationship. He took it well, with a philosophical laugh and a few words of French that she didn't understand.

Shaeffer released the Daimo. He made his way back to the castle alone.

Hawk prepared himself for the trip up the mountain. He chose one of the lower peaks to cross. He thought it best to wait on the mountaintop for the return of Ramos and, it was to be hoped, Alonso. For some reason, he had decided to go up there alone and reconnoiter. The presence of any danger above him had never crossed his mind. When Amelia begged him to let her come along, he happily conceded.

"Did you tell him?" he asked her as he helped her up the rocky slope.

"Yes."

"Hmm?"

"Yes, I told him."

"What'd he say?"

"He took it rather bravely. He loves me very much, you know. He's just out of his element here. He's a fine fellow, really. Oh, I don't know—I'm just glad it's over."

"Yeah." They struggled a bit farther. "How you feelin' this mornin? Seen old Lucifer any more?" Hawk laughed.

She smiled and bit her lip as she negotiated a steep ledge. "No. But I still think he'll come after me. I'm serious. Now I know that I won't give in to him, though. I'll fight him."

"Yeah, you're better," he said.

The sound of big guns thundered on the other side of the mountain. Hawk swung around. The straps of his helmet creaked and swayed with his turning head.

"Stay here," he said. He ran up the mountainside. Anti-aircraft guns were roaring at a raging gallop down along the beach. He reached the summit and saw the Japanese destroyer out in the sea, lying there motionless, like a hungry leviathan. Dozens of landing barges were being swished ashore by their gigantic airplane propellers. No expression showed on his grim features as he took in the scene. One could realize the helplessness that the victims of the Japanese juggernaut must have felt at the beginning of the war. Hawk realized and felt nothing, except that something new had to be done. He didn't see the three Americans who had brought the catastrophe to the shores of Tamara. He ran back down the slope, took Amelia's hand, and continued running.

"Trouble," he told her. They came down the mountain quickly.

"What's goin' on over at the beach?" Canlon asked. He had just put out the last campfire.

"Japs are hittin' the island. About eighty million goddamn Japs are swarmin' this way," said Hawk. He looked over the mountaintops and back at the jungle, then over to the old castle.

"What can we do?" Amelia asked.

"I don't know. Run like hell, I guess," said Hawk. His eyes scoured the mountaintops, searching for a way out of the trap. He only had a little time.

"That's about it," said Canlon. "Ramos'll never be able to get through all that shit. We just gotta hide out."

Hawk considered returning to the temples. He would have done it, too, if he hadn't already spread so much neighborly good cheer among the natives. That avenue was definitely closed. He resolved to go north along the foot of the mountain range. It looked as if it might be easy to hide in the rugged peaks that stabbed the sky in that direction. Unless the island was larger than he thought, those peaks probably leaned out over the northern ocean, and he would be able to watch for his rescue boat from that vantage point. If it ever came.

* * *

CALICOTE, Gill, and the third survivor, Carson, ran for their worthless lives. Carson was spent before they reached the mountains. Gill was in good shape; he could run this way for another half hour. If he hadn't been so scared, he could have run for hours. There was no limit to how far Calicote could run. Carson fell on the soft earth. He was neither athlete nor animal. He breathed heavily. His chest was on fire, his limbs trembled, his mouth was filled with bile. He was through. Gill and Calicote knelt over him. Gill's side was about to burst and his head reeled.

"This is what comes from going against our own," Carson wheezed. "This is what happens when you set out to kill Americans." Gill looked fearfully at the living jungle around him. They had lost their firearms in the sea. Gill was in no mood for a sermon.

"Get up, you bastard!" he roared. "Get up or we'll leave you here."

"You gonna make it, Gill?" Carson laughed. "You gonna find those Marines? You might, you know—if the Japs don't cook your stinkin' hide for breakfast."

"You're goddamn right, I'm gonna find 'em," said Gill, getting to his feet.

"It's not right," said Carson.

"Carson, you was made to be Jap bait," said Calicote. Carson snatched his knife from its scabbard and swung it weakly at Calicote. The Kentuckian grabbed his wrist and took the knife away. He plunged it repeatedly into the dying man's chest.

"Let's go," said Gill. "I gotta get Hawk before the Japs do." The two renewed their blind dash into the depths of Tamara.

Carson was still alive when the Japanese found him. The words "Sergeant Hawk" were on his delirious lips.

"Sergeant Hawk," one of his discoverers repeated. The enemy soldiers looked at each other. The renegade American Marine had attacked this man. The mad outlaw was on Tamara. The officer in charge led them away. He resolved to put an end to this legendary evil-doer who killed for the sake of killing. Carson died a short while later.

* * *

HAWK LED the platoon along the foothills of the mountain range. The range cut across the entire middle of the island, forming a natural barrier between the most convenient landing beach and the old Spanish castle. He could have tried to reach the east coast—it was the farthest from the invaders—but he would have had to go through the country of the Tamara tribesmen. It would have been a long, dangerous journey.

Mrs. Jennings and Bival were not up to any prolonged flights. Hawk realized that the enemy could easily overtake them once they knew that they were here. Among so many enemy troops there would be a few soldiers with the stamina to hunt the Americans day and night. The Marines had long ago used up their stamina; they were operating on guts alone. Fortunately, the island was not as wide as it was long. The march north was a short, untrying one. Hawk had no way of knowing Gill and Calicote were leading the invaders to the exact same locale he had chosen.

They started an upward climb when they reached the slope closest to the sea. In short order, they scrambled up to the summit of the mountain that was connected to a cliff hanging over the pounding ocean. A land bridge of loose stone connected these two formations. The bridge was nothing more than a pile of crumbled rock that filled the gap between the two slopes. Lesser peaks were before and behind the mountain; they jutted up on all sides, some looking as thin as the pages of an open book standing on its edge. These flat formations were impossible to climb and served to block the view of the mountain chosen to hide upon.

The cliff that abutted the ocean was a little distance below the summit of the mountain. Hawk and Canlon surveyed the breathless drop. The ocean was empty on this coast.

The sergeant ordered fortifications erected just below the mountaintop. Pits were dug out of the mountainside, and rocks and trees were stacked across the front of them. During the construction of these makeshift caves, an enemy column was sighted threading its way through the badlands at the foot of the mountain. The Marines crawled quietly into their caves and waited until the Japanese had passed. The endless column crossed the mountain range a few hundred yards to the south and proceeded toward Tamara's castle. This brush with the ominous Imperial forces made Hawk realize the severity of his predicament.

He sent Shaeffer back to the cliff to seek out an avenue of escape to the ocean below. He decided that he himself would go to a lesser elevation and see if he could spot the enemy and find out what their overall plan was going to be.

Conceding to the frailties of mortal man, he took George Phillips along with him. If enemy troops were sighted, at least one man should be able to make it back with a warning. Calvert asked to go along, too. Hawk knew he would be nothing more than a nuisance. He also knew that Calvert only wanted to redeem himself in the eyes of Amelia Jennings. For some reason, the sergeant felt obligated to allow the man this much. Perhaps the reason was to prove to Calvert that redemption would do him no good. It was an unprofessional decision, but Calvert was with them when they left the caves.

They struggled down the northern slope lest they be spotted by the Japanese before they had a chance to do any spotting of their own. When they got to the bottom of the slope, they circled the base of the mountain in a westerly direction. By this time Calvert was getting tired. He had been walking all day. Hawk would not consider a rest.

They were confronted by a sparse grove of trees and Hawk split them up. Calvert and Phillips were to flank the grove and he would go through it. They would meet on the other side. Thus it was that poor George Phillips haplessly ran into the jackal, Calicote, all by himself.

Calicote had separated from Gill. The two soldiers were both afraid of having to help each other, and so they gradually drifted apart. Morally bankrupt in the best of circumstances, Calicote had been reduced to madness by fear. He was not obsessed with capturing Hawk, as Gill was; he was obsessed with caring for his own hide, and killing was second nature to him.

"Hey, you there!" Calicote shouted when he saw Phillips rounding the grove. "Hey, Gyrene, over here!" Calicote fell exhaustedly to his knees. His wide eyes narrowed as he spied the rifle Phillips carried. The Marine turned white in alarm when he heard the nearby outburst. Then he saw the lanky body, the red beard, and the remnants of a GI uniform.

"Advance and be recognized," Phillips dutifully called.

"Cut that shit out and c'mere."

Phillips did so. "Who are you?" the Marine asked.

"Sure is good to see you." Calicote smiled a hideous,

insane smile. "Did you know there's a division of Japs chasin' me?" The kneeling soldier held out his hand. "I'm Jack Calicote. Give me that rifle, Gyrene."

Phillips shook hands with him. It didn't look like the other man, or creature, intended to let go. "Why?" George Phillips asked.

"To defend myself with," Calicote grinned wildly, "why do you think?"

Hawk heard the two men calling to one another. He was certain the noise would alert every Japanese within five miles. He couldn't imagine who Phillips could be yelling at unless it was the missing Merle Stroot. With the element of caution already compromised, he screamed for Calvert to join him. The two of them walked together toward the left flank of the grove. They didn't see, nor would they have expected to see, Amelia Jennings running down the mountainside after them. She was excited to tell them the news that Shaeffer had found a trail that somehow led to the sea.

When Hawk reached Phillips he was already dead: stabbed once in the ribs. He knelt over him and rubbed his aching forehead. Calvert watched the trees. He carried an Ml. "Goddamn Japs are here. We better..." Hawk began.

A scream sounding something like steam escaping from a boiler hissed in Hawk's ears. He looked up and saw a long-legged maniac running toward him. Calvert made no attempt to fire his rifle. He stepped back so that the assailant would have a clear path at Hawk. Calicote jumped on the sergeant and the two of them went rolling in the grass. Calvert had a clear shot at the attacker, but again he didn't fire.

Hawk kicked the entangling creature away. It was a

man with a bloody knife. A man in Army fatigues. At least some of the blood on the dripping blade was Hawk's. He had been slashed in the back and blood saturated his shirt.

"Here now, buddy," said Hawk from one knee as the man stood over him. "Who are you, buddy? We're Americans. We'll take care of you."

The long knife cast a shadow across Hawk's eyes. Calicote didn't answer. He made noises like a grieving dog. He jumped on the Marine again and, squirming and slashing with the lightning reflexes of insanity, he endeavored once more to kill him. Calvert stepped back even farther, lest he be injured in the untidy melee. He wanted to run. He was afraid of this creature; but he wanted to make sure that it killed Hawk first.

But Sergeant Hawk wasn't ready to die. He caught the naked blade with his bare hand and ripped it from Calicote's steel grip. The two men sprang simultaneously to their feet and faced each other. Hawk began circling him. Jack Calicote was mad, but he wasn't stupid. He turned and ran for the same gloomy forest that had produced him. Hawk was about to give angry chase when a crushing gush of pressure collided with the bone at the base of his neck. Calvert had hit him from behind with the rifle butt. Hawk fell groggily to one knee and another blow skidded along the side of his head and dug into his shoulder. But the Marine wouldn't fall over. With head bowed, he tackled Calvert and dragged him down.

Pain usually triggered Hawk's short temper. The second blow had nearly ripped his ear off. He grabbed Calvert's neck and stood up and picked him up by the throat and shook him. He lifted him off the ground and continued to shake him by the throat. He might have intended to kill him.

"James!"

Startled, Hawk looked over his burning shoulder. Amelia Jennings stood watching with open-mouthed astonishment. He threw Calvert down into an inglorious heap on the ground.

"What are you doing here?" Hawk roared at her. Adrenalin pounded through his injured body; rage was in his voice. "Get away from here!" He stood, breathing heavily, his bloody arms dangling like those of an ape.

Amelia backed away. She stared into the deep-set blue eyes with the dark leathery trails beneath them.

"It's him!" she whispered. It was Teer, and he had come for her, just as she thought that he would. "Daniel, run! Run!" she cried. Calvert needed no encouragement to do that, only the strength. He staggered to her side and took her hand. "It's him, Daniel," she said matter-of-factly, "we have to run." She cried out once more and ran for the mountain. Calvert followed without looking back.

Hawk fell bleeding onto the grass, holding himself up by one arm. He felt very little like the Satan belched from hell he was supposed to be. But, within a few minutes, when he had replaced his helmet and slung his Thompson, that was exactly what he was. He slouched steadily, unhurriedly back up the mountain.

When he returned, Joe Canlon met him at the cave defenses. "We got the woman and that Calvert guy hid out—so don't go lookin' for 'em," said Canlon.

"What do you mean?"

"Just that."

"I went lookin' for 'em through the middle of the

whole goddamn Jap army. I can find 'em now if I want to."

"I know you can. Just don't. It won't do anybody any good, including you."

They glared at each other for a moment. Hawk turned away and looked down the grey mountain. He could see the light-green glade where he fought Calvert. Beyond this was the dark-green forest.

"Awright," he said.

"Let me see your back. How'd you get scraped up? You're hand's cut up..."

"Get your goddamn hands off me, you son of a bitch." Hawk spun free of his prying hands.

Joe heaved a ragged sigh. "Okay." He sat down against the front of a gun pit. "Ramos got through with a boat. It ain't the boat we come in on. It's one of them Jap airboats. I don't know how he found us, but I got a feelin' the Japs are gonna hunt him and trail him here." Hawk nodded solemnly and Joe continued, "Shaeffer found a trail down the cliff to the water. When he got there, he found Ramos hidin' the boat. Pretty good, huh?" Joe held a hand over his eyes and looked through the fingers.

"One boat?"

Joe nodded. "They're big old boats though."

"You gonna let me and Calvert get in the same boat?"

"Look, Hawk, we're locked in here with a couple thousand Japs; this island is gonna be so crowded there ain't even gonna be room for an American to stand up. Why don't you act like you got good sense?"

"Because I ain't, I guess."

"I think we oughta start takin' off before they find us," said Joe, ignoring the comment.

"They done did," Hawk answered.

Joe stood and followed his eyes. Several columns of enemy soldiers were crossing the glade below. One could tell by their upturned faces that they had spotted the Marine position. They wore peaked caps and there were a lot of them.

When the enemy found the body of Phillips lying in the glade, they knew that they were on the trail of the infamous Sergeant Hawk.

"Show me this trail," Hawk said in a low, resigned voice. He took a broken cigar from his pocket and lit it. Canlon led him through the men and across the land bridge of loose stone to the cliff that hung over the sea. No one spoke to Hawk; no one acknowledged his presence.

Canlon lay on his belly at the edge of the cliff. "Look here," he said. Hawk lay beside him. Ten feet down, jutting out from the sheer drop, was a ledge that ran in a forty-five-degree angle to the sandy beach behind the mountains.

"That's a pretty damn rough way down," Hawk acknowledged.

"Pidge made it. Calvert and the girl...uh...made it."

Hawk nodded. "How'd Ramos get back?"

"I don't know. I didn't talk to him. He's down there. I guess Bival's friend brought him and dumped him."

"Did they make it down without ropes?"

"Yeah," said Canlon. "We just let 'em down by hand."

"Okay." Hawk got to his feet. "You know we'll be sittin' ducks if they case us in patrol boats? Them shallow draft barges wasn't meant for the open sea. Ain't a man here that knows how to sail a course." Canlon bobbed his helmet in agreement and shrugged. What choice was there?

They heard shots back at the rifle pits. They ran across the land bridge and back to the mountain. A tin bugle was blowing a spine-chilling charge. The Japanese were already climbing the slope. They had started the firefight and the Marines returned a cautious volley. Hawk looked all around the circumference of the base of the mountain. The enemy was rising toward them,

slowly, steadily, and in great numbers. He knew they couldn't hold the impending flood.

"Looks like we're too late, Joe," he said. "We can't make it down that goat walk at the rate they're comin' up. We'd get shot to pieces on the side of that bluff."

Hawk and Canlon took up a position in a rifle pit on the sparsely manned left flank.

Shaeffer loosed a burst of submachine-gun fire into one of the foremost enemy climbers. The stricken man screamed in surprise and went sprawling down the rock-strewn slope in an avalanche of dust.

Intermittent twenty-five-caliber shots cracked from below. Seconds later they whined off the rocks of the summit. The Japanese climbed, stopped, fired, took cover, and repeated the whole procedure. The fire remained light because of the enemy's preoccupation with climbing. Enough of the swishing bullets and meowing ricochets were sent upward to force the men to keep their heads down. If one were to close his eyes and listen, he could discern the gradual intensifying of the enemy fire. With one's eyes open, this went without notice. The spectacle of the rising tide of men drowned out all sound and thought. Canlon took off his helmet and ruffled his sweating hair. He could see the strained expressions on the faces of the climbers. The child's bugle whined at the Americans from somewhere close by. Hawk lit a cigar and threw the burning match down the mountain.

"Let's run for it!" Canlon gasped.

"We gotta fight," Hawk answered.

"Marine! Marine die!" came a scream from below. "Get you, Marine! Get YOU, Marine!"

The Marines screamed back at the horrible attackers, using every form of raging obscenity they could conjure up. But they were afraid.

"Sergeant Hawk," a passionate wail came from below in a Japanese accent. "Sergeant Hawk die! Get *you* Sergeant Hawk!"

The men looked at each other. The Japanese were calling for Hawk. They knew he was up there. Hawk peered down the mountainside. Absolutely no emotion showed in his face. The bugle made an abortive toot and then blared loudly.

"I hope Ramos has enough sense to get the girl outa here," Hawk finally said.

"Yeah," Canlon whispered. "What about us?"

"We're dead."

The climbing stopped. The Japanese remained in place and continued to fire up the slope. This went on for several minutes, then they broke from cover. It took away the breath of the waiting Americans. Every rock disgorged two or three Japanese soldiers. They bore down on the summit, screaming and firing and stumbling. The rocks seemed to be giving birth to full-grown warriors.

The Marine muzzles spat a line of red-orange flambeaux from the dark caves. The attack stalled halfway up the slope and the enemy retreated. The rocks swallowed the horde as quickly as they had produced them.

"Get them grenades ready," Hawk shouted. "If they get any closer, we'll use 'em. Make 'em count, now, goddamn it. They're the only thing that'll keep you from gettin' buried." The men were busily changing their clips as if they expected to survive the nightmare. No one had yet been injured. "Pidge!" Hawk shouted over the clicking of the clips and bayonets. "Over here. Davis, get that BAR over here." Hawk and Canlon stacked rocks higher across the mouth of their cave. The next attack was so sudden it had crossed half the distance between the two opposing forces before a shot was fired.

It looked like the end had come as the silent charge ended and roared to life. The Marines sensed there was no way to prevent being overrun. They were going to have to grapple with their foe and probably die in the process. They frantically turned their sights from one fearless assault trooper to the next. Canlon panicked and ran from his threatened cave to one on the right flank. Hawk stood up and put a leg over the barricade he had been using for cover. He poured an unrelenting deluge of riddling fire into the oncoming tanks. Men fell and rolled into one another, but the charge surged upward without hesitation. Shaeffer and Davis climbed beside Hawk. The chorus of automatic fire slowed the attack on the left flank, but over on the right, the enemy were already clawing their way into the caves. The annoying bugle was honking from somewhere on the mountaintop now.

Canlon had picked the wrong side to flee to for safety. He crawled behind the struggling men, gathering grenades. He heard them grunting and crying as they tore into hurtling human beings. Joe began throwing grenades indiscriminately. He knew that he was jeopardizing the lives of the Americans on the right flank, but they were as good as dead anyway. They couldn't hope to stall the attack with their bare hands.

Shaeffer and Davis both hit an empty clip at the same time. A spearhead of Japanese rushed up the moment their fire slackened. The left flank was going under. Hawk was knocked down; he saw a flurry of enemy leggings, then he struggled back to his feet with his weapon still blazing. The Japanese piled over the barricade. Davis collapsed in front of Hawk and rolled out in front of the cave beneath the feet of the attackers. He looked as if he had been doused with a can of red paint. Shaeffer and Hawk slung muzzle and stock at the angry faces that surrounded them until it looked as if they might be able to drive off the attack. They had been carried by the screaming mob over the barricade and out onto the open slope, where they continued to swing and kick at them. Four red fingernail marks ran down the side of Hawk's face. Shaeffer turned and jumped back behind the barricade. He caught a bullet in his spine for the effort. Hawk rolled over the rocks and into the cave beside him. Grenades thundered on all sides, shattering their eardrums. When Hawk looked out of the barricaded cave opening, the Japanese were gone.

The American grenades had taken their toll. The

Japanese had tossed their own bombs upward, but gravity was against them; their grenades had rolled back down the slope and into their own ranks. This had cut off the major portion of the attackers, leaving a few isolated around the Marine positions. Those were all killed. The attack was crushed for the time being. The enemy retreated down the slope for regrouping.

"You okay, Pidge?" Hawk asked. Shaeffer lay in a pool of blood at the bottom of the pit.

"I'm dyin'," he answered. His rough voice was finally filled with terror. "I'm...dyin', Hawk."

They looked at each other.

Hawk heard a wounded Japanese moaning. He was draped over the barricade. Hawk took out his knife and rammed it home.

"Pidge, I shouldn't have brought you here. I... know...that."

"Forget it." Shaeffer forced a roar. "It's done."

Half of the Marines were dead. All the caves were filled with blood and bone and suet and organs.

Canlon had been forced to kill most of them himself, to protect the fallen right flank. Joe was in shock. His mind had been blown out of a cannon and he was trying to pick up the jagged pieces. He stared with wide eyes at the smoking caves and the men he had annihilated with the grenades. He looked on the other side. Hawk's cave was silent.

"Hawk!" Joe sobbed at the top of his lungs. "Hawk!" Hawk had led him into this and now he had abandoned him. *"Hawk!"*

Hawk knelt over Shaeffer. He was still. The smooth face, the delicate features were motionless forever.

"He was a good man." Hawk nodded and slumped

against the side of the pit. "He was damn good." He heard Canlon calling him, but he didn't answer. His wounded back was stiffening on him. He looked up at the ceiling of the blood-spattered pit and shook his head. A bitter laugh slipped from his throat.

"Hawk!"

"What? Goddamnit, Joe, what?"

Canlon dove from his cave and ran to Hawk's. Bullets followed him, pinging off the rocks above his helmet and spewing white dust at his face. He vaulted the barricade and landed beside the body of Pidge Shaeffer.

"Let's run for it," Canlon whined, begging.

"Ah...shit...I don't know."

"Ramos is waitin' on us; I know he is."

"I hope not." Hawk silently considered the possibility. He sighed. "Okay," he mumbled under his breath. He dragged himself to his knees and looked outside. The teeth of Calvin Davis were tightly clenched in his dead skull. The teeth looked the same as when Davis had been able to use them, except that now you could see all of them. The uppers jutted out over the lowers in the bloody white skull. It was a sight that would remain with a person forever. Hawk immediately dismissed it from his mind. "Come on then," he said.

They quit the cave amidst a ravenous barrage from below. They scrambled and crawled through the positions on the smoking right flank. Hawk gathered all the remaining men together. They listened in numb silence as he spoke.

"I brought y'all here. It was mostly my doin' that got us into this. But I want to tell you men somethin' General Kravanart was tradin' with the Jap general in

Porkeet. Kravanart sold him American supplies for Jap gold. The Jap stole it from the Filipinos and he had to get rid of it—launder it, you see. So he bought our supplies and sold 'em off for Jap cash. That's what we found in the jungle out by Liloila that day. That's why Kravanart wouldn't take the town; him and this Jap did all their tradin' around there. The Japs must have took some of the stuff off to different places. They used this pirate as a go-between. He mighta sold the stuff on consignment, I don't know.

"Anyway, when Kravanart found out we stumbled onto his game he got scared. He tried to kill us—a whole company of us—and he almost did. He wanted us dead so nobody would know about it. I figure the bastard's crazy. It looks like him and this Jap general were old school buddies." Hawk relit his dead cigar. "Now, I'm tellin' you all this—not to excuse myself for nothin' I done—but just so's you'll know. I figure he'll still be tryin' to get you outa the way, if you get back to Lamare. But I got proof of what he done." He pointed at Bival's briefcase. "There's a purchase order or a bill of ladin' directed to the Jap, and Kravanart signed it. It's all in there. If anything happens to that, there's a copy down in them shrines where Pidge killed Collins. All I ask is that you don't let that murderin' bastard get away with this shit. I can guarantee you that I wouldn't." Hawk sighed.

"Now, something else," he said, "Pidge and—a few others, I imagine—reckon that I done this to y'all myself, and for myself. I'll tell you this and you can take it or leave it. There weren't no way we coulda got back to our lines alive. The Army was gonna shell us and the Japs had the water taken care of. We never could have got around Lamare. I knew that. I knew we'd just have to wait till the Army whipped the Japs or the Navy cleared the waters. I never told you that. I told you we was goin' back as soon as we got the women. Maybe I figured it'd be all over by the time we got 'em back. I don't know. I guess I done wrong. We couldn't have got back any sooner, but we coulda hid out on Lamare—and we didn't. Well, that's all I got to say."

The men remained silent.

"What do we do now?" Canlon asked.

"Y'all are gonna make a run for it. No sense sittin' here and just *lettin'* them bastards kill you. I'm gonna get back on that bluff and try to hold 'em off. They can't get more'n two or three men across that neck between the mountain and the bluff at a time. I can hold 'em until you get out to sea. I don't know how you're gonna do once you get out there, though."

The men turned sullenly away. Lasker came up to Hawk and told him he didn't consider any of the situation the sergeant's fault. Hawk thanked him, and he went and joined the others. Canlon stood beside the sergeant.

"They know you, Hawk. They want you bad," said Canlon, awed by the thought of the nameless, faceless enemy actually knowing a person's identity and hating him for it. They were vicious enough when you were anonymous.

"Yeah," Hawk laughed. "Everybody knows me. Everybody wants me. But, you know—they always change their mind when they get me."

The men began the dash across the land bridge to the high cliff that hung over the sea. They had to act fast. There was no time to think about it. One by one they lowered each other to the ledge and to the trail that descended the cliff. Canlon was the last to go.

"I'll stay with you," Joe offered.

"Naw, you best stick with the men. They ain't got too much sense. I figure this is the best place for me. There's too many hands against me."

Canlon nodded. He figured it was the best place for him, too. Before Hawk tried to kill Calvert, Joe never would have left him, no matter how scared he was. Canlon now had the same feelings about him that the rest of the world had—he was an unrestrained, cold-blooded killer. He belonged on the cliff, doing the one service he was capable of—killing.

"Things just didn't work out." Hawk smiled.

"You can't change people," said Joe. "Nothing can. They're gonna do what they want to do. You can't even change yourself."

"Get goin', Joe."

"Yeah. Well, so long, Hawk." The sergeant lowered him over the brink. His toes hit the ledge and he released Hawk's hand. Joe looked up at him and then went on down the trail.

Sporadic shots could be heard on the mountain. It wouldn't be long before the Japanese discovered it was empty. Hawk gathered the BAR, Shaeffer's Reising, and a few of the rifle grenades behind a flat rock on the cliff. He scooped a shallow burrow behind the rock and stoically faced the land bridge. The enemy would have a tough time crossing that bridge. They would scramble in its loose stone like spiders trying to climb out of a sand trap. A grim smiled touched his lips. He would get a bunch of them. He actually enjoyed sitting there waiting for them. Maybe he *did* belong here.

Why did he belong there? Why did violence and death follow him so easily? He sighed heavily. He could have changed, given the opportunity. Fighting was all he knew. He had to get around things like healing and families and birth. He had to get a new respect for life and not be so quick and intent upon destruction. He could have changed with a little more time. But how can you change when everybody's trying to kill you? He took out a block of chewing tobacco and tore off half of it. No point in saving it. No point in saving anything. It didn't matter.

The Japanese were taking their time. Expecting a trap, they climbed cautiously up the quiet mountain. But the Japanese had a way of advancing steadily, even when they were advancing into a known trap.

To hell with them. Hawk stood up and walked over to the edge of the cliff. The green and white sea slapped hollowly at its base. He could see Ramos to the east, helping the Marines onto the barge. He saw Amelia and Daniel Calvert already seated in it. Amelia was looking up at the cliff.

Amelia was startled when she saw the disheveled apparition on the rocks above her. It was him. Ten feet tall and bigger than the mountain—it was him.

Hawk turned away. There might have been tears somewhere between his chest and his throat, but his eyes were just as dry, dead, shiny, and cold as on the day he killed his first man. He went back to his burrow behind the flat rock. He sat there quietly, suffering, trying to get interested in the struggle that was to come.

The gash in his back sent out tendrils of pain that encircled his body. "Damn, that hurts," he whispered. He spat over the top of the rock.

He heard the motor of the barge revving up. He heard it pulling laboriously away from the beach. With a sigh, he got up and went back for another look. A sad white wake streamed behind the barge. Joe Canlon was trying to steer the awkward craft. Joe was supposed to know something about sailing. Old Joe.

Out of the corner of his eye he sighted two more barges on the surface of the vast empty ocean. They were gliding rapidly around the southwest corner of the island, coming from the beach where the Japanese had landed. Each had a skeleton crew of Japanese soldiers aboard. Without a doubt, they were chasing the Americans, but they were so far away they could never catch them, unless it be after a prolonged pursuit on the open sea. He thought of getting the BAR and taking a few shots at the two barges as they passed under him. But it would be a while before they came close to the cliff, and he probably wouldn't be there—or anywhere—by that time. At least the destroyer wasn't after them. It could catch them in short order. They had a pretty good chance. He spat down at the ocean.

"Hawk!"

The loud, drawn-out cry caused him to spin around. There before him, between him and the burrow, stood an American soldier. He was of towering height and massive build, completely unarmed, and with a strange look in his puffy eyes.

"I'm Malcolm Gill, Hawk. General Kravanart himself sent me here to kill you."

"Hey, now, look here, buddy, there's a few hundred Japs climbin' this way. I could use a little help. I don't know who you are or what your story is, but you need me as much as I need you." Hawk knew he was crazy.

He knew that the man who had attacked him in the glade must have been with this one. They must have all cracked up.

"I don't need you, Hawk. You are Hawk, ain'tcha?"

He could have denied it. "Yeah. That's me."

"I knew you was." Gill flexed his tree-trunk arms, whipping them behind himself like he was trying to make his elbows meet behind his back.

"Like I say, I could use some help."

"I'm gonna help you into hell, Hawk. I'm gonna kill you."

"You ain't killin' nobody, shitass."

The man was closer to the weapons than Hawk was. Yet he made no attempt to grab one of them. Apparently he was relying on his great size to overpower the Marine. Hawk misunderstood this. If *he* were trying to kill a man, he wouldn't be playing child's games with his hands. He thought that he might yet enlist the aid of the madman against the Japanese. So it was that Hawk made the mistake of not reaching for the little pistol he had in his jacket, the pistol he had taken from the sentry at Porkeet. It was not until the man had launched himself, and the two of them were locked in combat, that the Marine realized why the man was so confident. He was an exceptionally skilled boxer.

Blows thudded on both sides of Hawk's head, seemingly at once, and two more crashed into his chest, driving the wind from him. Hawk disentangled himself from this dynamo and fell to circling the man.

Gill was somewhat surprised, too. His adversary withstood the punches better than he should have. Gill's fists felt like they had been rammed into a fencepost.

Hawk heard a scream come from behind. He had

heard that insane peal before. Calicote was on his back, screaming and waving his knife. Hawk saw the blade slide down his right arm, followed by a stream of red that melted across his heavy muscles. He didn't know where Calicote had come from, but he knew he had to get rid of him. He staggered backwards with the flailing burden still clinging to him. Gill was watching in surprise and disappointment as his prey stumbled away from him. But his disappointment was not to last. Hawk knifed his elbows back at Calicote again and again, shattering his ribs and forcing him to let go. He rolled off into the loose stone of the land bridge, still screaming madly.

Hawk's temper got the best of him. He threw himself at the flat-footed Gill. The Marine's killer instinct took over. His arms came pounding into Gill's huge face in hard, overhanded, windmill blows. He leaned his entire ailing body into the blows and ignored the accurate, scientific punishment the boxer returned.

Gill's arms came at him in slow, crushing arcs. Hawk's fists tore back at him like pistons fired by lightning. Gill waited for the round to end, but it didn't. He waited for someone in his corner to stop the fight, but no one did. Then his numbed brain realized what it was really up against: death. He came to the final truth: if I fall down, he'll kick me to death. Terror gripped the recon patroller, but he fought on like a trapped rat, clawing and kicking and forgetting all about his manly art.

Blood spurted from Gill's eyes and nose. He found himself backing away from the cutting punches. Hawk pursued, and the two of them fell to trading blows dangerously close to the edge of the precipice. Gill was rallying. His opponent's eyes were glazing. Hawk had just about burned himself out. Now Gill's conditioning would pay off.

Hawk got a leg behind the Staff Sergeant and pushed him over it. He didn't realize that he was also knocking him over the brink of the abyss. The Marine pulled himself quickly back. Gill seemed to hover there in midair, then he let out a thunderous scream of terror. The scream continued until his body splattered across the jagged rocks in the sea below the cliff.

A gust of wind kindly caressed Hawk's face. It whistled in his ears and rustled his long hair as he stood looking down.

"Crazy son of a bitch," he growled. Breathless, beaten senseless, he turned back toward the burrow and his weapons. He settled behind the rock and laid his forehead on his bloody right arm. He rocked it back and forth and tried to catch his breath. Painfully, he looked up at the cloudy sky. What a hard place this world was.

He picked up the Thompson and waited for them to come for him. He would still get a few of them. His strength was gone, but it didn't take much strength to pull a trigger; only guts. And he would always have those, till the Japanese ripped them out of him.

They began coming across the isthmus of loose stone cautiously. Behind them somewhere, a bugle blew enthusiastically. He looked at their faces. They thought he was dead. He smiled and propped an elbow up on the flat rock.

He shot them coldly, happily, and using very few bullets. They continued trying to cross the bridge in ones and twos, and he blasted them down the mountainside, methodically, calmly, unerringly. He did not hurry. He arranged each man's death carefully, without congratulating himself after the arrangements proved successful. The Japanese gave up and fell to tossing grenades at him from the heights of the mountain. He was too far away. He fired rifle grenades at them—they were not too far away for the candlesticks. He was doing the job efficiently.

This devil frustrated the Japanese. They knew who this animal must be. Whenever faced with a tactical frustration, the suicidal bravery of the enemy took over. They massed in a human wave and charged the land bridge. Many were knocked from the narrow span by the pressing throng, but the rock formation was soon filled again by the men behind them.

Hawk mowed them down, bowling them over, splashing the rocks with endless blood and carnage. He held back the trigger of each gun until it was empty. Hanging grimly onto each successive weapon, he guided the wildly vibrating muzzles across the animated faces arrayed before him. He saw them sweating and grimacing as they cried out and fell over one another. They fell back as he ran out of ammunition.

The mountains grew quiet, as if even they were weary of trying to wrest the life of Sergeant Hawk from him.

"Sah-jint Hawk!" came a deep yell from above. "You see you, Sergeant Hawk!" The cry echoed over the sea. There, in a crevice, just beneath the mountaintop, was a head on a pole. It was being waved about in a ludicrous manner. It was the red-bearded head of Jack Calicote.

"Cute, Jap," he whispered hoarsely. He was more

intimidated by their vantage point than by their prize. And they had foolishly given their position away. He reached into his jacket and took out the tiny pistol of Kirijo's sentry. He wanted to kill as many of them as he could, so their victory party wouldn't be so crowded. He had a single grenade left. It would go last: He would let them gather around him and take them with him. They had taught him that trick. Fear did not cloud his thoughts. He planned it all, coldly and well.

It was then that he had the stray thought of jumping from the cliff. One way or the other, dead was dead. There were no degrees to death. Though, if he jumped, he wouldn't get the chance to take any of them with him, and that was important to him—killing. He laughed to himself. But there was a chance that he could beat all the odds and make it. If he pushed off hard and made a clean dive, he might be able to hit the ocean. He might also end up a mangled heap beside Gill. There would be no opportunity to stand on the brink and judge the leap. He would have to get up running, and risk a bullet in the back at that. Still, he had all the confidence a man hated by the world must have.

This new idea soothed his stiff back and his burning arm. He tucked the pistol back into his jacket. The Japanese began another push across the rocky isthmus. He let them fill it to capacity before he pulled the grenade's pin. Counting to four before he threw it, he didn't look to see where it landed. It was thrown like a pitcher throws a fastball, right into the face of an attacker.

In a single motion with the throw, he was up and running. He bounded, bird-like, from the edge of the cliff, off into total oblivion. He tumbled in the air and plummeted feet first.

The mighty drop took his breath away. He had jumped into a few bayous from high bridges as a youth, but nothing compared to this awesome height. The dive was far from clean, and when he hit the water the impact was so sudden that he was certain he had struck rock. Bubbles gushed before his eyes as he plunged deep into the sea, like a bullet aimed downward. He continued to fall in the black water, meeting no resistance from it due to his great velocity. He became mired up to his knees in the ocean's silty bottom.

The fall from the cliff had been a mere blur before his eyes. Thus it was that he didn't see the two Japanese landing barges chasing Canlon. They had finally come abreast of the cliff, and had nearly been struck by the hurtling Sergeant Hawk. Barely avoiding him, the prow of one barge rammed broadside into the other. The stricken craft began to sink rapidly, and its crewmen clambered over to the other boat.

Hawk kicked himself free of the tenacious mud of the ocean floor. He was swallowing water. He fought for the surface that hovered far above him. He saw the dark hulls of the Japanese barges resting on the lighted cellophane surface of the sea. He had the presence of mind to recognize them for what they were and he had no intention of trying to avoid them. If he made it to the surface without drowning, he was going to take them.

The prow of the sinking craft was already dipping beneath the choppy waves. A thick hand reached up from the ocean and pulled it deeper into the sea. Hawk brought his head up slowly. Water coursed off his long hair. He was behind the sinking barge; the men in the other landing craft couldn't see him. He looked up at something that was casting a shadow over him.

A twenty-millimeter machine cannon was mounted in the prow of the injured barge. Its ring-coiled barrel was already kissing the lapping waves. It was secured to a flimsy iron bracket. Hawk latched onto it and stopped treading the water. He had greater use for the weapon than as something to prevent him from sinking. He took the gun in both hands and, twisting it like the horns of a bull, bent the malleable bracket down until the machine cannon lay almost on its side. He kicked his legs in the water and the wreckage of the sinking boat gently careened toward the remaining barge. His breathed hissed in and out along the gyrating surface of the ocean.

The enemy soldiers were still gathering their wits. They were talking rapidly. They had been shaken by the surprising collision. They didn't see the gaping mouth of the machine cannon swing below them. Behind it was the merciless Sergeant Hawk, hanging onto the gun with both hands, teeth clenched, hate for the whole human race surging through his lacerated veins.

The armor-piercing twenty-millimeter shells could penetrate a thick layer of steel from hundreds of yards away. Hawk was only inches away. He twisted the bracket a bit more until it was just right. He watched his victims over the pronged cup of a flashguard that was on the tip of the cannon's muzzle. The sinking wreckage drifted closer.

A maelstrom of erupting fire and steel exploded beneath the Japanese. He pumped round after devastating round into the stumbling men, tearing flesh from their bodies, shredding them, hurling them through the air and into the ocean. Several shells hammered the armored gunwale of the barge, knocking massive chunks of wood from it and leaving only the smoking and splintered steel on the side. When the burst was over, a helmet was still whirring through the air. It plopped in the sea a hundred yards away.

Hawk climbed into the bloody boat. No one was left aboard, living or dead. The motor idled in the stern. He dragged himself back to it. After studying the controls for a moment, he threw it in gear and gave it full throttle. The giant airplane propeller pushed the boat suddenly forward. He caught himself with a hand on the deck. He seized the tiller and aimed the prow out to sea.

Shots clattered over the combined roar of the motor and the sea. The men on the cliff were shooting down at him, but he was already out of the range of their poor rifles. He looked over his shoulder at them, his scratched and weary face without expression.

15

WITH A LITTLE HELP, CANLON'S PARTY REACHED LAMARE in two days. A PT boat picked them up about a hundred miles off Tamara and delivered them right to the doorstep of General Kravanart. Canlon was manacled and led to the Quonset hut HQ, where he was told he was under arrest. Kravanart grudgingly accepted the fact that the Marine was alive. He couldn't shoot him right there in his office. Something might happen to the corporal later on. It would be a while before a trial could be arranged. Accidents can happen in a war zone.

The civilians were allowed to go free with their meager baggage. Ramos and Bival remained in southern Lamare, at a refugee center near the HQ. Calvert and the Jenningses were in San Francisco within three weeks. They sent Kravanart a nice letter, thanking him for their deliverance from the Japanese. Mrs. Jennings, Amelia, and the general had had a fine time talking about the old days in California with Amelia's aunt. He was the nicest man.

Under rigorous questioning, Canlon reported the

death of Sergeant Hawk. Later, in the privacy of his office, Kravanart breathed an emotional and physical sigh of relief. Thank God the bastard was dead. It was all over except for a few minor details. His secret was safe. The rest of the Marines were isolated in the brig. He resolved to cease trading with the Japanese and to disassociate himself from Garrotero. He had a complete moral rebirth because of the incident. Kirijo's death might have helped in the metamorphosis; close to two million dollars in a Swiss bank didn't hurt.

Even the poor Japanese were happy. Their propaganda boasted of a change in the course of the war. They had recaptured Tamara, the first island they had ever retaken from the Americans.

It looked like there was going to be a happy ending to the whole sordid affair for all of the unfortunate participants. But it wasn't to be. An unexpected, singularly ugly thing came to pass. The vile Sergeant Hawk rose from the dead.

No one had rescued Sergeant Hawk. Alone he had sailed his fragile airboat through the raging open sea. He followed the rising sun and was carried straight to the shores of Lamare as if the devil himself were guiding him; for who else would? He landed on an uninhabited beach and walked to the HQ.

He went to the hospital tent and found one of his Marines there. With that man's help, he was able to locate Bival. He took the briefcase from the Filipino and walked another two miles to the headquarters of Lamare's Marine Corps figurehead, Colonel Heller. Things were quiet at the colonel's office, for he had no men, and the campaign was over anyway. Heller's secretary let the beastly sergeant into the officer's chambers.

Heller stood up. Though the thing before him had just stepped out of a nightmare, he recognized him.

"Hawk! We thought you were dead." Heller indicated a chair opposite the desk behind which he sat. "Sit down, boy, sit down. You're in big trouble, you know."

"Yessir," came the deep, jarring voice. "But not as big as some."

"What do you mean?" Heller asked, a little irritated that Hawk didn't behave like a cowering fugitive.

Hawk told the Marine colonel the whole story—of Kravanart, of Garrotero, of Kirijo and the contraband — of the "friendly fire" on the Americans—even about Gill. The heavy voice grew softer as it told the tale. Heller sat dumbfounded as he listened to it in its entirety, without once interrupting the young man.

He noticed the black-crusted line on Hawk's arm. "Looks like you're hurt, Hawk. Let me get you a drink. Here, just sit there." Heller got up and went into another room to get a bottle. When he came back, he saw the other black-crusted line up the sergeant's back through his tattered shirt. He put the drink on the desk. Hawk made no move for it.

"Those are pretty grand allegations, Sergeant," Heller said sternly, "and you have some heavy charges against yourself." He tried to assume the tone of the angry schoolmaster officers use when addressing lesser creatures. He stared smugly at the long-haired, bearded wreck that was seated before him, as if he had just dismissed all of its allegations with his tone. But the tone wasn't that good.

"Yessir. And I can prove it," Hawk said wearily. "I got papers in this here bag to prove it." He dropped the briefcase heavily onto the desk.

"Incredible!" Heller's tone changed as he thumbed through the papers. He couldn't read Japanese. "I'd like to see Kravanart get what he deserves after the way he stalled my attack. I don't think there's been anything this big since Benedict Arnold."

"No, sir. I expect not."

"And I'll see to it personally that your name is cleared, too." Heller smiled efficiently, and added, "At your court-martial proceeding." He continued to smile and put the papers back into the case. "Now you go stretch your legs, boy. I won't call the Shore Patrol just yet. But, you know, eventually you'll have to go to the brig and await trial."

"Yessir. I imagine."

"There's still a lot of charges against you. Your men are already there. I'll hang onto these papers, though; you'll come out all right." Heller smiled some more and clapped him on his filthy shoulder and led him to the door. "Don't worry. I'll take care of you."

"Yessir." Hawk saluted and left. The door clicked weakly behind him. It was quiet in the outer office; you could hear the birds outside. Hawk scratched his eyebrow with a wrist still as thick and hard as a two-by-four. He heard the colonel crank the field telephone on his desk.

"Kravanart!" Heller brazenly shouted. "You almost lost your ass. I've got something to show you." Unused to caution, Heller continued to shout. He told the general about Hawk. Kravanart told him to drive himself over to the HQ alone as soon as possible. Heller took the briefcase out to his jeep without summoning his driver. He drove through the jungle to Kravanart's

HQ. It was well known that there were still snipers in the area.

Heller never made it. Snipers killed him along an overgrown stretch of the desolate road. A surgeon dug several Baby Nambu shells from his body. The Baby Nambu was a Japanese pistol. The killing was a vicious one.

Heller knew about the snipers in the area, but he had braved it alone. He was courageously delivering captured documents to the general. A silver star was awarded to him posthumously. He would have liked that, for up until then, Lamare had been a blot on his record. Intelligence picked up the briefcase. They were to go through its contents with a fine-toothed comb. General Kravanart would never see the briefcase; of course, he already knew what it contained. It was left to Major Clements to explain the documents.

Hawk, still on foot, stalked back to Kravanart's HQ. He finally realized that there was only one way to settle the matter, so he would settle it that way. Men began recognizing him as he neared the Quonset hut, but no one stopped him. They knew who he was and what he'd done, and some of them knew that he was already dead. No one who had just survived the battle for Lamare wanted to confront even the ghost of such a man. No one stopped him as he walked through the staff room, or the secretary's office, or even when he savagely kicked open Kravanart's door.

He found the General already lying across his desk. His papers were stained with little pools of his blood. He had shot himself in the head. Hawk turned and left the building. Later, he threw the Baby Nambu into the ocean.

A LOOK AT BOOK THREE:
UNDER ATTACK

ISLAND MASSACRE!

When Sergeant James Hawk's Marine battalion gets wiped out by Japanese submarines off the war-torn province of New Guinea, he—cut off from all hope—boldly takes command, knowing that survival means locating and destroying the deadly base.

His bloody drive through wild and dense forests are swarming with Japanese and vicious savages. The fatalities are high, and the air strikes relentless. But as a wounded Hawk pushes on, he begins to realize...this is only the beginning.

Will Hawk prevail all the hell war has to offer before his ultimate and final battle?

AVAILABLE JULY 2022

ABOUT THE AUTHOR

Patrick Clay was born a fifth generation Texan, in Galena Park, Texas, and went to a Catholic elementary school there. He attended St. Thomas High School and graduated fifth in his class. Patrick also received a scholarship to the University of St. Thomas and graduated cum laude from there. He then graduated magna cum laude from South Texas College of Law, where he was fourth in his class and a member of the law journal. While attending law school at night, Patrick operated his own locksmith shop. During the time he waited for the bar results, he began writing fiction. He began his second novel, *Sgt. Hawk*, in February 1977, and finished it in six weeks. Patrick had a well-known agent, who tried to sell it to major publishers and television. It was finally sold to Leisure Books in 1978, and by that time, Patrick had finished *The Return of Sgt. Hawk*, which was published in 1980. *Sgt. Hawk Under Attack* and *Sgt. Hawk Tiger Island* followed in 1981 and 1982, respectively. The titles of the latter two books were selected by the publisher, Leisure Books, as they originally had different names. *Sgt. Hawk and The Firebolt* was written in 1982 when Leisure Books went bankrupt, returned the rights, and never fulfilled distribution. Patrick had by then begun a solo law practice and gave up writing. He worked in a poor neighborhood, with plenty of wonderful clients, but not much compensation. So,

Patrick became a captain in the Civil Air Patrol and was Houston chess player in 1990, more for his tournament directing ability than playing skills. After fourteen years, he gave up the private law practice, and worked as an attorney for the federal government for the next thirty years. The podcast, *Paperback Warrior*, rekindled his interest in *Sgt. Hawk*.

Patrick met his beautiful wife at Astroworld in Houston, the first year that the amusement park opened. When he began writing in 1977, he had no children, and by the time he stopped writing in 1983, he had three daughters; he now has nine grandchildren. His father, a disabled veteran, and six uncles served in the South Pacific during World War II. Patrick was named after one of them, Patrick Clay, who was on a U.S. Navy ship with four battle stars. Another one of Patrick's uncles was at Pearl Harbor when it was attacked.